PRAIS … URSELF'



'I was immediately … my brain, letting me put r … ead it.'
– Cassian Lotte Lodge, *Poly in Pictures review*

'One of those books whose concepts stood out head and shoulders above the crowd.'
– Matt Mason, *Sweat, Tears, and Digital Ink*

'Barrett's writing is descriptive and often poetic, rendering characters and setting so vividly that I become immersed in Blondee's world.'
–Mary Maddox, *Ancient Children*

'Barrett beautifully describes society … a turn at every corner.'
– Amy Shiner, 'Find Yourself in the Book Forget Yourself',
*Modern Poly review*

'… a fascinating look into a dystopian future … greatly recommend it.'
– Rebekka K. Steg, writer

'Barrett does an amazing job in transporting the reader directly to this wasteland and engages all senses.'
–Amanda Amaya, *The Eclectic Bookworm*

'… exciting, fascinating, extremely chilling and startling…'
–*GA Bixler Reviews*

## PRAISE FOR 'THE GIDDY DEATH OF THE GAYS AND THE STRANGE DEMISE OF THE STRAIGHTS'

'An oddball and one-of-a-kind romantic comedy'
– Lambda Literary

'Love conquers all, especially such trivial things as monogamy and sexual orientation, in this polyamorous romance…a sprightlier comedy of modern manners.'
– Kirkus Reviews

'Redfern Jon Barrett's second novel is a fantastic ride through the lives of these Swansea residents…. The Giddy Death of the Gays and the Strange Demise of Straights is recommended to any library that collects popular fiction.'
– GLBT Roundtable of the American Library Assoc.

# forget yourself

REDFERN JON BARRETT

LETHE PRESS
MAPLE SHADE, NEW JERSEY

Published by Lethe Press
118 Heritage Ave, Maple Shade, NJ 08052
lethepressbooks.com



ISBN: 9781590213643



Cover and interior design
by Inkspiral Design

Library of Congress Cataloging-in-Publication Data
Names: Barrett, Redfern Jon, 1984- author.
Title: Forget yourself / Redfern Jon Barrett.
Description: Lethe Press edition. | Maple Shade, NJ : Lethe Press, [2016]
Identifiers: LCCN 2015045333 | ISBN 9781590213643
(softcover : acid-free paper)
Classification: LCC PR6102.A7749 F67 2016 | DDC 823/.92--dc23
LC record available at http://lccn.loc.gov/2015045333

# part one

I AM LIVING IN A HOLE. I am living in a hole in the ground. This is where they put me, though I don't really know who I am and I will be someone else pretty soon.

Tarp above; mud below. I am less of a nuisance here.

It is important that you know: I love you.

Of course I have no idea who you are.

But I have no real idea who I am either, so it seems fair to me.

Will you think of me, holding you? I have blonde hair that reaches my shoulders and I am of an average stature—though of course my definition of average will be misleading. I have the long fingers of a thief.

I love you because here, in this hole, that is all I have. Love and earth and rainwater. Perhaps you aren't real. That doesn't matter.

I will still hold you.

Will you let me?

I am not dangerous.

Tomorrow I will wake up someone new. The same damp earth will be under the same toes; the same fingers will clutch the same food and bring it to the same lips. But someone else will taste it.

The same eyes with someone else's vision.

The same brain with someone else's thoughts.

For me,
for Blondee,
this is the end.

I have tonight. Tonight is all I have left.

These hours are for me, for my story.

About how I broke the world.

# this is everything

IT STARTED WITH A BREAKUP—I imagine that to be common. The book tells us how breakups should happen.

*If one person cheats, the other breaks up with them.*

It's simple enough, and happens to be the first proverb on love in the book. Page 15, written in purple biro. Someone I didn't know had remembered it and written it down.

I had loved her, as far as I could tell; but she couldn't believe it. She lashed her tongue to all who would listen: Blondee is cheating. Blondee is cheating with Tie. Even after he was dead—especially after he was dead.

'Never cheat', says the book. What exactly cheating *was*, well, that was not so clear. My body—my full hips and thighs and too-small breasts—those I had shared only with her.

But my mind?

Tie had been there from the very start.

When people arrive here—awakening from a death-sleep which was the end of their old life—they are named by the clues they came with. I had nothing. Nothing but mid-length blonde hair. I was naked. It was how I came into the world.

So I was called Blondee.

I remember a small crowd. I was in the courtyard at the centre of the compound; a single water tap, some broken flagstones, and three-dozen old vacuum-tubes hammered into a row to form a fence. I wanted to know who I was. My skull throbbed. I had memories, but none of them were personal, none of them were really mine, and they were flat, two-dimensional, meaningless. I knew what bread was, and how to clean my teeth. I knew what a city was. But there was no detail. I didn't know my favourite type of bread or what colour my toothbrush was or even the name of a particular city. When I thought of a city I conjured up tall buildings and empty streets, a lifeless, pointless shell. Those were the memories we were left with.

Tie was the first person who blurred into view that first time I forced open my aching eyelids. He was smiling in a kindly way. He was disturbing. I tried to cover my breasts, left with the pointless, heaving memory of shame. I was declared a minor-theft. Like I say, I have long fingers. A lot of the others were there, though I can't recall which ones, and they were bored by my arrival. My terror was banal. Tie gave me a blanket, and someone said 'Blondee'.

We're here because we've committed a crime—that's what we tell ourselves. I didn't look so bad, so my crime must have been minor. Due largely to my fingers, I must have been a thief.

That was a long time before Ketamine came into the world. She had also been dropped in with the rations, her mind blank, a carrier-bag of possessions straddling her arm. She was thinner back then, her eyes so innocent you'd hardly have thought she'd committed a crime at all. She was declared a minor. She was pretty, with her long black hair; clearly a seductress. So her crime, she was informed, must have been minor, and it must have been sexual. In the bag was a t-shirt, the word 'Ketamine', white on black. That must have been her name. It was added to the back of the book with the others.

We fell in love and she came to live in my triangle hut: a large window propped up against the outer wall of the compound. That first night she'd lain next to me, trembling and confused. She trembled on her last night with me as well.

I knew it was over one day in particular—one of the days just after Tie's death. We were in our triangle-home. The crisp cut of scissor scattered another flurry of tufts to the floor.

She was cutting my hair.

The hair gently meandered over the smooth brown-and-yellow pattern, carried by a breeze that no number of rags stuffed between gaps could ever really get rid of. Another snip and the draft caught the yellow strands at knee-height, carrying them away from us and to the edge of the lino, which I had cut into shape and used as a rug to hide the worst of the dirt floor. Korma-flavoured noodles and home-made fuck-me-fuck-me perfume wafted through the air from next door, mingled with the tinny music from an ancient player. Ketamine's nipple had rubbed against my arm as she leant over my neck, la-la-ing along as she inspected her work.

I must have looked unhappy. I was thinking of Tie. Tie rotting.

"Are you done yet?" I swept my hands down myself, my skin all tingled and itchy, the stool pressing wood and metal into my arse.

"No, no, no," she sang, the notes matching those caught on the air.

It had been my idea that songs should have words, but it wasn't something I'd be able to prove. The sun shone strong through the glass. I needed air.

I stood up, showering my warm feet and the cold lino with hair. I almost hit my head on the shard of mirror which hung from a string.

"I'm not done," she squawked.

"I am."

"You're still thinking of him. Aren't you?"

"I am."

"He's dead. He's dead and you're still wasting your thoughts on him. You're with me, Blondee. You're with me."

"You're so young, Ketamine."

That did it. We had argued before, but not like we did that night. All night. She told me I didn't love her. I said that her gossiping had given me a reputation: no-one trusted me. She countered that she had only told the truth. What could be wrong with the truth?

*When it ends you have break-up sex once.*

This entry comes later. I don't know who remembered it, but they wrote it down in the book in coloured crayon smudges.

My eyes were still wet and my throat still swollen and raw as Ketamine ran trembling fingers over my breast, pressing her face into my stomach with desperate trails of snot and tears. Short black hair tickled the spaces between my fingers so I used my hand to brush at the humiliating tears, first on my face then on hers. We had tried to make it work just to avoid this, to keep ourselves behind private glass, where other people's memories were irrelevant.

"Ket—" it wasn't my voice, really it belonged elsewhere. Ketamine moved her face a nose from mine, wordless and crumpled, dripping onto my collarbone.

No kissing, no kissing, went written words, a bullet-point below the proverb. No kissing. Break-up sex is pleasure, not love.

*When it ends you never see each other again.*

Really, this is the most impractical of rules. The world is only twenty minutes long one way and sixteen minutes the other. Ketamine and I would see each other again, as did everyone who broke up. But the book reminds us how things are done outside the compound. We have to try and act normally, even if really, we can't. If we saw each other we'd avert our eyes or whisper 'good morning' at most. Eventually it would become normal. That was how everyone on the outside must have done it.

The triangle hut was mine. She moved out.

I didn't remember anything about love so I had nothing to add on it to the book.

*You keep something of each other.*

This is the nicest of the love proverbs. I had no idea who had remembered it, but I truly wished I did. I wished I had been there when they wrote it, so I could gently kiss them on the ear as they pressed blunt pencil to rough paper.

I got the t-shirt, cold and wet. She got some of my hair—the only blonde hair in the tiny world shared by a hundred of us.

And so goes the code of love.

# a minor corner

THE SUN FELL HEAVY upon my face, grimy and uninvited. The 'Ketamine' t-shirt was too small for me but I was wearing it anyway, hidden beneath a thick blue woollen jumper which frayed at the edges. The t-shirt was damp and squeezed me. I was perched on a small pile of bricks outside my home, watching the eleven houses around mine: each house in this section was as small as any other, but each was unique, made up of loose timber and old car doors, or maybe metal grilles and plastic tubes. It was too hot—everyone was indoors, sleeping over soft and dirty mats. All I could hear was the glistening hiss of the heat.

Ketamine had taken her few belongings and they had been replaced by a void. It filled my home, a void somehow larger than hut, eight steps long and three steps wide. I had tried to fill the space with clutter but it was swallowed up as soon as I turned my back. So I watched the world instead. There was no danger of seeing her in this corner.

"Get me away," she'd spat. She'd asked to live far away, amongst the moderates, and they'd allowed her. Something about her was special. She was newest and prettiest. She was belligerent and...

I needed to stop thinking about her. I would go for a walk.

I lived in the corner for those whose crimes were 'minor'. Around our corner are walls. The walls are yellowish grey, high and rounded. My triangle was in almost the very corner of our corner. I walked along by the wall, running my fingers down its length, swerving 'round to avoid the occasional house, propped against the perimeter like mine. The air was soaked in heat but the wall, the wall was always cool. There was never any clue what lay beyond it—forests or fields—perhaps we were on a platform in the ocean, or in the very middle of a city, sound-dampeners hiding the rush of waves or people on their way to work. Whatever, it didn't matter.

At the start of the world, apparently, people threw things over the wall, but it made no difference. They didn't know much at the start of the world.

More huts, one had ornaments outside—

*A tidy garden means a tidy mind.*

Though not many even in that corner could afford such luxury—what items we had generally went indoors, where we could enjoy them. Outside was too unpredictable, when days of snow could follow the hottest evenings.

I came to a hut made of bookshelves, piled atop one another and roughly-bound with sealant. It would be cool in there, a windowless box of bare wood. I ran my fingers over the dark grooves and varnish-coated contours which were warm and sticky beneath my fingertips.

There was a giggle inside. My hand snapped back, my fingertips brushing the scratchy fabric of my pullover. I moved my hand between myself and the hut, hovering between the two, before pressing my palm flat onto the exposed wood once again.

A giggle again: longer. I eased my palm away, feeling my face ache into a smile. Once more—once more I would touch it. I gripped the shelf, my fingers turning white, the sealant cracking slightly, a small cloud of dust spat toward my torso.

"What the—", a voice, soft and startled.

"Is someone there?" Another voice, this one rough and battle-ready.

Saliva filled my mouth and choked my throat. I walked on, quickly, not daring to run. A few feet away was the bush, an expansive shrub which served as the only foliage in our corner. I hid beneath it. I slid in and down toward the dusty grass. The bush boasted tiny dark-green and deep-red leaves woven together, jostling against one another with the slightest breeze. Sometimes, when it was cold, the red leaves would all flutter to the floor. Sometimes, when it was too warm, the green leaves would turn brown.

I was almost at the border, where our lives ended and the lives of those whose crimes were 'least' began, with their fine houses and tremendous luxury. Between us was the courtyard, beyond that the land of those whose crimes were 'moderate', who had stolen from children, say, or sent an old woman to hospital. Of course our crimes weren't that detailed but those were the clearest memories we had been left with—of violence and anarchy and deviance.

There's something important about our memories here—fact and theory become lost in one another, entwined, meshed together like berries and bruised vegetables.

Take plagues. I have an idea of a plague, of suffering and blackened skin and crosses-on-doors. Whether one has ever really happened, or if only the possibility remains, I don't know. The same is true of war—I can see soldiers, in smart-rough uniforms above heavy-booted feet, but whether soldiers have ever fought one another, well, I couldn't say. Take earthquakes that crumple cities, take acts of bravery, take extraordinary kindness, take mass celebration—if these are facts or ideas, in truth, is a pointless line of thought.

We've been left with small acts of unkindness, of suffering that we must have caused, that we've known from the beginning, of crimes which turn the stomach and hide those who must have been guilty of the worst—the very worst—to the far corner, away from us, at a distance that can eventually become bearable.

*People are punished for their crimes.*

The first page. But there are variants on it in every single section of the book. *People who inflict suffering are removed from society.*

Lifestyle. Page 69.

*Criminals are confined.*

Bodies. Page 84.

*Criminals don't get the pleasures most do.*

Food. 99.

It was Tie who had first explained my crime to me—poor fat Tie, bulky and heaving and sweating. I was shallow: my skin prickled in horror at the sight of him. Even so I had to ask: why was I 'minor-theft'? 'Minor-theft', 'minor-fucking-theft'. What did that mean?

Tie had told me that it meant I wasn't the best, but not the worst either.

I asked him what that fucking meant.

Tie had told me that everyone here committed a crime. My crime was minor—it did someone, somewhere some harm, but they'll have recovered.

I asked him who the worst were.

He took a moment before replying, gazing at me through small sad eyes, and told me that the worst were the 'severes', but that I wouldn't see much of them. Then the moderates. Then the minors, such as myself. Then the least, like himself. Least meant that whatever they did can't have been too bad.

He went on to tell me that I was a minor-theft. That meant I stole something, something which was probably important to someone and the theft of which will have hurt them.

His eyes rested on my fingers.

I have the memory of theft. Not my own, but of children crying for lost toys, of men and women teary-eyed and forever-lost items. My body ached with what I still had to grow used to. My body ached with guilt.

I asked him what his crime was.

He told me his was least-sexual.

I asked him what that meant.

He stared at his own chubby hands.

Was it like rape? For moments after asking the question my own guilt ebbed away.

He told me it was nothing like that: he was one of the least. His face turned so red it look as though it would blister and he wrapped his hands heavily over one another. There was a pause, a pause which lasted and lasted.

My breathing was steady and he was calm. I had to ask: when do we get to leave?

# the blank rations

A SINGLE SHADOW sliced the courtyard in two. Above it stood Pilsner, leaning on the water tap. Pilsner never slept in the day and never liked being alone. He was the earliest here who was still alive. He was one of the least.

"Blondee."

"Pilsner."

He slowly shifted his gaze over me, running his eyes up and down, seeing through the tattered jumper. "It's been a difficult time for you."

I couldn't say anything back. The heavy wrinkles around his mouth moved as though he were still talking. The air was stirred with the hefty metallic clatters from Frederick's project. Neither his nor Pilsner's homes were far away—none of the least were far from the courtyard. Of course as a minor, I had never been near their houses. They were left to my imagination.

"I've seen young Ketamine," he uttered, pushing the words from dry lips. He didn't mention Tie.

"Excuse me," I moved forward, placing my bucket beneath the water tap.

"It's dry right now." His words were matched by a thin trickle. "I have some you can use, if it's urgent."

"It's not." I sat down on the rough stone.

"You two couldn't have worked. Like it says, you can't tie a young thing down."

*You can't tie a young thing down.*

Page 67. And what did that even mean? Only a least would get away with writing something like that in the book. It was under 'lifestyle'.

"I suppose not, no," I lied.

I had driven her to the other side of the compound. My lungs felt a tenth their size and breath came in brutal gasps. The air was brittle.

"Careful, careful. Breathe. Breathe long," Pilsner's voice was always flat. He reached out to me, stopping his arm a finger away. He couldn't touch me: he wasn't my lover. I nodded and drew in shuddered breaths. Pilsner collected a trickle of water in a cup and placed it on the ground. I grasped it.

"Thank you. Thanks."

Pilsner stood and resumed his leaning on the water tap.

He had been alone since I could remember, since I had arrived at this courtyard for the first time. I had heard that Pilsner had partners once; but it was common knowledge that he couldn't or wouldn't—more likely couldn't—have sex. That Pilsner had no cock. As I sipped at the water I couldn't help glimpsing at the bulge in his trousers. It seemed normal.

The sky darkened a little more and Pilsner's shadow doubled.

Frederick's clatter grew louder. His projects always made noise. Pilsner said it was because he was young—young and youthful like Ketamine.

Frederick, by all accounts, was an artist.

He was the one who remembered that word, or so I was told. He had salvaged a memory of those whose only job was to paint and break and sculpt. Perhaps that was what he had been before—perhaps not—but it was what he was now and he seemed to enjoy it. He was immune from the restrictions of movement, restrictions which meant I knew the minor-corner like my own body, but that the rest of the world was a mystery. As an artist he wandered where he wanted, drawing inspiration from the tattered huts of those beneath his level. With his new profession had come a change in status—he went from least-violent to least-disruption; artists, he had said, caused controversy and not violence. And so it went in the book.

"Hello there, Frederick," Pilsner hailed.

"Mmm. Mmm," Frederick nodded nervously at the two of us, a rusted bar in his left hand, jutting at his shin in rapid, uneven jerks.

"Answer him, Blondee." Pilsner shot me a look, baring his teeth slightly. I lowered my head.

"Hello, Frederick."

"What brings you here?" Pilsner asked.

"The delivery. The rations," Frederick responded, making a clear effort to force the words from his mouth.

"Bit early for that. You'd best come back later."

Despite Pilsner's advice Frederick nodded and lay on the ground, anxiously watching the sky, his small eyes darting from cloud to cloud. His hair and scrap of a beard were the same muddy colour as the flagstones. He was camouflaged; only his mouth, nose and eyes stood out against the dust beneath him.

"I suppose the others will be here soon enough." Pilsner aimed his flat statement at me, but I kept my eyes on Frederick and the flagstones. It might have been Pilsner's right to talk down to me, my crime might have been worse than his, but I didn't have to like it. I could detest it if I wanted to. He noticed my anger and chuckled.

Slowly people filtered into the courtyard, an excitable mixture of least, minors, and moderates, exchanging glances of warmth and suspicion. Once in a while everyone met in the courtyard, waiting for the rations. An even space was left in the middle. The severes arrived last, hanging to the edge and watching us from the sides of their eyes.

I looked for her. I could smell the rank perfume of the man who lived in the hut next to mine. I could see the tall frame of the man who lived by the bush.

"Blondee." Tanned's voice stood firm against the clamour. Tanned was a minor too, with darkish skin and darkish eyes. Even one of his front teeth was dark, darker than the others, though like I say I am no judge of character.

"Tanned." Tanned was my friend. Friends were unusual, though not unheard of. Friends inspired jealousy. Friends were the reason for my reputation.

"How're—how've you been?" Tanned asked.

I paused before answering. "Not bad."

"I'm sorry I haven't seen you earlier, but, you know."

"I know."

*Leave your neighbours to their grievances.*

The handwriting was messy and etched in pencil. Somehow I don't remember the page. 'Home is a castle' is on page 115 so I'm fairly certain it's near there.

"Perhaps we can meet for a while tomorrow?" Tanned asked.

"Sure. I'd like that." I nodded. I wouldn't be able to complain of the company. We waited side-by-side.

The rations come into the world the same as people—with a blink. The centre of the courtyard is empty, then it isn't. You can focus, focus all of your attention on that centre, but your mind wanders and then the rations are there.

And there it was: the large metal box.

"Blondee."

It was my turn. It was dark. Casio was rationing this week. My legs ached. I hated waiting until all the least and half the minors had had their turn. Casio had the book in his hairy-slender hands and read my name without passion.

"Blondee. Single. Six large vegetables, seven small. Three bags of carbohydrate. Two proteins. Four desserts. No spare sugar or salt this week. One item of furniture."

"Thank you." I took my cue and stepped inside the large box which was flooded with stale light. The vegetables were the same as always. I watched the least walk away with food in colours I had no memory of. This time I'd stock up on orange things, orange things felt right. Six pumpkins, three oranges, two carrots and a banana. I placed them into the stiff bags provided, bags I would return tomorrow. I picked up two of rice and one of chips. A box of eggs and a small block of cheese. Then a yoghurt, a trifle and two rice puddings. The bags felt strangely empty: there was only one of me eating now, and the rations for a couple add up to more than the sum of their parts.

The furniture was a luxury. None of it was ever complete, not by my turn, but it was useful. I placed my bags in the corner and gently picked through the remaining items. More tubes, some planks, torn fabric and a great deal of foam. New foam would be good for my bed but I caressed the fabric between my fingers. It was striped—gold, orange and purple, and smooth as infancy. Patches were stained black though none came off on my hands—maybe it could be washed. I pictured it in the triangle home.

It was Tie who had given me my home. It was funny how no-one ever mentioned the dead, even though Tie had the biggest heart in all the world.

He called me Blondee.

I hadn't been used to the name and the fat man's hand was heavy on my shoulder.

He pointed to where I would live. It was an empty space, lying prostrate beneath the wall. A space at the edge of the world. It was covered in dandelions. Fuzzy yellow heads poked through grass and patches of sand.

I had turned to him, ready to fire a hundred questions from the weighty throb inside my head: what does he mean? How could I live there? Why can't I leave?

He had grinned at me, large jowls framing a small mouth. He motioned to a large window which was lying by the wall. He told me he had no use for it, and that it was mine. Behind it were bundles of junk. It seemed like punishment. I had yet to learn kindness.

I asked him how I could live in it.

He'd suggested I prop it up against the wall and close off one side with some wood, the other with heavy sheeting; it'd make a decent enough door.

This was to be my home? I didn't remember any particular house from my old life, but I remembered what a house was. It was more than this. This soon-to-be hut, this makeshift hovel.

He'd offered to help put it together with the same hopeful grin on his face.

Casio called my name. My time for collecting rations was up. I draped the gold-orange-purple striped fabric over my shoulders. It spat dust into both my nostrils. I placed it in the bag above the pumpkins.

I took in some deep breaths before leaving. The box smelled of fresh plastic.

# mushed teabags

THE YOGHURT WAS SOUR. I ate it anyway, savouring the sharp back-of-the-throat flavours. Blueberry and curdled milk. I stared at the trifle and rice puddings in the squat plastic containers, willing them to be fresh. Perhaps I should eat them today, I reasoned, the weather being so warm. Something smelled bad, like decay.

My elbow still ached from scrubbing at the blackened stains on what would be my orange-gold-purple striped curtains. I remembered curtains, it was a memory everyone had, but they were rare in this corner, where fabric was used for clothes and bedding. I was frightened of being closed in without light or protective glances—but I didn't have to cover the whole window. It would be elegant.

It was time to meet Tanned. There had been no tea, coffee or milkshake this fortnight so we'd have to drink hot water. The water tap in the courtyard had been flowing freely. We would meet at the bush, as was usual.

I arrived to find Tanned with his lover Burberry, both perched on deckchairs. I squatted on the floor. We nodded in greeting. I hadn't expected Burberry to be there, though really the two made a visually pleasing couple. They looked like siblings, with the same dark skin and well-proportioned frames—though Tanned's long hair was straight, whilst Burberry had dreadlocks painted around her full, warm features.

Ketamine's gossiping had made lovers wary of me, but Burberry was the best of them. Her jealousy was muted next to most, and now and then I would be able to grasp at some time with Tanned, or the two of them together. She had nothing to fear, though since I had lost Ketamine her wariness had grown, something she made as clear as she could.

"You're looking well, Blondee," Burberry said, an artificial smile drawn over her face.

I thanked her.

But I couldn't blame Ketamine for my reputation, not entirely. She made things worse but she didn't start them. How people look here is important. Everyone has a sex drive, and it influences their actions. Most people found me attractive when I arrived, and I enjoyed their stares, their gaze a soft lingering caress of brief intimacy—intimacy which I missed badly, but of which I also had no recollection. People were nice to me. I was a decent face bordered by butter-blonde hair.

It didn't take long to learn that the way I looked *limited* intimacy.

I would talk to wandering eyes and slight-smiling lips. I'd been excited about making friends, it would distract me from what I had decided was my death, and from the squalid hovel I'd been housed inside. But angry partners kept their lovers from me, jealous and afraid that I would steal their soul mate away, steal away their only possible achievement in this world. They never said it, but each new friend would eventually avoid me, softly-whispered excuses covering the harsh stares of their beloved. Almost everyone in the compound was coupled and it didn't do to talk too much to those who belonged to another.

So I had spent the first ages in the new world alone, not sure what to do with myself and sleeping most of the time. The only break had come in brief visits from Tie, who would come to make sure I was doing a little less miserably.

Tanned and Burberry never mentioned Tie either.

"Would you two like a drink?" I offered. "I don't have much but I can fetch some hot water."

"We've got some tea," Burberry offered, two mushy used teabags balanced on her hands like old testicles.

"Sure. I'll boil some water. Back soon." The bucket was full enough for three cups and I carried it over to the fire tap.

Each of the four corners came with their own fire tap, and as a result fire was more plentiful than water. There were no explanations there, nothing the book could tell us about them. Four fire one water. Our world was mysterious, set in place by a people to whom we had once belonged but no longer remembered. All we had was this: four fire taps and one water. They had always been here.

What did the world look like at the beginning? It was no secret—

"Here you go," a nameless neighbour offered me the tap and kettle, accidentally sloshing some of his lukewarm water onto my knee as he left, noticing but remaining wordless.

I returned as Tanned and Burberry pulled apart from an embrace. Tanned turned to me and unleashed his news: Ketamine had a job. I offered them the two cups of hot water, whilst Burberry plopped the bags in, scanning my face for a reaction.

"You'd have found out if you'd been meeting people. You should get over to the courtyard more." Tanned flashed his teeth at me, which gleamed white against dark skin, the one tooth a dirty brown-grey.

"Right."

"Don't you want to meet anyone?" He took a sip from the broken mug he clutched. "Anyone at all?"

"I don't know."

Tanned looked concerned. "You should get back on your feet, soon as possible."

I hadn't heard that before, but it sounded familiar. Tanned squinted his eyes in thought, trying to pull something from his mind. Burberry turned her intense gaze toward him.

"Do you remember—"

"Wait—"

"Do you remember something?" she ventured.

"I don't know. It'll come to me if it comes to me," Tanned replied, turning attention back toward me. "The point is you can't remain alone."

"Pilsner does." I wondered how he could be so relaxed about the possibility of a memory.

"Well, you know about him—"

"Oh, stop it." I snapped, failing to hide my amusement. "You can't talk about him like that."

Tanned released a sharp, hard laugh. Burberry scrunched her face in discomfort, so Tanned pressed his lips to hers. She parted them, allowing entry to his tongue.

I couldn't resist asking.

"What's her job?"

"Huh?" Tanned mumbled into Burberry's mouth.

"Ketamine's job?"

"Oh." He stopped. "She makes recipes now. She'll write down what we can cook."

"That's a job?"

"Apparently so."

"Right," I murmured, unsure. A quick breeze stung my bare arms and more cloud threatened the sky, churning it into the threat of rain.

"Her crime is the same. She didn't want it moved."

"Why?" I asked, but Tanned didn't need to answer, so he didn't. The smell of pumpkin sliced through the air. Someone was cooking. Mine had started to mush. Perhaps I should find someone: food was better with a partner, after all. Another pause and more clouds gathered, hovering above us, intent on useless showers. Water always pooled at the foot of my bed, drips which would tickle my feet and make me giggle.

"Look, she's gonna be hurt and looking for something to do. Maybe she remembered something, but it'll be the shock," Tanned offered.

Burberry stirred.

"It's getting late, we should be going. Goodbye Blondee," she called, elongating the syllables of my name. Blo-o-onde-e-e. Sing-song. Si-i-ing so-o-ong. She shifted her thin frame up from the deckchair, slinging it over her arm. Tanned followed. Burberry kept h[illegible] as she left, so I smiled at her, willing friendliness. They'd taken their tea with them. I watched them vanish before returning to my hut.

The fabric was still soaking in the bucket. I pulled it out and went to pin it to the window frame. As the slanted window was also wall and roof I had to use eight pins to hold it up. I left one third of the window uncovered. The curtain would provide shade. Light shone orange, gold, and purple over my hut and I rested the changing colours on my skin, basking in the glory of light from wet fabric. I noticed there were two colourless circles cast, one on the resin box I used as a kitchen and the other on my pillow.

There was little else to do. I had no job, and all those anyone could remember were already taken—like Frederick the artist, and Rings who sewed things. I was unemployed, which meant little except boredom—I had no idea what I had enjoyed before this new life. Did I read books? What were they about? I thought of books on a shelf, an endless array of smart blue spines, gold lining without words. They all looked like our book, our one book. Perhaps I sang, but how did singing work, when it can't be proven that tunes have words? Ketamine had been unemployed as well. We had enjoyed each other.

That evening I awoke, huddled under a collection of clothes and blankets: the night was cold. The noise drifted toward and away, a blunt thud thud thud, dim like blood pulsing through my ears. I lay on clammy foam, wondering if the dull clanging noise was real or not. The darkness was heavy. I had so much space. I didn't want it. Promises of sleep seemed to slip away.

It was my time with the book tomorrow. Thud, thud, thud. Was that noise there? Through the window I could see the crisp moon. It drifted toward and away.

Then I saw it, as clearly as with my eyes.

*A woman made of stone. A woman made of stone with an arrow in her hand and a dog at her feet. The stone woman's lips were painted berry red, her cheeks flushed pink. She looked at me.*

*The stone woman.*

*The stone woman was poised in elegant action. Her arrow was raised above her head, a bow strapped to her back. She was hunting, hunting some unknown creature.*

*Behind her were dogs, a dozen of them, all racing, bounding, snarling forward; all hard, all immobile.*

*The woman was looking back at them now, face frozen in wide-toothed grin, eyes fixed and alert. Two dogs were ahead of her, frozen, unmoving.*

*Her mouth was open. She unleashed a cry in silence. Her bow was in her hand.*

*Her bow was aimed high, the stone arrow tense, ready.*

*The arrow was gone.*

*She and her dogs were gone.*

It was a memory and it was mine. I tried to hold onto her, to grasp at her, but her image faded and she'd come away in soft wet clumps between my fingers, fizzling away into the sweat-soaked air.

All that was left was me, the bed, the hut and the compound, thick arching walls to keep the world away. I had remembered something, however strange and wordless. I had remembered something.

The foam coiled around my skin, hugging my ears and hair, sticky and tickling my arms and my legs. It was too much. I carefully shifted myself from my bed, to my sheet-door and into the night air. The moon coyly hid itself behind rapid clouds, occasionally flashing me, spreading glimpses of naked light over the ground. Crunched sand and dry grass massaged my feet as I made my way past silent huts. With each step my eyes grew heavier, my limbs more leaden.

There was a whiff of fruit-filled stench, of decomposing, of decay and entropy.

Then it was gone. All I could trust were my heavy legs, carrying me toward—carrying me toward the courtyard. That's what I wanted, to rinse my face in water. That's what I wanted.

# the book

THE BOOK LAY PEACEFULLY before me, my fingertips gently pressed against the rough paper. Slices of sunlight worked their way into the magic of the book's very own hut, worming their way around sheets of corrugated iron. In here it was always cool and dry. In here, far away from life and houses, it was quiet.

The book was serene.

It knew it could rest before me, that I would never have a chance to befoul its pages with ink-tainted memory. I had no pen. I wouldn't be writing my memory of the stone woman. I was just going to read as always.

"You're just going to read as always."

That's what Pilsner had told me. He'd found me in the courtyard, prone, slumped over the water tap. The sun had stabbed at my eyes with the hot anger of day. He'd been stood above me.

"Can I get to the tap?"

"Tap?" It was wrapped in my arms and pressed against my chin. My neck ached. "Oh, right. Sorry."

"No problem," his shadow moved toward me as I uncrossed my stiff arms and brought myself to my knees, eyes stuffed with sleep.

"So. Did you sleep here?" Pilsner asked.

"No." Pause. "I suppose I did."

I couldn't tell if he was laughing or tutting in response. Either way it was better to keep my lips pressed shut. They were dry and kept sticking together.

"Have some of this," he'd offered, thrusting a cup with a mouthful of water to me.

"Thank you," I waited for him to ask what I had been doing there.

"It's your turn with the book today."

"Right, there's actually something—"

"Why were you sleeping here, then?"

Words caught in my throat. I wasn't sure I had an explanation. I just had the floating-fuzzed image of the woman, which perhaps I'd never even seen.

"I had a memory."

"Really."

"I did, I saw this—"

"Are you sure you had a memory?"

I examined him through narrow eyes.

"It's just," Pilsner spoke to me slowly, "well, she who lived with you only just had a memory herself and—"

"No, not—"

"If you'll let me speak," his still voice hardened. "It's natural you would want a memory of your own. It doesn't make it real."

Real. The least decided what was real from our old lives, though why they'd have better memories or a better sense of judgement than anyone else was unclear.

Tiny scraps of dust danced around the book. Pilsner had searched me, making sure I had no hidden, secret pen, or pencil, or crayon. I knew he was there, outside the door, old ears straining for the sound of ink scratching paper.

I flipped each page over, delicately, as though they were made of crystal. I wanted to see if anything had changed since I had last been there. Ketamine's memory would be in there, I just had to find it.

New words were written in red pen, squatting at the end of Love:

*You should get back on your feet at soon as possible.*

It was Tanned's. Page 16. The letters were neat, carefully looped at the tips. He had taken his time. Underneath were bullet points, less neat, written by someone else. 'Don't mourn a break-up for too long', 'It shouldn't take longer than the next ration', 'You leave your house the next day'. Next ration had come, next ration had gone. Fine, I told myself. I would smile and move my lips in sync with words on how everything was fine. Changes weren't unusual. Eventually it would all be perfect. Eventually we would live as we had before.

I closed the book and opened it to a random page.

*Criminals go to prison. They're told how long by a judge. Sometimes they're put to death.*

Page 137. One of the more informative passages, actually telling us something about the outside world, though the information was useless in ours, where no-one ever committed a crime other than what they started with. But these were popular, the ones that didn't mean everyone had to change the way they did something. But what had we done that was so wrong we had to lose our minds?

Our old lives, ourselves. If this was a prison it wasn't like the flat image I had been left with.

I flicked through the next pages with less care, watching the cascade of coloured words crash about one another. Large blue letters called my attention. 'Entertainment'. A few more pages and a smaller heading, again in blue. Songs.

*Songs are a melody, with more than one instrument. Bands play together and make songs.*

I always said songs were more than that: they had words. Another false memory. Really, really I thought they just didn't want their notes sullied by voices. That was understandable.

More sections. 'Bodies', 'Disputes' and 'Food'. Food. I flipped the pages more slowly.

*Food is grown in farms, covered by plastic sheeting, lit by bright bulbs.*

*To be healthy you need protein.*

*MSG and large quantities of caffeine are illegal.*

And there it was. I had never seen her handwriting before.

*Recipes are invented by someone, who gives them to others.*

It was ugly, twisted, angular, each letter built of broken joints. Page 111. There were no bullet points underneath. Instead the words sat above an ocean of black space.

I removed my jumper, which was thick and heavy. I carefully folded it and placed it on the bamboo floor. I lowered myself onto it, my eyes level with the hefty binding and dainty-thin pages of the book. I stared.

I stared until my eyes lost focus.

The book held such a beauty, but it wasn't in the words.

So many people here had poured so much into it. I saw tears hitting pages, hands trembling, shards of old lives crumbled onto paper.

Others would come and feel the soft, rough pages, wishing for memories of their own, to have something of themselves back. Everything that was our old lives was in there.

I stared until the edges were gone.

The book gently glowed.

# a new corner of the world

LIFE HAD SETTLED, all but the brutal tic-tic-tic of forgotten water, seeping through the walls of the compound from outside. A small pool of it gathered beneath the bed, which I would swab and stab at with filthy cloth, sloshing stagnant liquid around. The bad smell returned, the smell of decomposing: I turned the hut inside out trying to find the source. I thought of Tie. Of course I thought of Tie.

Rain had been met by rain, and sand-strained mud gathered at my feet as I walked from hut to courtyard, or hut to fire tap.

The rations had been good this fortnight, they always seemed better when the weather was worse—as though those mysterious providers knew, as though they knew and were trying to compensate. I had crisp breads, and butter, I had curry and milkshake. I had fresh coconut milk and cream-noodles. I cradled the crumpled recipe-paper in my hand, covered in ugly spider lettering. I had Ketamine's instructions, and had saved pasta shells and curry powder from last fortnight, in case I'd have the ingredients to cover one of the recipes. I now did, for the first time.

*boil the pasta shells until soft then sprinkle five pinches of curry powder over the shells then mix them in mix a slosh of coconut milk and a handful of cocoa powder in a bowl until the milk is a rich brown then pour it over the pasta*

It didn't seem correct, but she was the one who would know. I traced my fingertips over the snapped-limb letters, letters which were unfamiliar and not at all like her. Right, it was time to cook, enough thinking. I gathered the ingredients into a clumsy bundle in my arms and made my way to the fire tap.

"Tanned."

"Blondee."

"Nice, look—you're cooking the same thing I'm about to make."

"Ah."

"It looks almost ready," I pointed out. "Are you not eating with Burberry?"

"She was tired. Rain makes her sleepy."

"Right."

For a moment there was silence. "Go on then," I gestured at his food, "try it."

The mud-brown pasta shells glistened as Tanned poured them into a bowl. He handed the pan to me, which spat and sizzled as I poured lukewarm water in. The air was damp and warm, as though it had itself been cooked. Tanned shovelled a mouthful of pasta into his mouth and swallowed quickly, his eyes resting first on me and then on the hard shells I was pouring into the pan.

"Are you not eating more?" I asked.

"It'd be rude. I'll wait for you," he smiled. The pasta boiled over the silence. I felt the paper in my pocket and remembered the book.

"Oh, I saw you wrote down a memory." My voice bubbled with enthusiasm.

Tanned nodded.

"That's a good thing, Tanned."

Tanned shook his head. "It didn't turn out quite how I wanted it. It doesn't matter."

Water still dripped somewhere, but aside from the blobs-and-hisses of cooking it was the only sound until my food was ready.

"Looks done," Tanned offered. I poured it into my own bowl, clutched at my spoon and placed it into my mouth.

Sniggering and then laughter met sweet and sharp and gut-pulling taste, spread over my tongue and down my throat.

"Grogh," I heaved.

"Nice, isn't it?" Tanned laughed through wide teeth.

We both resumed eating. Food couldn't be wasted. It was easier with each mouthful. We had almost finished when Burberry arrived to collect Tanned, muttering and murmuring to him and keeping her eyes off me. She had pulled her dreaded hair back and tied it with plastic-twine. Wet little balls of sweat rolled down from hair to chin. Her skin shone and beads rested on her pouted lips. Once or twice I leaned over gently, trying to gaze down her lightly-woven top without her noticing.

Tanned interrupted my thoughts. He jabbed his finger at his near-empty bowl.

"Either we're just broken and really not meant for the old world, or this," Tanned hesitated, "isn't how people would eat."

"It's how people would eat, really I'm sure of it," I replied.

"Ketamine might be wrong."

"It's how people would eat."

It's how I ate, for the next handful of days. The air did its usual trick of switching violently from hot to light to heavy or cold. Rain and sun battered our world at random. Again my hut was cool and my stomach full—once more I ate one of Ketamine's recipes, which would have to pass quickly over the tongue but which settled satisfyingly on the stomach. Thick. The food always seemed thick.

She was inside me. I told myself that, over and over. Of course that wasn't strictly true, but it was penance. She'd been scared. I couldn't have been angry or scared or betrayed. I'm too old to experience such youthful emotions. Strays of grey light delicately landed on my skin from the window. Colour collapsed to my sides.

The world darkened. She would leave my body again, she would leave my body and once more I would have nothing. From next door floated the familiar ambience of perfume and chatter and music-notes. I leant against the hard concrete edge of the world and closed my eyes until voices and perfume and lights were gone.

*The woman with the dogs was racing, still as stone. The dogs were ahead, front legs suspended in mid-leap, back legs poised. She was behind, charging onwards; fury in her face, her crystal eyes, her blood-red lips.*

The world was black. I could hear an even thud, a thudding from the distance, rhythmic and angry. Thud-thud-thud, pounding through my skull, thud thud thud. I threw off my tattered blankets and charged after it.

The compound was still but my body pulsed, limbs phantom-racing from the dream. The smell of rotting—rotting meat?—was back, and the damp ground had hardened into swirls of frozen mud. I pushed my thoughts down into my feet, paying attention to the contours of the ground against my toes. My soles met patches of slicked-down grass and grit, then the smooth flagstones of the courtyard, where I raised my head and looked around. The moon lazily lit the air as everyone slept.

I followed the thudding. It was coming from the unknown place.

I had never been to the moderate area before—it wasn't even visible from the courtyard. To get there I would have to wander up the embankment which hid their lives from us. Over there they were burdened with privacy.

The embankment was easy enough to climb, the earth crumbling beneath me. At the top I stood and looked around. I could also see some moderate huts now, tattered and misshapen and crude.

I was surprised, though not really sure why: of course they would be inglorious—they had to wait until after us to gather rations. Their food boxes, if they had any, would be crammed with mashed fruit and mouldy-at-the-edge cheese, and potatoes growing insect-like fingers and milkshake from near the bottom of the drum where it was curdled. Perhaps they didn't even have beds, not even crude beds.

I had to see.

The thudding was everywhere, coming from the ground, bouncing through my bones, pounding in my chest.

I half-walked half-slid down the other side of the bank and staggered to the nearest hut. It was darker here than I had ever seen. I trod lightly, my nerves inflamed by mischief. The hut was mostly made of cloth, a few poles holding the fabric up. Was this where Ketamine lived now? I had to see inside. If I was caught it would prove my crime had been more severe than they thought. I would live here, with the moderates, eating mouldy-mushed vegetables.

I ran my fingertips over the cloth. It was damp and rough. I pressed my nose into it, filling my nostrils with earthy smell. There was no stopping. I ran my fingers over it until I found a join, a sort of doorway, and raised it millimetre by millimetre, before peering inside. It was dark, really dark, but I could see furniture silhouettes. Nothing was taller than knee-height. No bed as I could see.

A snort. A snort and heavy breathing and I let go of the fabric, stepping backwards. I turned and made my way back over the mound of earth, over and to the courtyard, back into a lighter world. The sun was coming up and not a single person had seen me. No-one had seen me.

# Casino

Jay was playing a game.

It had seven dice, made of blue-tack.

The rations were spread before us in a barrage of colours. I'd had too much to drink. It had been so long since I'd been drinking. I might have never had a drink before in my life.

Chance and memory had met.

For the first time the rations had included alcohol—that was the chance. Bacardi, Bacardi, Bacardi. Everyone had gathered, gathered and chattered, chattered about what to do. What to do.

A moderate had stepped forward. I'd never seen him before. He said his name was Jay, and that he'd had a memory.

More gathering, more chattering and whispers into ear-hair.

"Let me tell you more about my memory."

"A moment Jay, you must be patient."

"Let me tell you more about my memory."

"A moment Jay, and you can write it in the book."

*People go to casinos, where they play games for money. Alcohol is served.*

Page … page? It was new and written in blue ink.

So Jay's hut had become a casino and he a casinoer—that was his word.

Everyone wanted to play. Everyone had gathered at once, disobeying written rules and rushing to the land of the moderates, desperate to play and drink. Crowds milled about the deformed huts, those better-off not even noticing the ruin surrounding them.

Everyone had gone to the land of the moderates. For that afternoon the rules had been broken. I'd felt cheated. They had robbed me of my transgression, of sneaking in mid-night to this area, of lifting fabric and peering into darkness.

As luck would have it, as chance would have it, that very hut I had found was Jay's hut. That very hut was to be the casino. Everyone had gathered there, stealing my crime.

The least devised a system: everyone would get to play, but only on weeks when there was alcohol. First would go the least, then the minors, and so on and so on.

The crowd dispersed. Everyone had talked. Tanned seemed thoughtful, whilst Burberry smiled and smiled.

Tanned was the first I had spoken to. I had scanned the crowd for familiarity. Of course I'd found him.

"Tanned."

"Blondee."

"Well."

"Indeed."

"What do you think about this? Is this memory real?" I made to poke him in his side, but remembered Burberry.

"It would seem so."

"Do you remember drinking?"

He just looked at me. Of course not. No-one remembered drinking. It would have been in the book. We only had the flat imprint of alcohol. I had seen the bottles, just for a moment. They were grimy and old.

"Blondee," a flash of a smile.

"Burberry."

"Isn't this fantastic?" An arm around Tanned.

"I'm not sure what to make of it. He doesn't seem too enthusiastic." I pointed to her lover.

"He's probably just stunned." Smile smile smile. I couldn't help myself and grinned in return.

"Frederick," I greeted his slender form from behind. He spun to face me.

"Blon—Blondee."

"I was just talking to Tanned and Burberry. They're minors, they live near me."

Silence.

"So what do you think about this, Frederick? I've never seen Jay before."

"He's—he's a nice—he's an attractive guy."

"I suppose," I uttered. Pilsner was a few steps away. "Excuse me a moment, Frederick."

"No problem."

I thought Pilsner hadn't seen me. I stepped behind him. He whirled round to meet my face.

"Blondee."

"Pilsner."

"Marvellous, isn't it?"

"I suppose—well yes, it is. People seem excited about it." I glanced over to Burberry. She was still smiling.

"Well I'll be in there like a shot, don't you worry. This is a turn up for the books."

*A turn-up for the books—miscellaneous phrase. Something went well unexpectedly.*

Page 237. The least knew the book well. They had the most time with it.

"So when will the first session be?" I asked Pilsner.

"Well it'll be soon Blondee, you can be sure of that. It seems that Bacardi has waited long enough." I wasn't even sure what type of alcohol Bacardi was. What types were there?

"Why have we only just had some now? Will we receive more?"

"Oh, I'm sure of that. We must have done something right, Blondee."

The back of Ketamine's head had flashed amongst the throng.

So there we were, Jay and myself and two others. We were strewn about the floor of Jay's canvas tent, a green-blue cloth between us, carrying both rations and game. This was where the Bacardi was served. There was a pile of sick in the corner.

I had felt dizzy and warm but the sensation was evaporating. Jay looked my age (or what I presumed my age to be) and was attractive, as Frederick had said. He had auburn hair, auburn stubble, and well-proportioned features. His shirt was open and every now and then he exposed a flicker of pale nipple. He was also drunk and clearly had been for the past several days.

The other two had introduced themselves: Gut and Green. Gut had a small beard and small round belly. Green had a bigger beard and no belly. I had seen them a few times at the fire tap.

"Bluey, it's your turn." Jay pointed at me, unable to keep his hand still, his eyes rolling. Green glanced at Gut and giggled to himself. "Don' laugh at her," Jay slurred. Both Green and Gut sniggered.

I rolled the dice. 67. I handed them to Green.

"Right, right, now hand 'em, hand 'em over to," Jay paused for a moment, trying to gather a lost name, "hand 'em to him." Green already held them in his open palm.

"I just did, I just handed—" I started.

"Look, don', don't argue just give him the dice."

Green and I looked at one another. I handed him empty air. We both laughed.

"Can I have another drink?" Gut asked, shooting me a stay-away look and motioned to the bottle between Jay's legs.

"You may have one," Jay replied. He sloshed the milky liquid unevenly into chipped mugs and wrapped his lips around the bottle, a trickle dribbling down his neck and over his chest. He placed the bottle to his side and slumped backwards, his eyes closed.

"Are you all right?" Green asked.

"He's not moving."

"Is he breathing?"

At that moment Jay snorted and began breathing deeply.

"I suppose that's it for the day," Green said, peering at Jay's empty expression.

"No point wasting this," Gut uttered, picking up the bottle, which was still a third full.

"Can we?" Green asked.

"I don't see why not," Gut replied, heaving himself up and feeling for the flap of fabric which was the exit.

"Can I have some?" I asked.

Gut sighed and, with an icy look, poured a mouthful into my mug.

"Until next time," Green said. He gathered the rations they had brought into a bag and threw it over his shoulder.

"Let's just go," Gut's voice hissed from outside the hut.

"Bye you two. Green. Gut."

I downed the contents of the mug with a swallow and a shudder. Jay was scratching his cheek vigorously, as though he was trying to remove a mask but couldn't find where it began and his face ended. I pulled myself up, gathered my food into my sack and stepped into the warm air of the evening.

This was my chance to look again. No-one could steal this from me—and if they asked I would say I was drunk. Still, it would be safest to wait, wait until night fell. Day and night, the only recognisable cycle in the world. I clambered back into the tent-hut, amidst heavy air being drawn in and out by Jay's deep breathing. I set down my bag and waited, watching his eyes flicker behind thin skin. Red marks were etched along his jawbone.

I had spent days avoiding the thought of her, her hair, her face when sleeping. Alone and sitting in fading light the thoughts returned, storming into my mind, angry that I had neglected them. I had to distract myself. I leant over the dreaming man, feeling the heureeeeeeur—heureeeeeeur of his breath on my cheek. Already it was stale. I leant back, watching his chest rise and fall, pulling his shirt back a little and examining it more fully. His skin was smooth and near-white, younger than his face. His only hair sprouted in red flecks around his nipples. I slumped to one arm and rested my head on his stomach, listening to the soft gurgle of shit in intestines. The fabric of the hut changed with the light.

What was I going to look for? Was it her? If I saw her I could apologise. In the dark. Uninvited. No, I just wanted to see how she lived, her new-new life. Perhaps I even wanted to explore, to wander these half-formed homes and think about how things would have been had my nose been a little longer, or fingers, or whatever it was which made someone recognisable as a moderate criminal. What had Jay done? I had heard someone mention his crime—moderate … moderate-disruption. That didn't exactly have to change with his new job.

It was dark before I decided it was safe to go. My stomach tensed as I sat up, sharp nails running beneath my skin. They spread up my arm as I pulled my bag over my shoulder, then down over my back. The air outside was colder than it had been, and prickles rode the surface of my body in rough waves.

I headed onwards. The ground scattered and crunched with every kick of a step. It was gravel—how had I not noticed before? It must have spread over this whole corner. Each step felt as though I were crushing a dozen insects, the only noise the scrunch-scrunch sound of my feet. I passed a tree which prodded through and brushed my hair delicately with brittle bones of bark. A metre of so behind the tree was another hut, this one also made with skin-like fabric. I brought my ear close.

Each hut was different—the first two were formed of canvas but the next were of broken chipboard, or sheets of plastic, or any number of furniture left over from rations. Some were silent, some cradled soft voices, others showcased violent rows. Some smelled of the air around them, some of paint, or the sweat of hefty sex.

A sliver of a breeze cut through my clothes, cold fingers working their way around me, shocking and unexpected. The breeze grew quickly, carrying away the heavy air and the smell of myself. I drifted through, a rush and whistle filling my ears. The claw-handed trees swayed a little, chips of gravel skipped about my feet. Everything had been so still and heavy and dead, and now it jigged to life, awakening with a dance. I passed a wire chain fence, criss-crossed into diamond-shapes, the division between the lands of the moderate and the very worst, the land of the severes. I didn't look beyond it.

In the distance was the far wall, the concrete border of the world. A dull ache spread through my head and I placed my hand to it. It felt different, it was smoother here.

Gravel crunched behind me.

I pressed my face to the smooth wall, rubbing my cheek against its bulk, which was always cool, even on this side. I poked out the chilled gravel like a dead tree.

Another crunch.

And again.

And again.

Whoever it was stood behind me, watching my secret embrace. I willed them away.

"Um. Hum. Blondee?"

So I was caught. If I became a moderate would I also no longer be a thief? I'd probably be disruptive instead, this sort of thing would probably—

"Blond—Blondee?"

I kept my face to the wall. "Yes?"

"Blondee," the voice wouldn't go away unless I turned around. I spun to face it.

"Frederick."

"What are you doing here?" Frederick looked confused. Twisted poles of metal dangled from his hands.

"I don't know. I wanted to see what it was like."

"Ah. Oh. I can understand." He looked no different than usual, though his shirt was draped around his shoulders, hair plastered around his chest, lean with the hint of a belly.

I stood and looked at him. He looked away, first up at the wall behind me, then to the sky, then to my right, his left.

"Are you going to tell anyone I was here?"

"No. I don't think so—I don't know why I would." His eyes returned to me. "Do you like coming here?"

I was thrown by the question. Answers darted back and forth, none of them escaping my mouth. I forced one through my lips. "It makes a change."

"Well come with me next time. We can go somewhere else if you like." He stepped forward and pressed me into a hug. He was only the second person whose body I had felt against my own.

He smelled like beetroot.

We left in different directions. All was silent through the moderate corner, as well as at the courtyard. As I got nearer my hut, however, a commotion grew. The rest of the minors were crowded around. People were scattered, in ones and pairs. Why were they at my hut? My skin prickled.

Wait—they were facing away, they faced the hut opposite mine. Burberry and Tanned stood there, hushing words into each other's ears. The same rotted stench filled the air.

"Burberry, Tanned."

"Blondee." They both uttered my name in a half-hush.

"What's happening?"

"Where were you?" Tanned asked.

"At the courtyard. What's happening?"

"The lady in the hut across from yours, she's dead."

"Oh."

So that's what the smell was.

# origin

And what was life like at the start of the world?

Everyone knows that.

I know it better, though, because I knew Tie, and he would have known what the start of the world was really like because he'd been there. He'd given me bits of the story and I've placed them atop the tale everyone knows, building it up, something like that. Making it three-dimensional.

And maybe it's wrong to call it the start of the world. The world was always there, as far as we can know. The walls, the ground with its grit and grass and gravel. The sky. But it was the start of us in the world. When the first of us arrived here.

There was Pilsner. There was Tie. There were two others, whose names are no longer important and who are no longer with us. They awoke in a patch of dry brittle ground on a scorch-hot day. Pilsner was the first awake. He was naked with black writing scrawled down his side. Pilsner. He looked at the others and wondered if he knew them. Why were they naked? One wore a tie around his wrist. Had he hit his head? He didn't remember anything, not anything about himself. He knew what a tree was and he knew rivers and femurs and all about atoms, but not his name, or his age, or who his cock had last been inside. Or whose cock had last been inside him.

And the others woke up.

And the others remembered nothing. They remembered some things and they listed them. They knew of Presidents and parks and agriculture. But they didn't know of any Presidents, or parks, and they didn't remember any particular farms.

They decided to walk, to find cities or leaders or farms. They walked in one direction, a tap here or there, with little logos of fire uncanny and familiar, brushing past the sway of trees and the crunch of the ground, until they hit a wall. They walked in another direction, over tufts of grass and shrubs, until they hit a wall. They walked again, slewing through sand and hot sun until they hit a wall. One last time they passed scattered bricks and a huge pile of rubbish and one final wall.

And they fought.

They fought a lot, about which of them had placed them there, which was a spy, whose fault it was.

Eventually spats and spots of rain petered down and pelted them until they stopped fighting. They had to make a shelter. They found the pile of debris and collected planks, and supports, and corrugated iron. They spent their first night in a makeshift shack.

There were the four of them, Pilsner and Tie and a woman and someone who could have been man or woman and is now lost in time. They huddled together in the shack they had built together and they cried together. They didn't know it, but they were doing for the first time what everyone would do when they first arrived, one by one. They cried for the lives they knew they had lost. Happy or sad, rich or shit-poor, they knew they had lost something. It didn't take them long to realise this was punishment: they had done something wrong and this was punishment. What else could it be, really? Tie had said it, after staring at the wall for hours and hours. Once said it was truth. That was that. This was punishment.

They huddled the night away together, exhausted. They woke up dark and heavy and thirsty, so went to the tap in the centre of the world, to the tap that would give them water. Each had drunk their fill before they noticed the box. It was metal and it was large, taller than each of them, taller than everyone in the world. It had a door and inside, inside they found food and drink and wood and more metal and plastic and tiles and this and that. They ate and drank and laughed. Whatever their crime it can't have been so bad.

When they were full they talked more. What else was there to do? They talked about punishment. What were their crimes? The woman pointed to Tie and told him his was sexual.

"What makes you say that? Why would you say that?"

"I don't know, I honestly don't know, it just feels right."

So his crime was sexual, though no crime was worse than any other, and they set about the rest of themselves. Pilsner's was disruptive, the woman's was violence, and the other's was theft. Those just felt right, but they could find reasons if they tried. Noses, fingers, eyes. Plenty of reasons. No crime was worse than any other, they were all in the same boat, and no-one need feel ashamed, no more than anyone else.

And so they lived and worked together, eating and shitting and crying and sleeping and building. They added bit-bit-bit to their shack, from the pile of treasure they had found and the rations every so-many-days. That was their world and they would live in it together and perhaps it wouldn't be so bad.

They'd found the book and the first memory all on the same day. Clearing away bits of homes and furniture from the pile Pilsner found the book, bound and blue and beautiful. It was full of clean white pages. It was fresh and new, the only fresh and new thing in the whole world.

He took it back to the palace they had made for themselves and the woman and the other stared at it. Oooh. Oooooh. It's so—new. They placed it in the centre of their home and they set about building it a table.

Tie rushed in, full of sweat and panted breath. He had run back. He had run back because he had remembered something. He had a memory, a real memory from the world outside. They listened and they opened a page in the book which felt right, and they wrote the memory down with a shard of pencil.

And every now and then memories would strike them hard about the brain and they would record it in the book. Memories formed around memories and clumped together in sections, written in pen and pencil.

This would help us live our lives. We could live as we did before we slept and forgot everything. We could live properly.

And they tried. That was all you could expect, really, to try.

Rations after rations and rations. Memories here and there, picked out from broken tiles and dirty fabric and plastic and planks of wood. Days were hot and cold, snow and rain fell amongst sun and heat-shivers.

One day there were bodies alongside the rations. They were naked and sleeping.

Why where they there? Six, there were six of them. They lay sweating and sleeping. One was wearing boxers: 'Frederick' across the band. He was so young. Another had a broken watch; one had ginger hair. That one had hair all about his shoulders. Straight away they could tell what they had done—violence, theft, theft, disruption, sexual. But that last one—something about him. Something as he awoke, something in his eyes. What he had done was slightly worse. It must have been worse. Probably not too bad, but worse all the same. It was violence, he had hurt someone. Something about the size of his hands.

They all awoke and cried and were shown the world. The hut was too small to fit ten whole people but there was plenty of wood and plastic. Plenty of metal. So they each built their own. The original hut was for the book.

But that one, the one whose crime was worse, who had hurt someone worse than anyone else had. Perhaps he should live on the other side of the courtyard. It wasn't too far away, after all—they'd still see him every day.

And that was the start of the world.

# part two

It rains. Thunder over the blue tarpaulin. I'm lying down now, staring at the ripples and waves of the plastic. I have mud in my hair. Water flows down into the hole, over my fingers, over my arms.

My eyes prickle with tears, tears of relief. I enjoy the feeling of them welling in my eyes, flooding over my face.

These are the last sensations I will have.

Tomorrow they will belong to someone else.

I think my last thoughts of Frederick. Secret hours together, sheltered from the world. Long and lazy hours.

The rain is falling heavier, the tarp beats like a dream.

Frederick.

# frederick

We explored together, he and I, we explored the land of the moderates. We retraced every step of their gravel-coated land, sneaking and slipping and stopping outside huts to listen to the conversations within. The conversations were simple—happy or angry or sad.

People talked about rations, people talked about if they were having enough sex, people talked about how hot it was today and how cold yesterday. People talked about how cold it was today and how it looked like it would be wet tomorrow.

As they talked Frederick and I would crouch or squat, fingers clasped together, or an arm over the other's shoulder.

One hut was made of actual skin—skin from a large and hairy animal, brown fur with grey splotches, sewn to another skin of another large creature, this one grey with brown splotches. Frederick had seen it before. He held out his arm to present it to me.

I asked him what it was made of.

He didn't know. The skin had been delivered with the rations long ago, but none of the least had wanted it.

"I—I was interested in them, even though I didn't take them—for myself. It was before I was an artist. I waited for a while, but I didn't—no-one left with them, that I saw."

I understood why. It smelled like death. We had enough of that amongst ourselves.

I expected it to be soft, but it was coarse to the touch, bristly, stiff with the weight of age. We heard someone moving inside.

I asked him if it was her. He shook his head.

The next day we found another hut; a pile of soaked, split cushions, furry with mould. It was held up with a series of bars, the large cushions draped over and around them, larger stiffer ones used to form basic walls. No-one lived there, and no-one had wanted the pieces of this failed experiment.

"The—well, you know they—the severes—they would want them, Blondee." Frederick put his arm around me, pulling me toward the crook of his neck.

Were things so bad for them? That they would want these warped and malformed cushions heavy with damp and crawling with insects? It wasn't something I wanted to think about.

"They don't have much, Blondee, they—"

And I kissed him, running my tongue over his lips, clearing away sad thoughts of the worst of us here, those who had committed terrible crimes and now lived terrible lives. I kissed him and he kissed me in return, his tongue meeting mine, dancing, flicking, plunging.

I don't remember who laughed first but we pulled apart, like every time, wiping our mouths. We couldn't kiss one another seriously. We had comfort but no passion. I put my arm around him, pulling his waist toward me.

So where did she live?

He knew where she was. He was hoping I would lose interest, that after a few visits I'd no longer have my strange desire to see the home of Ketamine. It wasn't that he was angry, it really wasn't: Frederick seemed below anger, as though he couldn't reach up for it even if he wanted to. Anger requires expectation, and Frederick seemed to have none of that, not for anything—people or rations or even his artist-pieces.

I told him it was simply something I needed to do, and then it would be over.

So he took me there.

He didn't tell me beforehand. It was evening and we reached a hut made of planks and rubber and he said, in a low-low voice,

"This is it."

I took some steps backwards, tripping over the heels of my feet. I couldn't hear her inside.

"Does it—does it help you, Blondee?" He was curious.

I didn't know.

"It helps," I said, lying about my certainty. "She's in a nice enough place."

She was a voluntary moderate. She had demoted herself, so of course she would be the first on their list, the lesser bad of the moderately bad. She still had less than if she'd remained with me, and I had more than her—but it was no longer my concern.

I wanted to leave her something, something more than a lock of my hair, something powerful, something protective. Something to keep her alive.

I asked Frederick for a moment to myself. He nodded and strolled away, almost beyond sight. I knew he was still watching, but I needed room, not privacy.

I would give her a circle.

Tie had told me that he knew a trick—one that would help me.

I asked if it would help me escape.

He told me it would, in a manner of speaking.

I asked him to show me.

He told me to breathe deeply, evenly, endlessly. He'd taken my hand in his. I'd flinched. He'd waited until my breathing settled into rhythm once more. I'd closed my eyes, the dark patches of colour flickering wildly, then settling, pulsing slowly.

He told me to point my finger.

So I did.

He'd pulled my hand toward the earth, prodding it by proxy, warm and deep. He'd pulled my hand along by the wrist, my finger tearing through the soft ground, on and on, my breathing and heartbeat and mind all steady.

He'd let go and told me to open my eyes.

We were in the middle of a circle, scratched through the dirt. He told me to keep my breathing steady. There was nothing but us and the circle, a tiny, peaceful, silent world. Everything was still. The crowded world was us.

Protection. Tie was gone but he had left me that.

I closed my eyes and kept my breathing even. The world melted. I pushed my finger into the gravel and drew a large circle around Ketamine's new hut, end-to-end. This was for her, this would keep her safe. I could let go.

End-to-end, I pulled my finger out from the ground and I pulled away from her. An arm reached around me. Frederick pressed his nose into my hair.

After the moderates Frederick had taken me over his own land. At first I argued: to go peak at the moderates was one thing, but to spy on the least? That was too much. But he had convinced me in his slow, stuttered way—the least are not so different, he had said.

He was wrong.

First of all, the opulence of the least houses was overwhelming. My mind couldn't comprehend the size—each home was three times larger than the courtyard, with windows and sturdy walls and doors in frames. They were lined with elegance itself: held together with nails rather than rope and glue.

All houses everywhere changed in shape, but there they changed in colour. Some wore pink-and-purple tiles, some were lavished with green paint. Each had a garden, ornaments jutting from the ground and marking a territory. Each garden too was draped in eye-clutching colours: red posts; blue ornaments.

One had pillars on either side of the front door—*front* door, Frederick had told me, there was very often more than one door. There were two small windows on either side of either pillar, glass gleaming in the afternoon sun. Frederick stepped to one of the side walls and pressed his ear to it.

I tugged at his sleeve. We couldn't listen to them, not in these rich homes, surely? But he folded his arms about my waist and we listened. They were quieter, those voices, muffled by their many walls.

Here was the second major difference: like the moderates they talked of rations and weather—but they also talked about the book and they talked far more of their neighbours. Frederick had smiled silently the whole time.

I enjoyed the warmth off his stomach.

Another house was clad in crimson boards and lined with small trees—living trees which were once scattered all over the world, which had been transported to the land of the minors. Frederick told me that this was Pilsner's home, one of the largest, one of the most elegant. We peered in through the window.

It was a palace. I'd had no idea how far it was flung, running backwards and backwards, at minimum the length of fifteen minor huts. In the centre squatted an actual coffee table with four legs. The walls were adorned with torn satin and silk. There were two unbroken mugs and a private water tap, which stood in the very centre of his home, surrounded by a mosaic of colourful chipped tile, proudly wrapped in orange rust. There were chairs, chairs which actually had backs.

I could see one of the mugs read 'World's Best Dad,' though most of the letters were worn. Why did he need two mugs?

"Do you live in a place like this, Frederick?"

He didn't reply.

He would come to my triangle hut, but always after it was dark or a little before the light—he would whisper my name through the fabric of my door, and I would whisper his name in return. Now and then he would enter the hut and we would spend time with our arms wrapped around one another, though that was the full extent of it.

We had spent some days exploring the land of the least before he turned up, a little before light, and said my name. He didn't enter—instead he asked if I wanted to see something truly new.

Of course.

We journeyed out of sight, in and around the backs of huts. He sped slightly, his bare feet kicking soil and sand in small flurries. His feet were burned black on the soles. We wound past more impossibly-large huts before leaving them behind. We came to a tangle of trees and bushes.

We passed through the scratched embrace of red and green leaves, pushing and shoving forward for space, clawed at, branches black against the dim sky. And there was the far wall of the least land. This was their edge, their limit. As I walked toward the wall I felt water curl about my toes, licking my toenails then up to my ankles. I stumbled and fell, a splash as water rippled around my wrists. My arse was wet.

"See."

The water stretched all the way over to the wall. He swept past me, small waves bobbing about his ankles, then shins, thighs, then his knees. I stood up and followed, watching him disappear from the bottom-up, waist then finally chest, up to the armpits.

"What is this?"

"Well, it's water," Frederick replied.

"Where's it coming from?"

"There's a pipe. Down there. It's not big enough to fit through."

"Can you drink it?"

"Would you want to try?"

I glanced behind.

"Don't worry—it's all fine—no-one ever comes here. And no, I don't—I just don't know why."

I swept my arms from side to side, enjoying the feeling of wet waves about my limbs, heavy in my clothes, spinning and feeling the slow movements of my liquid body. The water spread out through the fading light, an endless ocean wide and long. Frederick splashed his way back to land.

The water had a scent, a scent I couldn't place, one which crawled into my nose and stung my sinuses. I had smelled it before my death sleep, I knew that much. Frederick didn't seem to notice. He crouched with his back to me, examining the stone-scattered ground by the water. I waded over and knelt next to him, my knee scraping shards of rock.

"What is it?"

Sprigs of plants were sprawled and played between his fingers. They were red and green and tiny. I moved away and brought myself to the ground, kicking at the water with my toes.

"How many memories have you had, Frederick?"

"Well. I don't know."

"You remembered art."

"I did."

"Did you remember anything else?"

"A few things," he paused as he turned around, still crouching. He leaned his face into mine. I felt each word against my cheek. "I remembered having four meals a day. I remembered people have their hair cut evenly on all sides. I remembered sayings, like 'Any old iron' and 'Don't eat yellow snow'. I remembered sex, having sex when you broke up with someone—to say goodbye."

The last one stung. I slung a scatter of small stones over the water.

Frederick moved his head into my lap. I placed a pebble on his forehead.

"Did it all make it into the book?"

"What do you mean?"

"Did everything you remembered make it into the book?"

"Why wouldn't it?"

I didn't answer. I took the pebble from his face and flung it into the water. *Chlorine.* Where was that word from?

# purple

THE LIGHT WAS STRANGE from the moment the sun rose. It was a heavy bruised colour. I let in a sliver through the curtains. He lay half-dozing, half-awake, propped up against the wall as though it would collapse without him. Now and then he would snort or murmur, his arm resting gently against mine. The window was battered with heavy-falling droplets, falling in short bursts, tinny shots from the sky. I lay half-dozing, half-awake, one foot in the triangle home and the other somewhere else.

We were both slumped over stickly linoleum. I was careful not to place my hands upon the floor, instead resting one on Frederick's thigh, the other on my own. Sleep was edging away from me, being absorbed by him, into his young body which was clad in well-sewn green cotton. His breathing grew deeper and heavier as he drew more sleep from me, sucking it in through his mouth and nostrils. Perhaps if he took too much he would sleep forever, and I would be stuck with the weight of a young man on my lino. Perhaps I would have to feed him, move his mouth to chew for him, clean up after him when it came out again...

He opened his eyes and for a moment they rested on me, before slipping back behind half-closed lids. I ran a finger through his hair then pressed my weight on his thigh to push myself up. He gave a hollow grunt and leant forward, before leaning back into sleep.

I had slept with no memories. The days were flowing into one another so quickly and smoothly that I thought very little of the stone woman and her stern grimace. What did I even need memories for?

I went to make breakfast, pulling the plastic tray from under my bed. It was nearly empty—a dice-size block or two of bouillon-butter, slices of green-mottled cheese, firm rye bread, rice. There was little point in preparation and so I piled bread, butter and cheese into my mouth, forcing it down my throat, dry and unsatisfying.

"Blondee." Tanned's voice called through the doorway. He wouldn't be able to see Frederick, no-one had seen me spending all this time with Frederick. They would have said we were lovers, but we weren't fucking. We were physical, sure enough, but any caress was with arms, torsos, even legs: nothing below the waist, nothing above the thigh. The curtains were ever closed.

"Blondee."

I swallowed as quickly as I could. Frederick didn't stir.

"Tanned. I'm coming."

"You'd better," his voice sounded unnatural.

I stepped outside, the light grazing my eyes. Outside it was more vibrant: even the heat it gave was purple. It felt purple. The dusty grass was tinged with it, the wall was a gentle lilac, our skins dark.

"Did you ever see the sky like this?" I asked.

"I just felt like seeing you."

"No you didn't."

"I need to talk."

"Is it about Burberry?" I often imagined them as twins.

Tanned didn't respond, instead looking upwards, his eyes glinting an alien colour.

"So what's up with her?" I tried, "With you and her?"

With false reluctance he answered.

In all fairness I tried to concentrate. I tried to force my mind to focus. Tanned and Burberry fought, more often these days than ever, and the fights were usually the same and they were usually banal. Maybe it was just the way couples were, or maybe they really didn't get along and stayed together so as not to stand out in a world of partners. That was understandable.

"So what did she say?"

And Tanned talked about how she had been unreasonable and how he had tried to talk to her and how she would never really understand. And I nodded because it was friendly and fought the urge to glance back at the triangle hut.

Tanned told me how she had thrown old milk over him.

I wasn't unsympathetic, I felt for him. I could deal with the emotion but not the details. They were too familiar. I waited until he had finished talking and placed two of my fingers on his hand, as many as I could get away with. It was some restrained attempt at comfort.

"Talk to her."

"I will."

"You two will work things out."

"We will."

"Don't forget, you can always talk to me, if you need to."

*Talk to your partner about your problems.*

Code of love. Page 18.

*Problems can always be sorted out, don't give up on your love.*

Code of. Page 18.

*Don't forget, talk to Blondee, go to Blondee for sympathy.*

The last one wasn't in there. I meant it though. I waited until Tanned had disappeared behind the hut of the old-dead-woman before I returned to my own. Inside Frederick had slumped over, his beard stuck to the lino.

For the first time I ate cake. It was mostly icing, piled thick and creamy atop crumble-dry bread. Frederick had given it to me. He awoke and we ate it together: the sky was purple—that was surely a special enough reason to eat such a delicacy. We ate it quietly. I ran my fingers through the icing, piling fluffy clouds on my fingertips and licking them away.

"Blondee." A voice at the door.

"Tanned, you're back already?"

"It's Pilsner."

"Oh, sorry. Pilsner," I responded. Frederick gave a look of panic and tried to cover himself with one of my blankets. "I'll be out now," I called.

Outside the light was dimmer, less brilliant.

"What do you make of this then? I've seen nothing like it, not since the world began." Pilsner's voice was flat as ever.

"It's pretty."

"Well some think it means something. They're gathered now in the courtyard."

"You're not there."

"I don't think it means much, not really." There was a pause before Pilsner resumed pressing words through dry cracked lips. "Haven't seen you around there much. Not lately."

"I've been feeling private lately."

"Right. And have you seen anything of young Frederick? He also seems to have been feeling private."

His eyes darted toward the closed curtains of my triangle hut. In the purple light his face looked blue. Few muscles in his face ever seemed to move and right then he looked like a corpse. I wanted to get away from him.

He spoke first.

"I'll see you later."

I watched him stumble away, looking older than I had ever seen him.

Once Frederick had left I made my way to the courtyard. People were still clumped around, but any real conversation had drifted away with the purple light. Now the sky was a normal black-blue. Burberry was stood toward the edge, a cold stare at the mass of muttering people.

"Burberry."

"They were talking for hours," Burberry uttered, her voice soft and distant, her gaze fixed on the courtyard. I was thrown by her missing my name.

"Er, they were?"

Burberry nodded slowly.

"Are you all right?" It seemed everyone was acting oddly.

"I'm fine. The usual. Things have just been difficult. He'll have told you, I know he will."

"So what were they talking about?" I asked, ignoring the issue and gesturing to the mass of people.

This is what I learned: they had talked for hours, an excitable minor had babbled about the world entering a new phase, the purple light brought change.

'Shut up,' someone had said, over and over.

Most agreed it was strange.

Some had spent the day scouring the sky. Perhaps there had been some sort of sky explosion.

'Shut up,' someone had said, again and again.

Back and forth, back and forth, and the sky had begun to dim.

'Perhaps it's an illusion.'

One last 'shut up' and then there was no more. The sky went dark, the purple had gone and that was that. Slowly people had dropped away until there were only one or two people milling around the courtyard.

We stood there side-by-side, until Burberry left without a word.

# the first rations

Frederick had been building. Frederick had been building a building. Frederick's building was in the middle of his hut, which I now stood in for the first time.

The hut was large, though not quite as large as Pilsner's had been, and grand, though not quite as grand as Pilsner's. It was colourful, and the mosaic of the outside climbed through the windows and over the walls, jagged and bright. It was covered in bright shards of plastic, a clutter of landfill-spares. Furniture seemed to jut out the floor, as a part of the floor, and the windows were small—the whole place felt like a carefully constructed cave. I perched upon a silver stool.

"Your hut ..." I searched for something to say, yet he stood there ignoring my new experience.

"So, well, this is what I've been working on," Frederick gestured to the small plastic bricks piled atop one another.

They were arranged in columns: red, green, white. The columns were piled atop more columns, and tapered, more columns on more columns further up, until it reached knee-height.

It was a tower, of the flat and two-dimensional type I could conjure up in memory. An empty tower. I didn't understand it.

"Are you going to say anything?"

"Your hut—"

"About the work."

"It's—"

"It's actually unfinished, unfinished right now that is. There'll be more surrounding it," he waved his arms over it, a colossus towering over his creation, "it'll be a whole city, just wait, just wait." He stood panting and pulled off his shirt, then his trousers, his chest and legs shiny with sweat, before regaining his breath. I moved my face closer to the bricks.

"Where did you find these? Were they with the rations?"

"No, no, I found them near the place where the severes live, they were mostly buried, in this red box."

I stared at him. No-one had ever just *found* anything, not since the very first days. The shards of mirror around the small window behind him glinted, a shaft of light falling into my eyes.

I turned to face the door as it rapped three times. Bang. Bang-bang. I stood motionless as Frederick stepped over and opened it, but no-one was there.

Are there ghosts? I imagine there are ghosts. Flat white blobs with three black holes for a face. Where do we go when we drop dead? I don't know what anyone believes outside, but I know that out there, when someone dies, they do the same as we do. The old woman in the hut opposite mine was buried near the courtyard. Now there are fifty graves. Fifty graves and a hundred people. You just drop dead, no-one talks about it.

Tie is there.

A long time ago I'd asked Tie if I would meet someone.

As I had asked the question I laid back, my head balanced on a stone. It had been cold and wet and even snowy for the few days before—there was still a firm chill to the air.

He told me I already knew the answer: of course I would.

I thought on it for a moment. A speck of rain landed on my forehead. I hadn't wanted the conversation to end. It was long and comfortable.

I asked him if he had ever met anyone.

There was a pause. He told me that there was someone once, but that it was rushed and thoughtless. Then, in the morning—

He stopped and drew in his breath, heavy and wavering.

I asked him what happened.

Four beats and an answer.

He said they didn't want to see him after that. Not like that.

I'd asked him who it was.

But he didn't answer. I was afraid his face would crumple and his body collapse and all that would be left would be heavy sobs and I wouldn't be able to stretch him out again.

I told him I was going to meet Tanned at the courtyard later. And his partner, though I admitted I didn't remember her name.

He knew: Burberry. He'd known all the names. He'd known how everything worked. And he still brought me rations, right until it was time for me to collect my own.

And really, my very first trip for rations was intense. So intense my head throbbed and throbbed as though it would burst, bits of brain bouncing off the hot ground and bubbling in the light. It had been the hottest day I had ever known, and so many people wore bare skin, backs and arms and armpits exposed to the sun. Tie was different. He wore the same thick, heavy clothes he wore every day, the stench of sweat just slightly sharper.

Tie told me I was going to see a lot of people and hear a lot of things very quickly—that it's the fastest thing that ever happens, getting rations, except while you're waiting.

And I had nodded and tried to take in the blurry flurry of words.

He told me I'd get enough food to get by, if I just listened carefully to how much there was and how much I was allowed.

He explained carbohydrate, and protein, and everything else, and I nodded as my skin prickled.

It was the hardest thing I ever had to do and I would mess it up. Then what would happen? I nodded and nodded and nodded as he finished talking and suddenly we were in a mass of people, surrounded by bodies; chatter on all sides, a heady swirl of skin.

And then it was there. I had lost focus and it was there, in front of us all, as though the huge metal box had always been there.

Tie waited with me as lines were rationed out, as commands were rationed out and there was order. I had never seen order before. I stood watching, not daring say a word in case it was wrong. Eventually I was at the front, by the box, a stern-faced man opening and closing his mouth, four of this, five of that. I looked at Tie, panic wrapped around my body. He stepped toward Stern-Face and they whispered back and forth, and he motioned us inside.

Tie told me he was allowed in with me, to show me how it all worked. He'd pointed to vegetables and sugar and sacks of chips. He'd told me how many of each I could have and helped me choose each one, carefully placing them into bags with his big soft hands. With a small grin he'd even stolen a grape and held it to me, a small purple ball surrounded by fat fingers. I placed it on my tongue and slowly sucked away the skin, before tasting the pulpy flesh inside.

Clutching the half-filled bags we stepped back into the sunlight, shielding our eyes for a moment before pacing forward, away from the courtyard.

Once we'd returned to the shade outside my triangle home he'd informed me that I'd have to remember it all for next time.

I asked him why he couldn't come in with me every time.

He shook his head and told me we weren't in love.

And I'd laughed, perhaps cruelly, and asked him why ever did we need to be in love?

And he'd said you find a person, someone you love, and you stick with them. You love them. You live with them and you do everything together. You get the rations together.

I laughed again, less sure this time, and in a voice far too small for his huge frame, he spoke.

It's in the book, you'll see it soon enough.

Clack—clack—clack.

I pulled my eyes open. It was dark, save for tiny flickers of fire dotted about the room. The room was huge. I was sleeping in Frederick's bed: immense and comfortable. Frederick was placing more blocks atop one another, each brick clacking atop the last. A candle spat, mimicking the sound.

"Frederick."

"You're awake." He seemed excited. He was still wearing nothing but rough-stitched underwear.

"Did I sleep long?"

"Mmm," he grunted, his voice thick with ambiguity. "Come look."

I stumbled over to the bricks. There were two and a half towers now, at right angles to one another.

I still couldn't understand what he was trying to do.

# lost apples

I LOST AN APPLE, one of six.

I tried to focus on the game we were playing, keeping my eyes on my cards.

"He left me," her voice was low as the ground and sticky as the air.

I felt her misery infect me, seeping into my pores at every moment, little by little, filling me with an emotion which spilled from her without control. When we had finished placing our bets—near-fresh fruit and firm vegetables—her arm rested against mine. She didn't move it. Her skin was cold and smooth and I couldn't tell her scent from the sweet mash of rations in between us all and the scent of vodka and sweat which seemed to stick like beads to every surface. I felt dizzy. I leant into her. The noise of the new casino surrounded us.

The day before had been a rations day, cool and clear and dry. I went by myself, scanning the crowd as always for familiarity. There had been an excited clamour. When I saw Jay at the centre of the courtyard I'd realised what it was: there was booze again. The word was carried across the crowd. *Vodka.* I liked the way that sounded. I mouthed each syllable. Vod-ka. It was satisfying. I'd imagined it being thick and dark, a heavy heady liquor. Perhaps I would even win some extra rations, when Jay opened his casino again.

When it was my turn in the box my mind had been far from food. I thought of vodka and giant oceans at the edge of the world. I moved my hands and picked the food at random, carbohydrates and proteins and vegetables. There were a lot of apples, bruised and red. My fingers fell on waxy soft skin. I took three. No, I would take six, I'd reasoned, I would gamble them. Who doesn't like apples? There was no furniture this time. I collected thick milkshake and whispered to myself. Vodka. Vodka.

I lost an apple, one of five.

"I begged him, all throughout the breaking-up sex."

I watched Burberry with half my focus. She seemed deflated, as though someone had punched her in the stomach, knocking all the life from her, spilling it out her mouth and nostrils. I wanted to say something, something to ease whatever she was going through. I wanted to see Tanned, but I didn't dare ask where he was.

Instead I looked around the new casino. It was incredible. Not as grand or opulent as the huts of the least, but there were fragments of luxury, pieces of splendour, as well as modest furniture, dark and simple, and cheap rags scattered about the floor. It was as though all corners of our world had collided together to make this place, a little piece of everywhere. There were finely ornate mirrors, curved carvings caressing the glass. There were sturdy tables which already bore the scars of spilled drinks. There were dishcloths scattered about, some soiled some maybe-clean, all lit by a dim lamp. There was no sign of a home there though, and Jay stood as one of the accessories, and probably slept where he stood, filled with enough booze to make the days and night haze together. He was, of course, already drunk, and the game had begun around him. No-one had lost the ability to play.

Pilsner had been at the courtyard when I came out of the box, rations in hand. He hadn't smiled or greeted me.

"The new casino will be there. Just by that mound." He'd pointed to the embankment which led to the land of the moderates. "Can't have people trampling all over the wrong area."

"Are you looking forward to it again?"

"As much."

There was a silence between us—he hadn't been interested in talking, he just wanted to impart information.

"It's your turn with the book soon enough. No new memories today then?" He'd flashed a cruel smile. A nearby couple chatted noisily.

I'd turned and gone back to my hut, my leaden bags banging against my legs.

I lost an apple, one of four.

"I begged him not to go. We had our problems, true, but I begged him not to go."

A flurry of cards and another drink of vodka. Murmurs turned to laughter and we went unnoticed, balanced at the edge of the group. She pressed her arm harder to mine. I sipped at the drink clutched firm in my fingers, a taste more raw and bitter as any I'd ever splashed over my tongue.

The new tent had appeared as soon as the rations box was gone. This was the new casino; this was Jay's new home. I'd listened to the talk of couples as they stalked by. 'Look at it.' 'Look at it.' 'When's our turn? Did you hear yet?' 'He gets all the luck, that one.'

Did luck and casinos not go together?

They commented on its form, big and bulky, 'It even hides that mound', 'What mound?' 'The one that leads—well, you know, over there'. 'It's a strange colour.'

Well, that was true. I had never seen orange canvas before.

It squatted only a few metres from the courtyard. Once or twice I had seen Jay carrying bottles back and forth, dipping in and out of his new sun-coloured home, and I had waved. He had waved back, gently and carefully, the wave of someone who didn't exactly recognise who it was he was waving to.

I'd stayed at the courtyard that evening and kept my ears open. Least couples strode pair by pair into the orange mouth, held open by Jay, who was already swaying a little. I'd watched for Frederick and I'd watched for Pilsner, but neither Pilsner's slight-hunched build nor Frederick's careless form had made their way near.

I lost an apple, one of three.

"I'd wanted someone else," Burberry muttered.

And there was no game, no game which we were playing, the others were there, vying over our rations and my hands would move and press cards face-down as the pile in the middle grew into several uneven lumps.

I stared at her, trying to read her body for information. She felt me, I was sure of it, but I didn't stop. There was only her and the dice and mugs, the glug of the vodka being portioned. At first I'd thought it was water. It reminded me of the chlorine-pool. I felt the fraying orange-purple-gold edges of my top.

That morning I'd stitched together some of the spare fabric from the edges of my curtains, lining my shirt with colour. My home had smelt only of my own sweat, a thought which spread the dull ache of loneliness through my stomach. I'd knelt by my bed and inhaled, hoping for the earthy-beetroot scent left behind by Frederick's body, but there'd been nothing. I'd decided to do the rest of my sewing outdoors. I still hadn't heard from him. Perhaps he was making buildings.

It was almost dark and I had just placed the needle on the stone before me. I was admiring my jagged work as Burberry appeared. She was wearing shorts I had never seen before, hanging beneath her best shirt.

"You're going tonight, then?" I asked.

"I am." Her voice had been heavy. I hadn't asked where Tanned was. She leant over, neck resting on my shoulder. "Wow, Blondee, that's wonderful. I didn't know you could sew anything."

"I can't, but as long as it stays on for tonight."

It was Ketamine who had taught me to sew after she had watched Rings at work. It had been a long time since I had seen either Ketamine or the jagged shards of her recipes. She had slipped into memory like a dream.

"You'll look great," she'd said.

We'd left for the casino together.

I lost an apple, one of two.

"I said I wanted both of you, Blondee. I did. I wanted you. I'd heard the rumours, I heard them from Ketamine herself—you loved more than one person. It's possible for you. What if it's possible for me? That's what I told him."

And with her words falling softly into my ear the room fell silent and mouths pressed words through booze-dripped lips and cups chinked and dice rumbled but all inaudible.

There were only her words, and her skin—and her leg pressing into mine.

I didn't tell her that nothing was deliberate, that I wasn't even sure how I'd felt. I didn't tell her because I rarely told anyone anything—there had always been other people to do that for me.

My last apple vanished into one of the larger piles. I dropped my cards. The distraction was gone. I turned to face her, to see her staring at me.

"He left. He called me all sorts of things. I hate him." She looked thoughtful. "I think it's really sad that you can hate more than one person but not love more than one person."

I turned the words over in my mind as her lips met mine, full and thick and heavy. Her hands grasped at my arms as she pressed her body into me, her tongue further into my mouth. I ran my hand over her back, unsure of what to do.

Sound returned to the room
a flurry of gasps
and whispers
and a cheer.

I pulled my lips from hers, twenty faces watching us, some surprised and shocked, some looking to others to see what the fuss was all about. Somewhere I heard a voice, 'They broke up this afternoon,' and there were more grunts and hushes which fizzled all about us.

"If you want another drink, just give me your cup," Jay called to all from somewhere unseen.

And her words echoed through my head as she took my hand and led me from the moist grasp of the casino-tent. Hand-in-hand we wandered to my triangle home, where I lit a small candle and she watched me, until she spoke, as softly as she had amongst the clatter of dice and cards and drinks and gossip.

"He said you only love one person. Just one at a time. It's not true, Blondee, it's not true, I swear. I love you, Blondee—I have for ages. And I love—or loved—I love Tanned." Her words were soft but they were quick, and brushed over me like shreds of velvet. "It doesn't matter what it says in the book. We don't know that's right, *he* doesn't know that's right—perhaps some people do love two, or even three people, on the outside. He knew how I felt about you. He said that I should stay away from you and it would go away. That it was a crush and it would go away. But it didn't, over all this time it just never went. And I wanted to see you but he said I shouldn't."

She leant forward and kissed me again. I tried to untangle her words, to make sense of them as they still scattered about the air. She pulled back and continued.

"He told me to leave. He just told me to leave."

And I reached over and pulled her to me. Her head rested on my breast and I felt her. It was more than despair, it was a desperate mix of despair and desire that had built in her and flowed into me. She kissed me again, and this time there was no interruption, just a phrase which stuck to my mind:

*You love one person.*

And it was so early on in the book that it hardly mattered now.

# confess

THE NIGHT AT THE CASINO WAS OVER. Daylight clawed through the window. Our corner was vacant, a mass of bodies sleeping away the drink and dice and the dizzying air. It was cold and I was frozen, waiting for them to wake up and begin talking, tongues lashing tales of Burberry and Blondee, who had pressed their lips together and ran away, away into the emptiness of the night. The news would thaw and feed drip-drip-drip, until it built and welled, it would flood across our corner and over into the rest of the world, flowing over Tanned, flowing over Frederick. What explanation did I have? She loved me, and she loved Tanned, and doing so she had broken the rules of the world. There she lay, sleeping next to me. Grief and pleasure both infected her dreams and both made me lie back down and hold her.

The world would have to wait.

We were both naked, our skin smooth against rough blankets. Her breath was light and even, lightly stale, her arm slung beneath my neck. I ran my fingertips over her, from her face down the dark sweep of her neck, down further, down over her breasts, lightly over the soft circle of nipple, from there to her stomach, over the furry trail from her stomach to her tangle of pubic hair, through its coarseness, over the warmth of her—she mumbled and moved, turning over onto her front, pulling her arm free. I ran my fingers over the mount of her buttocks, down the back of her thigh, the light fuzz of her calf, to her ankle.

Did I think? I must have thought. I must have thought of her, not only of her skin but her heartbreak, her pain, its intermingling with her desire for me. Love. Did she feel love—or hard, driving, exhaustible lust? She had abandoned Tanned for me, however unwillingly. I wouldn't want her to regret that.

And how did I feel about her? She had always been an accessory to Tanned, an extra, an adornment—one which needed the other to function. But I wanted her. My body wanted her.

I don't believe I really thought of Tanned. At that moment he will have been intangible, a theory—unreal in the presence of Burberry's bare skin.

I will have thought of Frederick. If Frederick was unhappy that would be a problem—I needed his soft skin and simple thoughts. To hurt or anger him, to turn warm embraces cold—that would be too painful.

In truth, however, I don't really remember if I thought at all. I simply remember the dream of her, in the dusky light filtered through the curtains.

She slept, so I slept.

The tring of notes bounced about my hut. The little music player was on, knocking me awake.

"Blondee." Burberry was smiling. I sat up.

"You were asleep," she explained. "I still have some rations left—would you like some?"

We ate together.

We talked quickly.

She would move in, as was the way—she would move in before the day ended. I agreed: I was glad of someone to share the space. Now and then she would heavy-sigh for Tanned, she would light-sigh for me and I enjoyed her, savouring every taste and smell and sigh. Suddenly she had appeared, right there in my hut, as though she had always been there. I had let her speak, telling me of her now-ex, of how they had fought and he was gone, to another part of our corner. She asked me about Ketamine, how I could bear her leaving, and the thought of never touching her again. I found Ketamine's shirt crumple-balled beneath the bed and showed it to her. She drifted back into talk of Tanned and then on to how much she liked the triangle-hut.

Eventually I had to take my turn, to tell her about Frederick. I told her quickly, tripping over my own words.

"Oh. I didn't realise." She fixed her eyes on me.

"Well, we're not lovers, not really, we just ..." I let my voice drift away. There wasn't any way of finishing the sentence. What should I tell her? That he would come to my hut and I would draw him to me—enjoying him as I had enjoyed her—that there was no sex? I did my best. That was all I could expect from myself.

For a moment she drifted too, lost in thought, before reaching a resolution.

"Well, you should still see him. I meant what I said last night."

"I suppose so," I replied, but her voice was firm: there wasn't any arguing with that, had I even wanted to. I thought of Ketamine and saw her body with Burberry's head—then one half of Tie and the other of Frederick. Perhaps they had all been lovers, sex or no.

As Burberry went to gather her things I made my way to the courtyard. Somehow chunks of old pipes had snaked their way over the patches of grass and I hopped over each one, glad to keep my mind free. The pipes were thick and orange with rust, as though they had scattered from the large tent which edged into sight, itself sleeping away the day, a large orange tongue idly drifting back and forth.

The courtyard was empty. I knew where to find Frederick.

I made my way to the least-corner, walking behind bushes and slopes and keeping myself from sight. I passed right by Frederick's hut—he wouldn't be there. I headed for the very corner: to the giant lake which no-one ever saw.

The stench of chlorine hit me before the vision of the pool. I staggered through a maze of shrubbery and trees, pushing aside each one, each branch bringing doubt, each bramble scratching new fears: was this it? Was telling the truth an act of ending? It had been for Burberry. The truth had torn her and Tanned apart. Torn them apart and slung each piece into opposite directions. She had landed in my triangle, but where was he? If the truth did the same to me and Frederick, where would I land? And him? I ducked under an arm of bark, breathing heavy, the loss of Frederick beating down on me: warm touches frozen cold.

I stepped free of the leaves and faced the pool. He floated in the centre, his eyes trained on the sky, sky mirrored all around him, framed by the lake. All around the sun glittered, water blue and burning in the sun. His skin shone. My heart beat close to bursting: to watch him was delight, the tension unbearable.

I loved him.

I love him.

I love you Frederick, was what I wanted to shout, but instead I watched him in the water, gently floating toward me and away, bobbing without direction. He floated among the clouds, his skin shimmering.

He saw me—I was caught in the corner of his eye.

"Blondee," he called, plunging his feet through the clouds, to the bottom of the sky, before wading toward me.

"Frederick."

"You came all the way over here? You should have waited for me."

"I wanted to see you, I wanted—"

I let my voice trail away. And what was I to tell him? That I had been seduced by someone wrapped in misery, that I had enjoyed it? That I had enjoyed her as I had enjoyed him: but that we had actually had sex? That I had tasted her?

Frederick kicked himself free of the water and spoke, wary, his eyes turned to the ground.

"You're with Burberry?"

The world was small enough for him to hear. Gasps and moans sunk into curious ears, passed on and on by thoughtless tongues. Of course he had heard.

"Yes," I replied. I was. What could come next? I waited for him to shout or leave. He didn't do either. He rolled back his shoulders, shaking himself free of spare droplets, shaking words from his lips.

"I'd still—I would still really, really like to see you."

He pulled me toward himself.

My thoughts flooded with the book. I wondered if anyone in all the world really read it, really believed in how things should be. I wondered if anyone in the world wanted to get back to where we had been before, before we were thrown here.

"I'd like that too," is what I said back, my nose filled with his beetroot-scent.

And that was that, quick as anything. I had two lovers. By the time I returned it was dark, and my hut already bustled with Burberry's things.

# the real city

THE SKY WAS PURPLE AGAIN, but this time no-one said a word: the sky must just do that once-a-while. The open spaces of our world were crawling with people, all basking in the strange—but probably normal—light.

The courtyard was no exception. Busy strangers made their way to the tap, over and over again, filling bucket after bucket until it ran dry. Then they would come back every hour or every few minutes, to see if there was more water, an excuse to enjoy the purple day. Pilsner stood as solid guardian of the water tap, formally informing them of its status, a gruff 'still dry' to appease them. I sat opposite him.

"I wish they would leave this thing alone," Pilsner uttered, his face to the sky.

He coughed and leant against the black metal of the faucet, ready to resume his guard and return to his two words. Still dry. Still dry. I decided to stop him: anything would be better than that unceasing repetition.

"How are things with you, Pilsner?"

"It's best not to pry into others' affairs, Blondee."

*Do not pry into others' affairs.*

Near 'home is your castle', which I read last time I was with the book. They were both on page 125.

"I'm sorry," I replied, "I didn't mean to, well, to pry."

The word just didn't seem to fit. To pry. I thought of yanking Pilsner open with a crowbar, prying him open, prying ribs and secrets all over the flagstones beneath us.

"Well, if you need know, I've been well, thank you. Enjoying time by myself."

Enjoying time by himself? He had never really enjoyed time by himself—it was why he had always near-lived right there in the courtyard.

Perhaps he had changed. The world hadn't existed long enough to find that out. Perhaps people could change without as much as a warning. After all, we had all changed; we were different people before we were here.

"Good, it's good to enjoy time by yourself," was all I could summon as a reply. It was what we had had in common, our hatred of being alone, and now he had changed.

"Is it?" He shot the words forward, facing me, thinning hair clutching his scalp.

"I presume so." I didn't know what else he expected me to say.

It wasn't the right answer—it couldn't have been the right answer, as he went back to his guard. The only words which left his lips for the rest of the afternoon were 'still dry'. Still dry, still dry, still dry.

He was unhappy, but he, so I believed, simply needed an excuse: anger was the easiest emotion to deal with—anger wouldn't lead to your own death. He'd been angry, in fact, ever since he'd started asking about me and Frederick. Something was hidden. Secrets pried from a chest.

I had enough of the courtyard and headed back to the triangle hut I now shared with Burberry.

It was empty but the sweet smell of her body lingered. I made my way to the fire tap, a thin whistle of wind goading me on.

I saw my next-door neighbour, as ever dripping with perfume.

"You're the one with that pretty dread-locked woman. I'm Fluffed."

He lived right next to my triangle hut, right next to it, and this was the first time I had ever spoken to him. His own hut was made of broken bricks piled over rocks, all bound together with clay.

"Blondee," I introduced myself.

"Right, your hair."

"Why Fluffed?" It was an insultingly intimate question but it had been a strange day. I tried to subtly cover my nose, to shield it from the smell.

He laughed. "My hair too. Was big and fluffy. Even my chest hair was kinda fluffed. So we're both named after hair. Nice." He looked excitable, his eyes shimmering, his expression playful. I didn't know what to say and the perfume was starting to burn my nostrils. I made my way onwards.

Burberry was framed in dying purple light, her rich-brown clothes and pale skin soaking up the colour: her skin was bleached lilac, her clothes a deep violet. She had decided to cook, to cook one of Ketamine's recipes. I smelled the stomach-flipping combinations of thick-sweet and bitter, sugar and sour.

All of a sudden I wanted to talk to Tanned, who would laugh at the lists in the spidery-writing. But I hadn't seen him. He had changed too. I felt my whole body tighten. I pushed him from my mind and stepped toward the hot, heavy film of cooking.

"Burberry."

"Blondee." She sounded frustrated.

I stood just behind her, feeling ropes of her hair catch against my face, tossed about by the breeze.

She moved backward, her arse against my hip. I peered round her and saw her problem—the wind was causing flames to lick at the air, wild and aggressive.

"It's slow going I'm afraid."

The stodge of food which had burnt black and crumbled around the edges. Crystals of salt and sugar caught the dim light.

"It's good to see you," Burberry whispered, turning to face me and brushing her lips against my cheek.

"You too," I answered.

We returned to the hut and ate until it was dark. She slept facing the wall. The heavy mass of food clutched at my stomach as those recipes always did, though this time I swear I could feel each individual crystal of sugar and salt crawling around my gut. At first I worked my arm over her and pulled her body to me, which she met with a sigh, but soon our bodies huddled together became damp and wet. It was too hot. I turned round, pulled on a roughly-sewn shirt and stepped through the fabric into the night.

The world was smothered in darkness. I fumbled back into the hut to find a candle and matches, each clang and clatter of upturned boxes and scattered clothes prompting 'mmm's and 'raummm's and sighs from Burberry. At last I found them and waited until I stood outside before lighting it, shielding the tiny flame from the breeze with my body. Through the whistle and whine of wind I heard a noise I had forgotten.

Thud thud thud.

It might have been faint but it was heavy and metallic, distant, dull and dawdling through the darkness toward me. Somehow it didn't belong in my life right now. It belonged to when I was lonely and scared and hungry. My heart stopped as I felt it beat into me, a heavy rhythm, thud thud thud, each faint knock digging into me, spreading anxiety through my limbs. I had to move.

It felt like a long time since I had last wandered through the night by myself. The world felt dimmer than it had ever been and only the odd stick or brick stuck out by the tiny flicker-flame of my candle. I hummed to myself; as though it would beat back both darkness and dull thud of sound.

I arrived at Frederick's hut.

"Blondee." The voice came from the other side of his wall.

"Frederick?"

"You're here quite late. Are you all right?"

"How did you know I was here?"

"I heard you humming to yourself."

"Oh."

"Come in."

The candles mounted to the walls of his colourful cave flickered as I stepped through his door. I blew out my own candle and gently set it to the ground.

Frederick was kneeling on the edge of his bed, naked bar a pair of socks. Before him were tens of tiny towers, each arranged in squares, streets branching out from one another, a series of cracks surrounded by buildings. Frederick stood and carefully trod his way through. His cock hung half-limp half-heavy as he stepped toward me.

"I couldn't sleep," I muttered, casting my gaze down each lane and avenue.

"Well, that's—that's okay," he answered. "It's finished, more or less," he motioned to the new world he had formed.

We all remembered cities. Tall, empty buildings, long empty streets, faceless shop-fronts. This wasn't a new memory, but Frederick had brought our shared flat vision to life, carefully building a world we had lost but almost remembered, bringing it a little closer to reality. It was living, breathing evidence that we could re-make the world. I was drawn in further, over roof terraces and archways, around apartment blocks and over boutiques. Down back alleys and side-alleys and tiny lanes. This was the old world. It brought something back. Perhaps we had lived in those flats; perhaps we had worked in those offices and shopped there, or there, or there. Perhaps we had idly wandered at night around those streets, down that alley and along there, a million-million people around to keep us from ever feeling lonely. It did everything the book did and more.

I wanted to ask him something or tell him something but there wasn't anything to ask, there wasn't anything to tell.

"Lie down with me," he said.

So instead we lay down together amongst the bricks, bringing buildings to eye-level and streets within grasping-reach. I felt his cock press against my thigh and let the dry scent of beetroot cover me. I pressed my face into his neck, young and soft. He didn't make a sound. I was tired but waves rolled over my skin, tiny pins pressing themselves into me, curling my toes and pulling us closer. I lifted my face and saw the pinnacles of towers peering over his shoulder. He lay me down, pulled up my shirt, and ran his tongue over my breast, stopping at the nipple. I leant my head back and could see the base of two-storey homes, before they were obscured by his hair, his forehead, his eyes and broad nose and mouth. I sat up and took him fully-hard in my hand, his leg scraping a skyscraper, my leg drawn around him, his arm around my shoulders, my ear against his ear, and there we were, two giants, having sex in the middle of a real city.

# expanding

FREDERICK LED ME TO THE WALL.

I asked him what we were doing.

He told me we were to stand here and think.

"What do you mean?" I asked him.

"Don't talk Blondee, just—just think."

I thought, but I didn't know what to think of. I thought about the usual things: what I would eat, what the neighbours were doing. I thought I felt a little thirsty. Then I thought I was bored.

I told him so.

"Think Blondee. What—what do you think is on the other side? Right there?"

"I have thought about the outside before, Frederick."

"No, he said, I—I mean *right there*." He pointed at the wall.

"What do you think is there, Frederick?"

"A windmill." He answered straight away.

"A windmill?"

"Yuh—yes, a windmill."

He was sincere—he truly believed what he said. He felt that there was a windmill, not ten steps away.

"Why a windmill, Frederick?"

"It isn't something—something that I can explain. I feel that there's a windmill there. Can't you feel it? Don't you think so?"

I didn't lie. I had the need to tell him the truth. I told him that no, I didn't feel there was a windmill there, and that I didn't understand why he felt there was.

He told me that sometimes we could know things and not be able to realise why. That not everything was ordered.

"S—sometimes, Blondee, things don't make sense. They don't fit together.

And they don't need to. We can't—we can't explain everything, Blondee, and there's no need to try. Sometimes things are as they are."

I didn't lie to him. I simply nodded.

Later I relayed the conversation to Burberry.

"A windmill?"

She seemed interested, but she had her own opinions on the matter. She didn't agree, she said that the truth might be elusive, and that we might often get it all wrong, but it was there somewhere. Maybe we didn't have to find truth, but we certainly shouldn't pretend to know things we don't.

She was as sincere and determined as Frederick.

I knew they had to meet. I could never live with the two halves of me so separate. Each was new, and fragile, I knew that, but each time I explored with Frederick or felt Burberry's lips with my own I knew that they couldn't be kept apart. They had to meet.

I mentioned it to Burberry first. We were cooking together—she stirring and I watching—when it burst out. She listened to me with patience and a slight smile. She had no objection. She lifted the spoon from the pan, blew on it, and brought it to my mouth. We kissed.

Then Frederick. We were sitting drinking tea together—tea was plentiful for him—and I told him what I had said to Burberry. He stammered and his nerves were plain to see, but he agreed. I put my arms around him in comfort. I told him that it would be okay. There was nothing to worry about.

Now this was indeed a lie—I was worried myself. So I brought them together as carefully as I could. I met Frederick and drew a voiceless circle in the sand by the pool, end-to-end, breath steady, closed to the world. I gave him a hug goodbye and withdrew to my land, the land of the minors.

There was Burberry, and I took her hand in silence, leading her to the land of the least, to the pool—I forward, she in tow.

She did her best, forcing herself into focus, though once or twice the excitement of sneaking through the land of the least caused her to yelp in pleasure or grab at my arm in fear. Her head darted to and fro, she gulped down the sights before her: the unbelievable luxury of a hut painted rose pink, with matching pink windows with matching pink curtains; the opulence of private trees; the unbearable beauty of stones neatly arranged into swirls of a garden. I saw each of these through her, my heart and mind racing, the splendour of the land painted fresh. As we made our way through the shrubbery she wrapped her arm around mine.

We stepped into open space. There was the pool; the circle; there was Frederick. Burberry jumped away from me.

We said nothing.

Frederick stepped forward, the three of us standing in front of one another. We stood together in the circle.

We said absolutely nothing as the air changed around us, as the breeze moved to wind and calmed to stillness, as the sun sank and the sky darkened, as the pool lapped unending against its shore.

We said nothing but felt everything, us three: we poured anger into one another, spread fear to one another, spun jealousy and curiosity; hurt and hope. But no words. Movements were tiny, a flick of a finger, the barely-seen squint of an eye. A toe's length toward, a fraction away.

They lost sight of me. They saw only one another. I was lost. The sun vanished in a dance of colours and it grew dark. Burberry's arms opened a little, Frederick moved forward. The circle grew outwards, ever outwards, diminishing all before it, collapsing to nothing, it grew through the walls and out further, into other worlds, on and on.

*At its edge the stone woman, charging its boundaries, leading it forward, away into the darkness. All around the edge her dogs, pushing it, further, further, smaller and smaller, vanishing in all directions.*

"Blondee."

Frederick and Burberry were together, arm-over-shoulder; arm-over-shoulder. They pulled me toward them. We embraced.

The circle fell and everything returned.

# part three

THE WIND HAS STOPPED: everything is quiet. The ground is starting to freeze beneath my limbs. The hole is getting cold.

Frederick and I only had sex the one time. I loved him, I wanted him, I wanted to pull him close, to smell him and feel him. I did. But we remained how we always were: soft and dry and happy.

Burberry and I were different.

We had sex in the triangle hut

we had sex by the fire tap

in-between huts

and anywhere and everywhere whilst we giggled and came with her breath spread over my face. We were hard and wet and I was happy.

And when I came home from Frederick's hut, with its colours and its buildings and its whole-other-world,

there she was, smiling and biting her bottom lip.

I remember thinking that Pilsner had been right all along: I had no memories. I didn't need them. The world was how I wanted it. This was who I was, this was my life, I was Blondee and I loved two people.

It's coming. I'm getting tired. Soon I shall enter sleep. Soon I shall be born anew.

# two hundred eyes

IT GREW, FACELESS AND ANGRY, restless and slow.

The world had known I was with Burberry. Neighbours had stood by and watched as she moved her fabric, her plastic, her metal, into our hut. It had been such a short time since Burberry and Tanned had parted ways, but it was a shining example of the new rule, how we shouldn't dwell, how we needed to get over these things.

*You should get back on your feet at soon as possible.*

They were Tanned's own words, in Tanned's own handwriting. Page 16.

They all felt we were just a little closer to the outside, to how things should be, to how things always were. We even got a gift with the next rations: brown-and-black scraps of wallpaper, the dark colours dancing, driving one another to and fro in elegant swirls. Burberry wanted to place them around the hut. I piled them one atop the other and bundled them under the bed.

We weren't accepted, I told her, not really. I was with her and I was with Frederick. It was just that no-one knew.

Burberry giggled and without a word picked them out again, sticking them to the wall with whatever she could find. As I opened my mouth to object she covered my lips with hers and pressed me to the floor, covering my arms with hers, my legs with hers. The black-brown swirls were to stay on the wall, and by the time my limbs were limp with exhaustion and my skin slick with sweat it was like they had always been there.

I went about my life. With Frederick I wallowed in the chlorine-waters or quietly skulked about to spy on other people's huts late at night. No-one in his land knew who I was and I made sure never to be seen. Not until—

"Blondee."

I was standing at the door to Frederick's hut.

"Pilsner," I replied. He was leaving. I couldn't see his face, he stood in the doorway, light glowering behind him. He was a shadow, flat and featureless.

The evening had dimmed and no-one would be around. Only lovers saw one another at night—it was in the book. The more I seemed to see of the world the more I saw how people would pick and choose the rules, picking at them like loose strands of fabric, picking at them until there would be nothing left.

"How surprising you're here," he uttered, his voice as monotone as ever but softer, softer and quieter. He moved forward and on past me, fading into the dark.

Inside Frederick stood by his bed, confused and naked, his slight belly deflated and his cock limp over his balls, which hung even lower.

"He saw you," he stated.

"I guess so. Why—" and I stopped.

He raised his eyebrows as response. I knew why. Frederick had given in to Pilsner, or Pilsner into Frederick, moaning and writhing and sweating and kissing. We were sharing each other. That was how things were. I couldn't tell if it was simple or if it was complicated, and I thought of the softness of Pilsner's voice, something I had never heard before. It scared me.

"Is he all right?" I asked.

Frederick stared at the wall without an answer.

"Are *you* all right?" I asked.

He nodded.

At his motion we left his hut and walked foot-by-foot toward the pool, Frederick still pulling on his clothes.

"Why don't you just *be*—with him?" I hesitated as I wasn't really sure what the word meant.

He pulled a shirt over his head, sleek and shiny, a rare fabric. I stroked the sleeve.

"I, well, I did ask," he said.

"You did?"

"The—when it started, the first time. Mmm." Frederick stopped walking for a moment. "He said 'things are best left as they are', or something like that. I didn't question it, not really. We, we met—after that—and we wound up meeting about once every rations. That's how it's been for a while."

"Why didn't you tell me about it?"

At that moment I tripped, the rocky ground meeting me diagonally, a sharp stone in my knee.

"Fuck."

"Here," Frederick reached his hand and helped me up. A hole was torn in my trousers, the skin raw beneath. There wasn't any blood. I picked at the minute boulders lodged around the graze. I spent a few moments carefully lifting at each one and dropping them into my pocket. Frederick watched me. When I was finished I spoke again and we resumed walking.

"So, why didn't you tell me about it?"

Frederick followed me, two quick-step paces behind, his mind racing to keep up with his legs. There was another pause before he spoke, his words hushed and slow, pressed through dry lips.

"It wasn't—it's not—my place to say. This is his secret, his secret thing, not mine." He caught up with me. "Are you angry?"

"I don't know."

I wasn't, not really.

We reached the water. I took off my shoes and felt it lick at my feet.

"You can clean that up," Frederick said, bending down to take my calf in one warm hand and dripping water onto my graze with the other.

I stood over him.

"Why is Pilsner unhappy?" I asked.

Each droplet tickled my knee then raced down my shin.

"I don't know. I don't know why he's unhappy. Your guess there is as good as mine. He wanted me every now and then and he gets me every now and then."

"Why don't you talk to him?" As the words left my mouth he stared up at me, his eyes wide and white, not quite believing I asked the question. He was right, there wouldn't be any talking about it, not with Pilsner.

Frederick returned to dropping dollops and drips of water over my knee. I ran my fingers through his hair.

Not long after that the world had begun its watching. It was Pilsner. It was his doing, those eyes watched for him. Those tongues spread his gossip.

My pity twisted into anger.

I was angry. Ketamine had gossiped about me, certainly, but she had done so without thought. Pilsner did it from spite. I would have shared. I would have talked to him. What option had he left us?

Burberry did her best. She'd laugh or giggle or chew on her lip and tell me that the whole world didn't matter. What mattered was how I saw myself. What mattered was how we felt toward one another. 'And whatever you've got going with Frederick,' she added, flicking a dreadlock of her hair behind her ear and grinning.

By the next casino-event it was everywhere. Now the stares were everywhere, and they crawled all over my skin, an itch, a rash that they had thrown over me and which blanketed my body. I wanted them to go away. For once I wanted to be like the others, not watched or monitored, not made the subject of idle tongues. I'd had enough.

The roll of dice and huffy-shuffle of cards was familiar, though each time the booze had been different. Now it was 'Liquibuzz': an array of bright colours lit by candlelight, a flame placed behind each bottle, red and green and blue drinks shimmering. The glass clutched in my hand was slick with syrupy red liquid and my lips were coated with the sticky tingle of sugar. The bottle said 'strawberry', and I had never tasted strawberries. I didn't like them.

It was my third mug.

Burberry's glass was stained a heavy-inky colour, where blue and green had mixed together into a rich ooze. She raised the glass to her lips over and over, taking tiny sips, giving her hands and her mouth something to do.

The others would watch us just out-of-sight, talking from the corner of their mouths. Burberry had noticed them and glanced at me. Every mouth's murmur was about us, I knew it, and Burberry knew it. She gave up her sipping and downed the rest of her glass in one go, a dark dribble dangling from her lip.

My perfume-heavy neighbour, Fluffed, was one of the few not staring. He clutched a glass of yellow liquid, which cast a golden shimmer of shadow on the wall of the tent. He still had most of it left: he had been too busy talking to the attractive man by his side to swallow. He would be talking about something else. The rations had been meagre this week and the weather hot and sunny. He would be talking about those. Or perhaps he was uttering the words that would carry him into sex. I watched their lips, placing my thoughts into their mouths:

That's some shirt you're wearing.

Wanna take it off?

Of course.

Let's fuck. We'll fuck.

We'll fuck.

We'll fuck and it's okay, we have no ties, we never tried to love more than one person, just sex, just sex over and over—

Do you like my perfume?

Then there was Tanned. He was across from us, in a different circle, his head bobbing in and out of view. I watched his hand, to see what he had been drinking. Red, it was red—his drink matched mine.

A woman smiled and smirked by his side, a look broken only by each sip of green ooze. His new girlfriend. I had never seen her before. She was plain and her face too big and round, a plate of skin around tiny olive-eyes. She was nothing next to Burberry.

I gently moved my hand a few millimetres to my side, letting my little finger rest against her leg.

A woman with a blue drink stared.

A woman with an orangey-red drink stared.

A man with a blue drink,

a green drink,

a yellow drink.

When my eyes met theirs they glanced away.

"Don't worry about them," Burberry whispered, her melon-blackberry-sugar-breath buffing my face.

"I wish they'd stop," I said, meeting each stare in turn, one by one.

"They will stop. They'll get bored."

But how did she know that? The world was filled with little enough scandal. Others were more careful than us.

"Hello there." I jumped at the voice in my ear. It was Jay. I hadn't seen him. His breath smelled of every one of the sugar-fruits. "Don' worry about all the—" he gestured at the others, a sweep of his hand driving their gazes elsewhere, "all of that. You two jus' do what you want. Do what you want. Life is too short and the world too fucking small."

He waddled away. Burberry smiled and raised her eyebrows, relieved by the drunken display of sympathy. At the other end of the casino-tent he stumbled, staggered and fell into a pile of cards, drawing angry cries and one of two quick slaps to the legs as he kicked, trying to get up.

I had to leave. We kissed, her sugar-silted lips pressed to my mouth, and I stepped outside. I didn't stop until I was by my triangle home.

I planted my arse to the ground.

I closed my eyes and found a small stone. I clasped the stone, dry skin meeting dry rock. I took a deep breath. The breeze was scented with Fluffed's perfume and gently sounded of footsteps and clatter. Another deep breath, filling my lungs, deep against the darkness. Another long draw of breath and I gripped the stone securely. It was the only firm thing in existence. I drove it through the ground. I traced a long circle around me, switching hands halfway. There was the circle and there was me.

Images splashed through my head—Fluffed's hair, Pilsner's face. There was a city, miles upon miles of coloured blocks waiting for people to go to work, to fight, to have sex. There was a giant, lying dazed and naked between the towers. There were soft gently-wobbling breasts beneath a coarse shirt and there was the roll of dice and the tang of sour yoghurt. There was a stone woman, and there was a man, floating away in a chlorine-soaked pool to be with his new lover. There were flecks of blonde hair dancing about the floor and then there was gravel doing the same. There was an endless purple sea, a blank stare and the end of the world.

In front of me was Tie. In the old days I'd see Pilsner at the courtyard but Tie would come all the way to my hut, panting and sweating even in snow-flurried hail-pelted times. He'd bring me some of his rations. One day he'd brought me sugar and bread, which was fluffy and crunchy and spread itself over my teeth. He'd taken pity on me, he'd say, and he'd smile. Sometimes I'd punch him on the arm, which made him smile more. At first I was suspicious.

I asked him what he wanted: was it to fuck me? I couldn't bear to imagine his huge body crushing the air from me.

He had looked hurt, really hurt. He'd shaken his head and told me he didn't want to fuck anyone.

I hadn't said anything. What was there to say? He seemed to forget about it afterwards, I hoped he'd forgotten.

He'd listen to my early-day rambles. I'd think about how I used to be. It wasn't uncommon. I had no comparison really, so I used the neighbours as examples.

I suggested that I was like that woman, the one who sewed everything.

He said her name was Rings and said that I didn't know what she was like—I'd never spoken to her.

With some authority I was that she was kind: she had a kind face.

He'd indulged me and said yes, maybe I was kind.

Then I suggested I might have been like that man with the long white hair. He looked cruel, but like he didn't enjoy being cruel. Maybe I was like him.

Tie agreed: maybe I was.

I asked him what he was like.

He said he didn't know. He supposed he was fat.

I wasn't sure what to say. We'd stepped from my hut and were silent until we reached the courtyard, where Pilsner'd stood fiddling with the tap.

I did it again: perhaps I was rich. Perhaps I was wealthier than anyone. My words tore through the quiet.

Pilsner said it didn't matter. He shot the words at me in his unchanging voice.

Tie told Pilsner to leave me alone.

Pilsner said that whomever my body was before, they were dead. I was Blondee, and that's all I ever was.

Tie's voice swung like a lead stick: shut up, Pilsner.

Pilsner glowered.

After that I'd stopped wondering about my old life.

I stepped from the circle. It was too much. I had to confront him. It wouldn't wait. My hair, skin, teeth and nails felt dirty.

I hated him.

I hated Pilsner. I hated his condescending voice, his knowing everything, his gossipy words. I reached his hut before I even realised I had been walking. He was on the other side of the thin wall, I knew it, and I felt the weighty throb of anger. He had no right to talk about me, to talk about the life I had built—it was none of his business, and if he wanted Frederick he could have claimed him. The anger pulled at my arm, and I threw my palm at the wall, over and over,

batter batter batter,

my hand clenching to a fist,

clunk clunk clunk,

and soon he would be running out to me, his monotone voice flexed with anger, wanting to know what I was doing. And I could shout, I could shout at him, "Who are you, who are you to tell me what I am?"

cadunk cadunk.

The wooden board came loose and rattled against its neighbours. My anger built, spreading from my stomach to my lungs, down my arms and my legs till toes and fingertips trembled.

The door swung open, swaying on one hinge. Two eyes stared coldly. There he was.

"What do you want?" He was black-lined by the doorway.

"I want to talk."

"No you don't."

"What does that mean? Talk to me," I shouted.

"I mean." He spoke the two monotone words as though they were the beginning and end of his sentence. He spoke again, his voice faster, "You aren't interested in talking, Blondee."

I opened my mouth to speak before being silenced, overridden by the torrent of quick, flat, lifeless words.

"Blondee, you're interested in what you can get for yourself. You're interested in how you perceive yourself, who you are, what you are. You're interested in how others perceive you, in who they see you are, who they think you are. You're not interested in talking: you're not interested in thinking. You're just trying to make an identity for yourself, trying to build a person out of the lump of flesh and hair which landed here. It's exactly the same as all the others. There's nothing left but you, because you're trying to build a whole new person, and if that doesn't take the whole of someone's time, the whole of someone's mind, then I don't know what does.

"Of course everyone here needs an opinion on that, someone to test that experiment on. Someone to judge their achievement. So they get their little lovers and spend all their time impressing them. They try to impress them with this whole person they've built. But it's pointless, neither is paying attention, neither is listening because really all they can hear is themselves. Each person trying to impress the other simply so they can impress themselves. Eventually it fails because no-one is really listening to anyone and they get angry, or frustrated, or bored, and the only time the other person then exists is as a nuisance they need to get rid of. And so they do. They get rid of each other and continue their experiment, searching for a whole new person to be a judge of it and start the whole fucking process over again.

"Actually, I know I said a moment ago that you're the same as everyone else in the world, but that's not true, is it? Most people just need the one person to size them up. But you need two. Your project must be so big, so great to need two separate people examine the creation that is Blondee—"

"Will you stop, just for one moment."

"Why?"

"Just give me a moment."

"No. And I know what people have said about me. It's not your business, it's not theirs, but I chose not to have a partner. I don't want to work on building a person."

"What happened with Frederick?"

"It doesn't mean I don't want to fuck. But I don't need anyone to tell me how much they love me, when really they're asking if *you* love them, if you love what they've made of themselves, out of nothing. I suppose you've said it, right? To both of them? Let—"

And I started walking away, but he continued in his monotone voice, and the walk became a run, until his dirty metallic opinions were far behind me, at the other end of the world, far away where he could chew on them, where he could gnaw on them crumbling his teeth and shattering his jaw, his skull caving in and body snapping and folding in on itself and folding and folding until there was nothing left.

I stopped as I reached our hut. I heard Burberry inside—she must have left the casino after me—loudly singing to herself, la-la notes without words, and I had never wanted to hold her so much, to hold her and kiss her neck, hold her and kiss her neck and say I love you.

# gold

We were picking the rations together. It was one of my favourite activities. For the first time since talking with Pilsner I felt at ease.

"What do you think of this?" she asked, fuzz-furred peaches cradled by fingers. I smiled and nodded. She was choosing food, I furniture. I picked my way through large flat slabs of black plastic, large flat slabs of grey plastic, and small red foam disks. I felt at ease, easy enough to talk to her.

"I went to Pilsner's."

I fingered through sheets of foil. I couldn't see her behind me but I pictured her face, puzzled, maybe annoyed. Lines building around her eyes.

"You did?"

"I did."

"What happened?"

I paused over some small wooden blocks. There was a lot to choose from this week.

What happened? I didn't want to go over it, not what he said. I had spent the past few days limb-locked with Burberry and collapsed into Frederick, my mind picking up each word of Pilsner's. With Burberry's breath over my forehead I knew he was wrong. With Frederick's skin I knew he was a bitter old man.

"He's a bitter old man," I answered, turning to face her."Hmm, I'm guessing it didn't go too well then," she uttered, holding up bananas."I've not had these in a while—do you mind?"

"No. And no."

"So he's got a thing for Frederick but his cock was too limp to do anything about it. It's not your problem. It's not even Frederick's. What about these?" She held two brown furry fruits. I'd never seen them before.

"What are they?" I took them in my hands, feeling them tickle my palms. I brought my nostrils to the fuzz-covered surface and sniffed. They smelt sweet, an old woman's corpse rotting alone in a hut.

"You've not had them before? They're good. They're good, I used to have them with Tanned." Her voice trailed. I handed the fruit back to her.

"Do you still miss Tanned?" Of course she did. They had been together countless rations and had only been broken for two or three.

"I do." Her voice was soft. I stroked her arm.

A few moments drifted before we both turned and resumed picking and sorting and prodding and choosing. 'These?' she would ask and I would nod. 'This?' she would ask and I'd smile. I picked my way through the scraps of furniture but nothing was suitable. Soon she had her bags of food and I was stuck, unable to choose anything.

"Can I help you, madame?" Burberry asked.

*"Can I help you madam?" is a phrase used to demonstrate concern and offer assistance.*

"I suppose, sure."

"What about this?" she picked up three planks of sand-blonde wood.

"There's nowhere in the hut for them to go," I answered.

"They can go outside."

I nodded. I'd never placed anything outside. I thought of flagpoles and faceless empires. Names carved onto globes and tiny paintbrushes colouring the world the same shade.

This was the first time I had been unable to pick or choose rations, unable to claim any item as my own. She picked up the bags and placed one in my hand, gently brushing my cheek with her mouth and running a hand over my breast.

"I love you," she said.

"I love you."

The day ran by, it was rainy and so Burberry fell tired, stretching herself over the foam of the bed and letting her eyelids flutter. The boards we had collected were on the floor. I kissed and ran my hands over her, listening to her moans grow softer and softer, until they faded from her throat.

"I'm going out to see Frederick," I whispered. She half-opened her eyes.

"Okay."

"I'll be back tomorrow."

"Okay." The words petered and vanished before they left her lips. Her breath fell into even rhythms. I looked around for a bag.

"So what is it you want to show me, Frederick?"

He grinned, his eyebrows furrowed, a mischief I had never noticed before. He wouldn't speak, and so I jabbed at him with my fingers, each prod making him giggle.

There was nothing unusual about the chlorine pool. It was placid as ever, incapable of life but beautiful all the same. He wandered away.

"I don't see anything," I shouted after him. He knelt down a little distance from me, but when I stepped toward him he motioned me to stay. I lowered myself to the ground, bringing my face to the sky. The sun glowered fiercely, angry, furious at the fact that it must die, that it must leave us and cast us into night. The pale orange light the hot-tempered angered-red sun threw over us looked like urine, or gold.

I had seen gold once, in Pilsner's grasping hands as he wandered from the rations cube clutching his prize. I hadn't been in the world long and I treasured the sight—I had shared in the gift, having been able to look at it. Perhaps Frederick had seen it—it must have still been somewhere in Pilsner's hut, saved, hidden away. Ration after ration the image slowly faded from my mind and even the exact colour of gold left me, but right then I imagined it was the same as the sky.

"Will you be long?" I called. He gave no answer and I prodded at the water, circle-waves dancing around my finger, the gigantic epicentre.

"All right—all right, Blondee, you can come over."

Knees creaked and up I went. As I approached I could see he was surrounded. He was surrounded by a pubic mass of the tiny-trees, a mass of shrubs red-leaved, green-leaved. In front of him they spread, out and out, hundreds of the little trees gently swaying. It was a forest. Had I had that sight before? I had never thought about it. We were two giants once again, stood over the tree-tops and watching the hefty green-and-brown mass. They would be filled with birds, they would be crawling with insects, snakes hanging from branches which delicately filtered the sunlight.

He had made a forest.

"It's so far from the city", I said.

He smiled and told me that it would be okay.

"I went to Pilsner's," I said at last.

"I knew you would. I knew he wouldn't like it."

"He didn't."

"I know."

The leaves changed with the sky. The breeze died and they stood, silent and sturdy. At one time the whole world had been forests, I knew that much. Even where we stood, within the four walls in which we had been reborn, there had been an endless mass of trees even here. There were birds. I only had a single memory of them, and of course it was hollow: there weren't birds in our world. We could be in the middle of a city; we could be in the middle of an ocean. We were at the centre of a huge forest, all that is left of the outside, pristine, untouched, virgin and old.

*Keep your place in the world.*

It was early, it was page 2. I couldn't be sure what my place was—triangle hut or circle or pool or courtyard. Frederick knew the quote and said that he was an artist. He said it made sense, and that the ones who didn't keep their place had no sense of self, they had no centre and then, well, there were enough examples of that, there really were.

In his hut, in the dark, by his snores, I lay awake. Who was I? I was Blondee, and I had my own way of seeing the world, which no-one else could copy, or steal. Who was I? I was Blondee, with two lovers. I was Blondee, no occupation, no job, with enough time to sneak and wander and watch. But I didn't have a place, or purpose. I saw Ketamine, her spider-writing, her new task of feeding us all.

I don't remember when I fell asleep, but I did so telling myself who I was, doing my best to hide from the possibility that I'd never find an answer.

# an answer

*The stone woman was small. What had happened? She had been life-sized before. Now she was shrunken; the size of a hand. In fact, there she was, in a hand, clutched by clumsy fingers. Chewed nails. The skin was thick and rough.*

*She relented. She allowed it. Her dogs were glued to her sides.*

*The thick-skinned hands plunged her into water and she vanished down, down into the soapy sea, thick reams of foam obscuring her, head-sized bubbles bursting at the surface. The thick-skinned hands pulled her up again. Soap clung to her face.*

*Why wasn't she fighting? Why were her arrows sheathed?*

*She was shrouded in a dry cloth, rubbing at her, rubbing hard enough to rub away her colour, and what if those hands rubbed away her colours until she shone ghost-white?*

*"Stop it," I shouted. "Stop."*

*The towel was removed. Her colours remained.*

*The stone woman was placed onto a shelf. No, she was placed onto the mantelpiece. She stood above the fireplace. There were flowers either side of her—roses and lilacs, red as her lips, white as her teeth. The fireplace was the focal point of the room—our living room. Yellow wallpaper and a smart green-striped couch. Sanded floorboards.*

*My husband dried his hands on the towel, his eyes wrinkling in amusement.*

I opened my eyes, the blur of evening pouring through my eyelashes. I was no longer in Frederick's bed. I leant backwards. Humming, humming drifting through the air. It was Burberry. A line had been traced around me, so I twisted my neck to see where it went. It was all around, the two ends missing one another where it had begun, where it had ended. I was in a circle, a circle I had made. When did I get here?

"Blondee." Warm breath on my neck.

"Burberry," I leapt to my feet, stumbling beyond the lines, outside my circle.

"Blondee," she said, her voice low and slow, "where have you been?"

I had no answer. I had been outside the hut of my enemy; I had been in the bed of my lover; I had been in a house, a real house with a husband and a stone ornament. I bit my tongue as I remembered the word. Burberry planted kisses on my neck, ran her hand over my shoulder, and led me inside.

# remember

IT WAS THE MIDDLE of the next day by the time I reached a decision: I was going to rebuild the memory. If Frederick could build a whole city or dense forest, then I could recreate a living room.

I made my way to an empty patch of the minor corner: a place of bare, dry earth and some worms. I arrived with a plank of wood from the hut in one arm and a bag of my rations in the other. I set them down by the wall.

I had tried to remember more, to recall the name of my husband, to remember more of the words we had passed back and forth. To remember something other than the room with the fireplace. I had failed—the memory was already starting to blur indistinct. I had to hold onto it. It was the most detailed, most important memory any of us had. I couldn't lose it.

To recreate it, I told myself, would give me a chance of keeping it. Perhaps it would even spur more memories. If only I could make it solid, tangible.

I pressed my hand to the wall at the edge of the world. At this deserted section it was discoloured—an eight-step width was brown rather than grey. Perhaps my home, the living room at its centre, was just on the other side of that wall? Perhaps that was even where my garden began?

I pickled up the plank: that would be the mantelpiece. But it needed to be at shoulder-height, and how could I make it shoulder-height? I had no way of attaching it to the wall. Instead I placed two cans of milkshake on the ground, balancing the board atop them. It would have to do. I placed twigs upon it as substitute flowers.

For the stone woman I used a stone—that was simple. I placed her on the board, which wobbled then stayed more-or-less stable.

For the bowl of water I used my bucket. The water tap had been almost completely dry, so instead of a mass of foaming water I had a dribble. It would do.

For my husband I used the rest of the bag of rations, a cloth sack with clumps of food inside—it was much smaller than him but I had no other option. I had thought of asking Frederick or Burberry, but I already knew their faces, they had already made their own memories with me—it wouldn't work. Besides, I hadn't even told them about the memory yet. It was the bag or nothing.

But it wasn't right.

The sack-husband was lumpy and lifeless. The mantelpiece collapsed. I peered into the bucket, but there was nothing.

Of course, the stone woman belonged in the bucket—that was how the memory started.

So I took the stone and placed it into the bucket.

It still wasn't right.

I stood before the sack-husband and tried talking to him. But what could I say? I had no memory of myself. What was the sort of thing I would say as his wife?

"Be careful," I said, pointing to the bucket stone.

He didn't respond.

I gave up and sat down by the mantelpiece. I picked up one of the cans of milkshake and began to drink. It was sour.

I was the only one who remembered marriage. But away from my memory it seemed alien. Still, marriage tied people together. Marriage would stop people flying away.

I drew a circle, then pressed my eyes closed. I tried to go further. I uttered the words to myself, listening to the lull-lull of my own tongue, 'stone woman stone woman stone woman'. I tried to turn my husband around, to grasp him by the shoulder. But he couldn't be turned, he had no back. But he *was* my husband. I tried to open the door to the room, but beyond the door there were only walls, beige and prickled.

I could go back, back to that room, and stand and watch the yellow walls but there was no beyond, there was nothing else. Me, a living room, a husband. That was it.

"Have you had memories?" I asked Burberry, stepping back into the hut.

She lay with her back to me, her breathing even. I took her shoulder and turned her toward me. Her eyelids fluttered.

"Blondee."

"Burberry," I kissed her lips. "Burberry, have you had memories?"

"I have lots of memories, many, many, many." Her voice was churned with sleep.

"Really? What were they?"

"Well," she said, slowly pulling herself up, resting her forehead on my collarbone for an instant, "I remember kissing you. I remember holding you last night. I remember eating yesterday, I ate cold soup from a can—"

"You know what I mean," I squeezed her shoulder. She laughed, gently, slowly.

"Of before? Of outside the world?" She was toying with me, making me play for an answer. I nodded dutifully.

"No," she leant back. "No, I don't."

"None at all? Not ever?"

"No." She closed her eyes. It would have been quiet at that moment, but for Fluffed flitting around next door. Finally she spoke, licking her lips to keep them from sticking together. "No-one does."

"What?"

"I don't think anyone does, not really."

"What?"

"What else is there to say?" she asked.

"No-one does? No-one has any memories at all? But what about the book, what about—"

"And they're memories, are they?"

"They're memories of the outside, of the old world, how things were, of the world before."

"They're not memories." She sounded certain, spread before me as still as stone.

"Then what are they, Burberry?"

"Inventions. Stories. Creations." She was quiet for another moment. "I'm sure people think they're real."

I stared at her. She lifted herself up, propping herself on the foam mattress with her elbows.

"Or maybe they're real, maybe they're all true," she continued. "It doesn't really matter though, does it? We've got no way of knowing." She looked hard at me, as though she were trying to find a speck of dust on my face. "Why? Have you? Have you had any memories?"

"No."

The curtain-cloth had been pulled closed, its colours collapsing about the room. Burberry lay down and rolled over, her breath descending into even sweeps. I ran my hand along her back. In the book there are hundreds, hundreds of memories, and I had no way of recalling them all. Burberry was wrong.

I decided to make her breakfast, pulling the tray from beneath the bed, a small array of coloured boxes sliding into view, an old t-shirt bundled into the corner. It would be rations-time again soon enough, and all we had were powdered egg, jelly squares, salt-pepper-mix and rice. I was certain it wouldn't go together, but it would make for a good spider-lettered recipe. We had run low on food earlier than ever, but I had been hungry, and I had eaten more than my fair share. Today I would eat less. When I was single I would often starve for a day or two before the next ration. It wasn't helpful to gather rations whilst hunger gnawed at your insides. For a moment hunger looked to me like an animal, small and furry with huge teeth. I wanted to feed it. There were few animals within our walls.

I stepped from the hut, boxes bundled in my arms. A short gasp leapt from my throat. The sun had risen, throwing purple light over the sand and grass and mud and huts, purple as a raw throat, deeper and richer than before. Wordlessly one or two figures wandered, faces driven upwards, nothing to say or do but wonder at the sky. It didn't mean anything, the sky must have always played such tricks. But it was beautiful, that couldn't be denied—deep-red-purple to rich-blue-purple, the clouds scattered like fresh innards above our heads.

At the fire tap there was a queue, people trying to cook their morning meal whilst watching the scene above without scalding their delicate arms or burning their bellies. One man failed, and even those who rushed to help him as he shrieked and growled in pain couldn't help but witness the world above. His skin blistered in the same heavy hues.

Fluffed was there, not saying a word to me as he cooked tart chilli and canned beans, a scent which stung my nostrils almost as much as his ever-present perfume. I wanted to greet him, to say hello or smile, but I was cowed into blank-faced silence by the strange light. At my turn I cooked quickly and methodically, before leaving the food by Burberry's sleeping form. I didn't eat any.

Outside again I lay on the ground, my thoughts interrupted by the odd slow and unsure footsteps of those facing the sun. I knew my memories, I knew the world on the outside, I knew of marriage and husbands and mantelpieces. Watching his rough hands in soap water I knew he was mine. He was mine and he wouldn't fly away. But I couldn't marry twice, two separate people all at once. The hunger animal squirmed about my gut.

*Those who are lazy go hungry.*

The middle of the book.

I thought of the book, blue spine and golden lettering saying 'Notes'. I had to put my memory in there, I had to transform this memory into ink before it faded.

That meant I had to find Pilsner.

# Pilsner

He stood his age-old guard at the water tap. We were alone. He didn't greet me: he simply glanced at my approach and then watched the middle-distance. It was up to me to greet him.

"Pilsner."

Still he said nothing. He stood motionless as an ornament, one arm leaning on the tap, the other hanging limp at his side. I glanced around to see if anyone was approaching. No-one was.

"Pilsner," I repeated. Still he made no movement. He was waiting for me to leave. He was scared, I could see it in the tiny motion of his left eyelid. He was afraid of me. I wasn't leaving.

"I had a memory," I said, my voice rasping with frustration.

Finally he turned to me, the only movement his neck, still with one arm on the tap and the other to his side.

"You told me that, Blondee."

"I had another."

He turned away, back to his original position.

I stepped toward him, not stopping until we were a toe's length apart, the stench of his body filling my nostrils, the stench of mine filling his. I wasn't going to leave—I was going to write my memory in the book.

He spoke without looking at me.

"What do you want, Blondee?"

I was confused. He knew what I wanted. I answered honestly.

"I want to write it in the book."

I couldn't leave it at that. I would tell him my memory—he would be the first. If he heard what I had remembered then he would realise how important it was. This would change everything.

So I did. He stood rigid whilst I told him about the ornament, about the bowl of water, about the rough fingers and the mantelpiece. I told him that this man was my husband—I had remembered marriage. You see, I told him, two people get married and then they stay together. They don't leave, you keep one another. That was how things were done on the outside; that was how we did them before. I rambled and rambled until I wrung myself breathless.

He listened. When I was done he spoke. I jumped back. He was unmoving but his mouth contorted, his face reddening. His voice boomed.

"I hear you, Blondee. I hear you. I know what you want. You don't just want to rebuild yourself like everyone else here. You want to rebuild everything, all we have, all by yourself. But you'll destroy it first, there's no other way. Do you know that? You'll destroy it. I won't let you. How could I let you? You're destructive. We were wrong, so wrong to label you a minor. You're the worst of anyone here."

He paused for a moment to catch his breath. His voice softened.

"Blondee, I'm aware I'm angry at you. And you're angry at me. Neither of us will listen—anger closes the ears. But you must pay attention to me: stop this. Stop this whole thing. What we have now is fragile, more fragile than you realise."

"I had a memory, Pilsner."

"I will never let you write down a memory, Blondee. We write down our memories to work together, to add to what we've made together. You must understand—it doesn't matter what we did on the outside, or what we were like before. The book is important because it binds us all. You're not interested in that—you want to rewrite the whole thing to make the world as you want it. This marriage memory doesn't even fit with how you're living now—with your two. You want to change things and you don't even know how or why you're doing it."

He stood up fully and stepped away from his perch at the water tap.

"Blondee, I'm not letting you near the book again."

I held myself back, back from tearing and biting his skin, and not stopping until I reached bone. I wanted to hurt him. How could he say those things? The book was there to help us remember, to help us get back to ourselves. It was there to help us know what was real and what was pretend. He was a liar. He picked at the book and chose what he wanted to follow. I knew what the world was like—he didn't care.

"Don't be angry, Blondee. Anger's hard to get rid of. The world is too small."

I left him behind.

# a whole new crime

Tie would never have taken gold: he would have had no use for it. He would find a use for wood and metal and planks which could make huts. He would take his furniture rations and with a heart so full it would burst, he would lay the useful items to one side for someone else. He would save them for someone new, someone new who would arrive in the world with nothing, no clothes, no home and no hope. He saved me the window and the pieces which would make my home, pieces which I would never have had access to, not as a simple minor. I fell into the world and was caught by his generosity. He was never thanked.

I had been there for the next arrival, the one after myself.

The new one was scared, of course. He was scared; he was a minor; he was a sexual. I could never remember why. He cried a lot, even more than most. He was young but not so young. Tie guided the new naked man by the shoulder, over to the edge of the wall where he had been stacking new furniture. I had followed behind.

The man quivered and asked where we were taking him. He hadn't realised that we were fellow captives, not captors, and that we could take him nowhere but the world.

Tie, so matter-of-fact, told him we were taking him to his new home.

The man's voice rose and he stammered, this was not his home. Get your hands off me, spit mixed with tears, throwing himself from Tie and toward the wall.

I shouted at him.

Tie murmured that it was all right and walked over to the wall, to where the man had collapsed in a heap. I stood still and watched.

I couldn't hear a word, but at first only Tie's lips moved. I watched his mouth forming gentle words, trying to soothe the man who sat with his head between his legs, his back heaving.

There was a cry, the man leapt to his feet, the man struck Tie which his hand, across his face. Calmly Tie stood, and gently, so gently, took hold of the man's wrists and sat him down. The man's torso still heaved, but now his head was erect and Tie continued talking. Soon he joined him, and they talked for hours, oblivious to my watching. Eventually the man smiled and they stood, surveying the pile of treasure before them. I walked over.

Tie told me that it would be dark soon and the hut still wasn't built. He asked me if I would help.

The man wordlessly turned to me, his eyes shimmering. Hopeful.

I told him I would. I told him my name.

The man told me his name in return, but I forgot it since. Perhaps he died.

For the next hours we built, until his hut was complete, more-or-less. The weather had been cool and I had hardly begun to sweat, but salty water poured over Tie's bumpy face. We said goodbye after Tie fetched him some sheets and walked toward the courtyard surrounded by night.

I asked Tie why the man had hit him.

Tie replied that the man was scared.

I asked if he'd said thank you.

Tie asked if I'd said thank you.

I felt my face burn. I hadn't. I had cried for my old life, I had yelled and I had asked endless questions but I had never thanked him. There hadn't been room for that.

I said thank you.

He laughed and told me it wasn't the point. It didn't matter. The man, like me, needed a home so he gave one. That was that.

The night was the usual ink-blue-black, and I carried my anger, knotted deep inside me. It was casino night; though once again the tent was different.

"We can make three tents," someone had said, "least, minor and moderate, then we could all have a casino night at once, without waiting."

And there had been more talk, the tents were erected and the booze was divided: the least had half the drink, the minors a third, and the moderates the rest.

"What about us?" a voice at the edge shouted. No-one heard.

And where would Jay go?

I'll hop between the three, he'd offered, a noble glance at those around.

And that was that. A cheerful murmur and three tents later, there we were. The new tent for the minors was smaller, and at that moment quiet and subdued as we waited for Jay with the drink. I waited by Burberry—people were still staring at us, still whispering about us. What was there left to say? We could hear Jay's voice from the least tent, already speech-slurred and sloppy.

We were all huddled together, squashed into a group. I was pressed against Burberry and someone with black hair who smelt vaguely of smoke. It was too cramped to play games and so we waited for the drunken man with the drink: our only entertainment.

"Should we get him?" someone asked.

"Would you?" asked another. "If you want to go into the least tent then go ahead."

We heard laughter, then a voice from the other tent—Frederick?—who told Jay he'd better move along. Our tent was filled with a sigh and a chuckle of relief. Jay step-stumbled in through the opening.

"Jay," everyone said in unison. He looked drunk, dazed and startled, and began to make his way back out again until a hand—Tanned's hand—dragged him back inside.

"Come on then," Tanned held up his glass. The woman by him giggled. Jay nodded and filled his glass, then made his way around, pausing every few seconds to down a deep swig from the bottle.

Each chipped mug and glass was filled, emptied, and filled again until the room carried a healthy murmur. Burberry chatted idly away to someone whose face I couldn't see, and I leant my own face against the fabric of the tent, letting it caress my cheek.

"Go on, drink it," Jay instructed me, spilling bitter-cream alcohol into my glass and almost standing on Burberry's shin. I obeyed, raising the glass to my mouth and letting the thick gloopy liquid slide downwards into my stomach, hoping it would ease the knot of anger.

The tent grew hot, too hot, the murmur was a roar, the tart and bitter stenches of sweat and perfume and booze clogging up my lungs, which heaved and gasped for air. I threw myself from the mass of bodies.

Outside it was chilly and clear. I lay on the ground, head on the flagstones, gulping at the night air. When I had had enough I listened for familiar voices, but the conversations were so loud they all blurred into one.

How could he stop me?

How could he keep me from the book?

Couldn't I go right then if I wanted?

So I did.

Since the beginning no-one had knowingly committed a crime: sex-criminals had never had inappropriate sex, the violent ones had never harmed anyone, the disruptives lived by the rules and no thief, like me, had ever taken anything that wasn't theirs. To live up to the burden of the crime you carried would be to expose yourself. If anyone saw—if people knew—it would be terrible.

I was on my way to steal time with the book. No-one would be there. It wasn't my turn and if Pilsner had his way it never would be, but I would go to the book.

I hurried to my triangle hut for a candle. Everyone was still in the casino tents, but at every corner of the world their voices would be heard. A roar carrying the occasional burst of searing laughter. They were cheering me on, a hearty approval of my transgression. I found a thick candle under my bed and hurried back through the noise-encrusted night.

I made my way to the book's house. Glimpses of tin rusted in the candlelight. The noise of the tents found their way in through the doorway and round gaps between the wall and ceiling, bouncing from wall to wall. In the centre of the room, where it always lay, was the book. By night its blue covers were black, its pages grey and yellow. What was I going to do?

I was going to read. Wasn't that what I always did?

The book seemed heavier, first the covers and then each page weighted down by memories, none of which would ever be mine. It was too dark to read from a normal distance, the words a steady smudge, so I moved the candle nearer, then my face, a warm glow toward my forehead and age-ripe pages under my nose.

*They're not memories. They're inventions. Stories. Creations. People think they're real.*

Burberry's messy scrawl. It was wrong.

There was a scream and then a guffaw from each of the walls, which died into the usual murmur. I skimmed my eyes over the blue ink, the red ink and black, moving my face away each time I needed to turn a page.

*It doesn't really matter, does it? We've got no way of knowing.*

Burberry again. How could it not matter? How were we ever to find who we were if nothing we remembered was real?

Pages flicked between my fingers, brittle as thinly-sliced bone. Where did I fit in here? I had lived in a house, with a living room and a husband, not a hut. Where was I?

*You want to rebuild everything, all we have, all by yourself.*

Pilsner. The words were red as heat. Of course I wanted to rebuild, wasn't that the point? That was the book, that was its purpose.

A yelp and more laughing, the vibration of tin. Songs and dancing and crimes. I couldn't keep my eyes clear, and they flooded, my throat swelling, my breath a gasp.

*What we have now is fragile, more fragile than you realise.*

And the pages were blurred, but I could see them, as always, unfocused but clear. I saw desperate people huddled over blank squares of paper, needing to leave a mark, to leave something behind, something, anything to prove that they had once existed. I saw a girl writing her mundane memory of a weather report, her hands shaking, I saw a man forming words on soup, seasoned with salt-water from his eyes. I saw a rush of them all crowding inside the hut wanting to last forever. Anything, anything, anything but to disappear again.

*I'm not letting you near the book.*

The walls sobbed, over and over, tinged with laughs and chatter. The whole book an ink-black blob, a stain, a mistake.

I scrubbed my eyes and cheeks with my fingers, shaking angry hateful droplets to the floor. I turned the book to its first pages. Ink and pencil together told me how to love, who to love, when and where and why. Tin huts and lost-lover agonies, two weeks of pain and a fresh start, a lifetime of proving who you were to someone else. The words scraped against the flesh of my eyes, hard, sharp, and it would tear me apart, it would tear me into hundreds and hundreds of pieces, there would be nothing left, only the fragments desperate people could bear to pick up and rearrange. The tin walls snarled, and with one sharp rush the first page was gone. It lay limp and powerless in the tremble of my hand.

I was outside the book-hut, the smoke from the candle crawling up my nose. So I was a thief. They were right. More than minor though, oh, I was more than that. A moderate, perhaps even a severe, I had stolen one of the most important things in the world. The first page of the book. I had stolen some of the world's memories.

Standing in the cool gulps of air I felt nothing but concern—what they would do when they found what I had done? Fingernails scraping earth, I fixed that problem.

I buried the page in a circle—by my triangle hut, where no-one would ever find it.

# part four

The rain has died a little; I think I can hear footsteps.
I cannot tell. Perhaps, perhaps not. I'll shout anyway.
No, nothing.

So I stole: I am indeed a thief.
But I wanted to give also.
If you are prevented from giving, then what is left but to take?
Doing nothing was not an option. Doing nothing is death.

And now I'm doing nothing.

# theft

THE BOOZE-BROUGHT HEADACHES of the night before had kept everyone in bed, and there I was, at Frederick's, sitting quietly amongst the sleeping world. His back was pressed to my breasts, and I kissed his neck, wondering if he too slept.

"Frederick?"

There was no answer, but his head turned and lips met mine, soft, and again, soft. He ran his hands down my linen-coated arms, almost reaching my fingertips, nails caked in soil—dirt from my crime. The worst crime in the world. I pulled my hand away and ran it through his hair instead. He gave a light moan.

And the world jolted awake with a cry.

Mangled and anguished it called. At first they were garbled sounds, but soon they formed words.

The book, the book, the book.

Frederick rose, all I could see was his arse as he stepped toward his door.

"What was that?"

"The book," a wordless voice cried.

"The book? What about the book?" his back answered.

"It's broken, it's been damaged, it's gone—" the breathless voice called.

"Gone? Damaged and gone?"

"A page, the first page, the very first page, it's gone." The voice melted away, ready to spread the awful news to the far walls.

And at that Frederick turned, confused, as I tried to wipe my nails on my clothes. He stared at the coloured shards of ceiling.

"That doesn't sound good," he murmured. "You should go back to your hut. Better not give anyone any more reason to talk."

I nodded and I too stepped toward the door, an innocent kiss on his collarbone.

People paced to and fro. What have you heard? What have you heard? I waited for one to patter up to me, to ask what I knew. No-one did, and I was glad. I reached my hut to find Burberry standing outside.

"What've you heard?" She looked at me, her face tense.

"Someone's damaged the book, torn out the front page."

"That's what I heard." She sounded disappointed and stepped inside the hut, motioning me to follow.

"They'll be asking who did it soon." As soon as the words fell from my mouth I wondered if I should have said them.

"Do you know? Do you know that?" she asked, excited once more.

"No."

"Oh."

And we watched the world as it paced to and from outside the hut. 'Something should be done,' someone called. Then another, then another. 'They're ours, they're our memories, no-one should take them away from us. Not again.' One or two of them were crying, running from hut to hut. At first Burberry's eyes shone, then as the hours crawled on they faded into dull boredom.

"So what's the fuss all about? It's a page." And she stood to make some food. "Olives and rice?"

"Burberry—"

I decided to tell her—after what she had said, about the memories and the book, it would be safe. I could trust Burberry, she saw things differently to the others. So I told her, starting from my arriving at the book's hut, lit by my candle, about my rage, about my fingers flicking flicking flicking, then tearing. Her eyes grew wider, her tongue curling over her lower lip.

"But why did you do it?"

I didn't tell her about the reason for my rage, about what I saw on those pages, about the memory of my husband: she wanted something else—something more noble. Something vague.

"I had to."

And that was enough. She hugged me tight, told me that she would tell no-one, and that I must do the same. We couldn't know what would happen now—this was new. We had to trust one another.

It wasn't long before there was more calling: meet at the courtyard meet at the courtyard meet at the courtyard. Now.

And so everyone did. In ones and twos they ran to the centre of the world.

The least, minors and moderates gathered; we joined them.

"Be quiet."

"Look, just shut up, just for one minute, right?"

"He's talking."

Pilsner cleared his throat, ready for a monotone barrage.

Casio spoke instead. I kept my face hidden behind my hands, pretending grief, willing myself away from the chaotic chatter. Burberry held on to my arm.

"Everyone's heard about the book. None of you need telling then, but today it was noticed that a page was gone."

"Who noticed it was gone?"

"Who was it?"

"We can't tell you that," he ordered.

"It was me." A small woman's voice.

"What did you see?"

"Why were you there?"

"It was her turn with the book."

"Yes, it was my turn," her small voice called amidst the crumble of others, "I got there and the book was open. The first page was gone. It had been torn out. There was a little bit of it left. It was ripped."

Gasp groan shudder.

"Did you see who did it?"

"Did you see anyone?"

"No, there was no-one with a turn before me today. It was empty," she replied.

A jumbled silence a heartbeat long.

"Who was last yesterday?"

"Who the fuck was last then?"

"It was me." The voice belonged to Pilsner. He was above reproach.

"Who before you?"

"The page was there when I was in there yesterday." Monotone.

"It seems the page was stolen last night."

A murmur, and some minutes before I could pick out a single voice. Everything looked velvet-purple between my fingers. Suddenly everyone was suspect. We were all criminals, after all.

"... only left the tent for a minute, I had to piss. It was the booze."

"Yeah. Okay."

"Hey, I had to leave as well. I had to leave twice. If it could have been her it could have been me."

"I'm not saying it wasn't you."

"You've got a lot to say about this, were you there the whole time? I didn't see you."

"Me neither."

"Fuck you, both of you."

"Will you guys be quiet? Casio's trying to talk."

A yelp and a roar. The sound of feet moving and bodies jostling.

"Just fucking listen!"

"Look," Casio's voice. "Last night we were all at the Casino—"

"I know who weren't!"

"What?"

"The severes! They weren't at the casino. What if it was them?"

There was another pause, a low grumble. They weren't often mentioned.

"You know, it might have been."

"You don't know that."

"We'd have noticed them, I know I would have."

"And me."

"Look," Casio again, "Did anyone see anything? Did anyone actually see anything?"

"I heard something from over there, from the severes."

"When?"

"How should I know when?"

Pilsner cleared his throat again, before lifting his voice. "We don't even know when it happened. We won't ever know who did this. There's no point in blaming anyone. No—" a bleat from someone somewhere, "No. We remember what's on there. We can write it again."

"What on?"

Hostile murmurs.

"Does anyone have any paper?"

A smaller rush of feet, away, a breath, then back again. My face was hot beneath my hands.

"Here."

"Right." Pilsner's flat voice resumed. "We'll write it all down, right now. I'll read out what I'm writing. If anyone knows it as different, call out."

And so he read as he wrote. Voices carried through the air, uneasy, waiting for a chance to ignite. I looked up at his face, which flashed in and out of view between arms and chests and breasts. His face was crumpled, concentrating, his throat steady. Some people left. He remembered every word, word for word. My legs were light and my arms heavy, the cartilage of my knees trembling, my body sagging to the flagstones. I carefully sat down, resting on my elbow.

The new page looked uneven. It was larger that the others, and it was whiter—aside from a brown stain which chewed at the upper-right corner. It didn't fit, and a lot of people had noticed. I caught angry shudders of conversations, rattling against Pilsner, or the severes, or Casio. Once I even heard someone blaming 'that one with her two'. I hurried away before I was seen.

"Has Pilsner noticed?" I asked Frederick. He had told me earlier that day that he and Pilsner were talking again. I hadn't asked if their words had melted into slow and languid sex.

Frederick and I were in his cave-like hut, rolling a small rubber ball to one another.

"Noticed?" He caught it between his thumb and point-finger.

"People talking."

"I haven't asked. Probably, though. People talk a lot." He rolled it back to me, it bouncing into my knee and nestling against my shin.

"About the page."

"About it. Yeah." He caught it once more.

"Have you heard much?"

Frederick kept his focus on the ball as he rolled it back to me, his lips stuck shut.

"Frederick?"

"Of course. I'm not—I'm not sure there's much point paying attention to it." He nodded to himself and caught it once more. I wasn't aware it had left my hands.

"Have you heard them talking about me? About you and me? Me and Burberry?"

He nodded, gently bouncing the ball toward me. I missed it and left it to rest against the wall.

"I might have thought so," I uttered.

"I wouldn't worry."

"Why not worry?"

"There's—there's more talk about the trip than about us." He nodded again.

"Trip?"

"The trip. To the severes."

I stared at him so he continued. "You know—a lot of people are angry at them. They say they did it, they're the ones with the worst—you know. They—they say they're going on a trip."

"Who do you mean 'they'?"

"They. Everybody. Some angry people." He caught the ball again.

I was with Burberry when I saw 'they' leave.

We were at the courtyard—we had been waiting to see what would happen. At first we had been alone.

"Where is the page?" she had asked, running her hand over the water tap.

"It's gone," I answered.

"Where is it gone?" she enquired. When I didn't answer she continued. "I'm not prying, I just want to make sure that you'll be safe, that you've hidden it properly. I trust you, I trust that you've hidden it well, or destroyed it, and it won't be found by anyone. You just need to tell me that."

"It won't be," I told her.

Slowly 'they' began to arrive. A woman with a rope in her hands. A man with a shard of glass. Then more, a couple, a small group, a crowd. They didn't seem to notice us and we watched them in awed silence. More came.

Hostile murmurs grew into sharp words.

'They' were furious, they were shouting to one another, pulling to and fro. After a while I saw that they were two separate, shouting groups. One group held bars and pipes and—what looked like a hand-cranked drill—in their hands. The others simply raised their hands up, screaming at them.

"Don't go, don't go," they shouted. A man grabbed a woman by the arm, wanting to pull her home, pull her back to what was normal. She spat at him. Others pleaded, "stay here, stay here. There's no sense in what you're doing."

"We're just going to get it back," called the others. "We just want it back, it belongs to all of us." A man with a stick hugged another man. "It'll be fine. We should go, we should just fucking go," another bellowed.

"Wait, just wait a minute. We can't know who did thus. Please, stay here." Another lunge; more grasping arms.

"We're doing what we're doing. We're only going to look. Yeah, that's all." An arm held out: stay away. "They're the worst regardless. If anyone took it it was them."

"You'll get hurt. We don't know who did this. Listen to what was said."

"It'll be fine. We know what's what. We don't need telling that."

Eventually one of 'they'—raised bar in hand—started the trek to the land of the severes, calling as he went. His calls pulled one or two others, then three or four. Some stayed behind, dropping their tools on the flagstones with a clatter, falling into lovers' arms. One—who had been calling 'don't go'—picked up a rope and followed her lover. The exchange was over.

Burberry stroked my hair. Someone else would be punished for my crime. 'Whose crime is whose?' She had whispered it to me one warm night when beads of water kissed the window-wall. I had asked what she meant. She told me that perhaps we're punished for crimes someone else did. 'Someone else?' I'd asked. 'Somebody not here,' she'd answered. I hadn't asked more. 'We can't know anything,' she had added. I had wondered if Tanned had ever heard such words.

We stayed at the courtyard. I flitted from foot to foot, waiting for them to come back. There was no-one else around, they had all gone home to wait for the others. I wanted to see what had happened, to inspect their fingers as they returned; for blood, or even bits of brain. Perhaps they would be chatting back and forth, discussing what they had done, ready for my ears to catch. Maybe they would be silent, their deeds written in the gloom on their faces

There was a clatter, a hollow thud thud thud.

They didn't come, not all together. Every now and then I noticed one walking home, weapon slung by their side. There was no talking—they were each alone, and they didn't look excited or sad. I noticed the first, walking as though he were going to collect food or travel to the tap: not fast or slow or slumped or proud. He was everyday, unmarked stick swinging by his side.

Then there was another—was his hair roughed up?—the same, not even bored-looking, just average. Then one more, with a drill, as though she were going to fix one of the grander huts, off to her chore. There were no clues. Perhaps they hadn't done anything. I needed to know.

I wanted to see. I wanted to go to the land of the severes.

Burberry demanded to come with me, but I told her that I had to go and see it alone—this was my doing. "Besides, I said, it's better you wait at the courtyard so we don't miss anything."

She said there was safety together, but I told her I needed to go alone. She relented, slumping sullenly to the flagstones.

It wasn't dark, there was little cover, and there could have been anything up to a hundred people watching, but I went. It was the last part of all the world that I had never seen. I had to see what was left.

Now and then there was a bellow as someone returned home to their lover, one with a lurid pink top and a chair-leg in one hand, shortly afterwards one with knotted brown hair and the head of a shovel.

The ground was hard—it was concrete—with a thin layer of dust and sand over the top. It burned beneath the soles of my feet. There was nothing: no bushes or dead trees, not even any huts. I couldn't see anything but the flat ground and the lone figures marching back to their own lands.

I passed the woman with a rope, off from hanging a hammock, or a man who stole her memories. She didn't see me. Her gaze was fixed dead-ahead, her expression placid.

There was a clatter, thud-thud-thud, and it grew louder by the step.

There was the chain-fence, the one that divided their land from the land of the moderates, cross-cross-crossed into diamonds. I had seen it once, from the other side, in the distance, back when I had explored the world alone. Now I had to reach out and touch it, slide my fingers along silken-smooth steel. Knots of string clung to it in places, flitting in the breeze. I could see myself beyond it, wandering from the first ever casino tent, over to the far wall, meeting Frederick and hugging and smelling him for the first time.

There was one more of 'they' returning home, torn shirt, exposed body hair, weapon gone, more casual than was possible. He was the last of them. Then the land was empty, concrete and wisps of sand.

A sinus-stuffing must choked the air. I had smelled it on old couch-cushions. Mould and fabric and time. Then I saw it: a scrap-built hut, hanging to the far wall, a wave of smoke spiralling upwards. It was the only hut in all the land. It was where they lived: all of them. The walls of the hut were thin, stapled and bolted and glued together, torn sheets of flimsy plastics and shards of corrugated iron stained black-brown, a row of drainpipes duct-taped together, mouldy wood, mouldy fabrics, mould-covered felt boards, all holding up a thin roof of chipboard, smoke rising up from somewhere in the middle. The only hut in all the land. It was made from the dregs of the world.

There was screaming, and it came from inside. I stepped over ragged mounds of litter and shreds of fabric, sobs and screaming louder and louder, until I stood by the hut and rested by hand on the gritty wall.

The screaming stopped, revealing a slow sad hum of words, from over a dozen voices.

"Let him go Jonas, we need to bury him."

"Just let him go."

More sobbing. Long, hefty sobs.

"Have they all gone?"

"They've all gone."

"Let him go."

There was whimper.

"He didn't deserve it."

"But what if it was him? What if they come back because of him?"

There was a roar. The thin walls shook to yelps and loud cries, dust pouring from all sides. There was a clatter, thud-thud-thud, and it smothered every voice, it trembled every bone. The whole land trembled from the ground up, and I ran forward on unsteady legs, past the cross-crossed fence, over the stinging concrete ground, then to the deserted courtyard, on and on until I was home.

I crawled to the circle by my triangle hut, hands-on-earth, but the circle was gone, the line had weathered away.

I had to find the page, I had to find it. But what would I do?

Burned.

Watch the page curl and flicker, char upwards into smoke and downwards into ash. There would be safety, then I could forget, then we all could forget. A fire to call the return to how things were.

Buried.

Or I could check it was still in the ground and leave it there. Maybe bury it a little deeper into the earth. Someday it may be found; some day I will answer. Leave it to chance, to the mystery of the soil.

Fluttering.

Dig it out, hold it aloft, fluttering up in the air. Shout it: I did this, it was me. Calling my confession, my voice carried on the breeze. Everything out in the open, clean and clear, my punishment deserved.

Sinking.

Perhaps it would be best to go to the lake—walk, don't swim, walk until my head was below, release the air from my lungs, draw in water. Punish myself—it was common enough to fall dead, there would be no questions. They would be free of the guilt, they need never know they had wrongly harmed the severes.

I hadn't decided.

A tiny white corner protruded from the soil. It was the page, the page had crawled up through the ground. It was trying to escape. I pulled at the corner, pulling the paper up. The page came free, then another, then another, then staples, then more. It was a magazine. A woman smiled up at me, glossy-white dress and teeth stained by dirt.

# buried

*Beat the Brides: Ten Ways to Make Your Wedding Stand Out*

She smiled, a hundred hundred teeth all in a row, lined in red. They were the central focus of a pale oval face which boasted thick black eyelashes and crowned with Blondee-blonde hair. She smiled, but her thin wisps of eyebrows frowned, menacing, letting everyone know she could get what she wanted. Her full breasts bulged in her cream-coloured and now mud-caked dress, spindle-thin arms clutching severed flowers, red and green, red and green.

Beside her stood her new husband. He was taller, his face brushing the words 'The Big Dream', which were big and brash and purple. His hair was slicked smooth and black, a canopy for black eyebrows, themselves a roof for a small black moustache. His eyes were unrusted metal grey, his skin as pale and creamy as his new wife. He wore a meek smile above a black jacket with white trimmings. His soiled white shirt was open just enough to let a few strands of chest hair poke free.

They stood side-by-side, a rain of colourful paper strands falling from the sky, just for them. Below them words danced, inviting the reader to open the magazine up and find out who they were. Blondee obeyed.

*It's a Sizzling Summer—BBQ on the Big Day*

There was another woman, housed inside an oval, surrounded by an army of words. She was smiling, head cocked to one side, plumper and with smaller eyelashes than the woman on the front. Someone had scrubbed her eyes away with a pen. She had a long name, and she was an editor. She had some things to tell this month, just you wait, and this season's hottest wedding will be yours. Some words were larger, grander, and bolder than the others: 'Deck Chairs', 'Barbecue', 'Spicy Vows' and 'Margaritas'. At the bottom of the page was 'Julie' and then XXX, as though she had tried to cross out her own name.

Then came a list, all letters and numbers. Blondee turned the page again. And again.

*Grooming the Groom: Getting Him to Match*

More large words, 'Co-ordinate', 'Ties', 'Disaster' and 'Focus'. There was another man, choco-shake brown hair this time, a huge frown and sad eyes. His mouth was bent downwards. 'Take control'. You can spend years searching for the perfect match, only to find a clash on the big day! The page was lined, mauve and lilac. Keep track not only of what he's wearing, but his friends as well! Novelty ties.

Page-by-page there were pictures of the world, of the big world—the one outside.

*City Brides*

There were buildings, high as the clouds, spiralling upwards. Shops and offices and apartments blurred into the background, behind a smiling tan-skinned woman and her wife. They were each holding glasses with stems, tall and thin as the towers which surrounded them, filled with a golden fizz. The words here were stuck to a small white box. The month's hottest city, Barcelona, home to all the celebrity weddings. Honeymoon in the Spanish deserts, air-conditioning, bride-sweat, planning ahead. Sun-sets. Wedding-nights in luxurious mini-pools, six-star hotels, the only water for tens of miles around: all yours. All night casinos and real Catholic priests. Words without meaning. Round-the-clock caviare with real cod. Real love.

The women were watching one another, their eyes gleaming. They were both laughing as the sky hung in a dozen colours behind them. Nipples had been drawn on their dresses in blue biro.

Three pages over and there was a new woman, holding her arm out, heavy silver rings circled over her arm, 'Le Prins' huddled in curled letters into the corner. Her smile showed no teeth but it was wide, the edges of her mouth almost touching her yellow hair; hair which collapsed to her shoulders. She too wore a near-white dress, which matched her big smile.

*The Flowers You Pick Say Everything About You*

Pictures of plants in a dozen shapes and colours. Some curled around and around, blood red. Some drooped white-yellow. Passionate love, timeless friendship. Be careful what you choose. Don't fall for the tricks of the florist! Florist.

*Wrong Flowers, Wrong Function*

Turn the page again, glossy-under-skin, a group of women laughing together, stepping from a huge red car with rows and rows of windows.

*The Perfect Hen Night*

This is your big goodbye. Make it a send-off to remember. Not the night before the wedding, first-time-bride mistake. The street was slick-wet with puddles, flagstones shimmering in a hundred coloured lights chasing away night. No tacky discount-store accessories, give them something special. A broach or matching watches. Lists of bars: city, region, country. Don't drink too much, beware photos.

*Wear Your Feet*

A dark black page and a pair of pale feet, sparkling silver shoes hung on precariously.

*A Simple Touch*

A man and a woman were stood outside a smart small hut, walls white and elegant. She had a smile on her face, not too big, but showing enough teeth to bare her happiness to the world. He had a silly grin, which was unthreatening, somehow kind. A good wedding doesn't need to cost your house, as long as you plan it right. The key to your future, sincere vows. Select party. Securing your hopes. Her dress was cream-white too, but around her neck were strings of beads she made herself. A home-cooked meal for all the guests. Modern values. Her hair was brushed smooth and lapped around her milkshake-coloured shoulders. His hair was short, and finely tousled. They're both young, younger than anyone gathered between the pages so far. Both were staring directly at the camera, not pretending to look somewhere else. They held their hands together, matching rings glinting in the half-light of morning.

A few pages on and there were lists of vows, each one next to a pair of rings locked together.

The modern: I give myself to you whole, to you and to no other. To you I will be observant and tend to your every need. I will be your wife and you will hold and protect me in return. You shall stay strong for me and I will assist you as long as I shall live. A vow for proper roles, getting off to a good start. Ideal to raise a family.

Then the religious: In sight of God I take this sacred, solemn vow. To be with you eternally, that we may serve His will together, that we may shine in His everlasting glory. I promise never to give myself to another of the flesh, I promise never to break our union, I promise to live in purity until the day we dwell with Him. Spiritual. More and more popular. Exchanging chastity rings for wedding rings.

The classic: I take you to be my everlasting husband. My eternal friend, my faithful partner and my love from this day forward. Here before all I take a solemn vow to be your partner in sickness or health, wealth or poverty, in good times and bad. Forsaking all others, I will love and support you without limit, to honour and give respect to you and to cherish you as long as we both shall live. Longer, not for all. Requires both bride and groom to speak.

Which vows are right for you? None: fuck off, came the biro reply.

The next page was covered in more illegible words and an endless stream of numbers.

Then there were two more women, arm-in-arm. Choosing your chief bridesmaid. Your chief bridesmaid is there to help you up the aisle. She can handle any last-minute crises and cheer you on from the sidelines. A loyal, dependable friend. Someone you can count on. She should be unmarried herself, she can be next. A gown that goes with yours, but doesn't overshadow it. Sombre deep colours. Her own speech, at the meal afterwards, her way of helping you into your new life. Someone important, someone who wants what's best for you. Someone you know intimately. The two women were laughing together, like the women stepping from the big red car, but these ones had tears in their eyes, above wide crimson mouths.

The pages flicked by faster and faster, there was less room to take things in and the words were getting more complicated, more exotic and strange. Hire-carriage services. Specialist catering services. Professional make-up engineers.

At the very back there was another double-page with few words. Proposal. The scent of surprise. A woman alone in a street, in the dark. She looked scared. A hundred shadows were cast by the street lights and she was holding her bag with both hands, which were sheathed in delicate off-white gloves. She was alone. Little does she know her soon-husband is stepping from a car around the corner, flowers in hand, ready to meet her. Any moment, stepping from the shadows.

# drowned

I HAD TAKEN THE MAGAZINE and hidden it, beneath the lino, beneath the dirt floor, wrapped in plastic to keep it fresh. Beneath my feet the brides smiled up at me, sharing my memory. I had been one of them. I had worn a dress and recited vows and smiled a big big smile. How had I done it?

"Burberry."

"Yes my dear?" An arched eyebrow.

Had I donned my cream white dress by the ocean?

"I was just wondering—"

Had I recited vows in a forest?

"What were you wondering?"

In a city? Lights towering over us.

"Does it bother you?"

I and my love, my spouse, for better or worse.

"Does it bother you," I repeated, "when I go to see Frederick?"

Forsaking all others.

"I have a question for you," Burberry replied.

For the rest of our lives.

"Go on."

The rest of our lives, until we're taken and placed somewhere else, wiped clean.

"Do you love me?"

"I love you," I replied.

"Then no, it doesn't bother me. I love you, too."

Burberry left to cook at the fire tap—I told her I was unwell. I couldn't tell her about the magazine—she had hated the book, this would be worse. Really, I needed to keep it to myself.

I unfurled the lino, took the magazine and hid it beneath my fraying jumper, then stepped into the warm air. Rain fell in a series of flecks, weakly spattering my face as though it had run out of energy. Nobody had found the page, it hadn't been mentioned. It was gone.

Of course they hadn't found the page. They never would. Each line about the end of love had been wrong. There was no end to love. There were no tearful goodbyes, no shattered promise, no break-up sex. There was marriage, there was union, and it was eternal. The page had been wrong and so it had been corrected.

I took the magazine to my mock-living room, by the deserted, discoloured section of wall. The plank that was my mantelpiece still rested on the ground. I sat on it and flicked through the magazine once more.

*The Great Outdoors*

Another page, another wedding: the great outdoors. Endless piles of trees under an ever-blue sky. Two men: one older one younger, both handsome. Rows of words surrounded them from both sides. One was holding a pole with a wire dangling from the end, the other looking at him with unmatched adoration. The older one had thick eyebrows and set his eyes in the middle distance, toes on the edge of a stream which had frothed itself into frenzy. The ground was a neat carpet of wood chippings. For the alternative wedding, try the great outdoors. Fresh air, new love. The sky has faded purple-blue and clashed with the green trees.

The next page and another couple, her curly black hair was tied up above her head, her dress nearly-white. Him with a closed-mouth grin. They had their feet in water and were surrounded by sand which almost matched her dress. Red flowers scattered around them, swirled crimson shells. Tiny letters passed unnoticed beneath her feet, dress by Regina Ingrid Norman-Gotes. Exclusive. An ink-scrawled knife stuck into her gut.

Words filled the sky: the best beaches this time of year. Sand beaches, shingle beaches, or for the very edgy, post-urban beaches. Sand or pebbles or slabs of salt-water-soaked concrete. A new season of bridal gowns for the very thing. Disaster-relief styles. Louisiana chic. Chapel Wave Weddings will give a service in a water-lapped church, waves dancing by your toes and stained glass above your head. Celebrities.

Or the great outdoors indoors. A winter wedding. Actual snow. A projected sky, you won't know the difference. It's the great Alps of our parents. Ice-themed accessories. A couple in matching copper-toned ski-gear.

I stopped reading. Burberry would be wondering where I was. I buried the magazine beneath the mantelpiece and left.

There were footprints everywhere. All around the bush, all around the courtyard, to and fro. One line of craters were half the size, someone sprinting on their toes, trying to be somewhere quickly. The footprints were crossed by another pair, slow and sure, feet firmly planted. What could they have been so sure of?

I followed a series of them to the fire tap.

"Blondee," my neighbour greeted.

"Fluffed." I hadn't seen him for a while.

"I haven't seen you for a while," he said.

"What's been happening?" I asked. "Why are you naked?"

"I came out to keep an eye on things. It's all been pretty strange lately, you'll have noticed. Not that things have been especially normal at yours, eh?"

"What?" I asked.

"Well, your two—"

"Oh." My two lovers. The crime seemed least now. I watched a drop of water crawl from his temple, down his face, zigzag through stubble, cross his jawbone and ride down his neck, through the light hair on his chest and down over the flat surface of his stomach. It rested in the curve of his belly button.

"Blondee, what're you looking at?"

"Nothing." I moved my gaze to his face.

"It's been crazy", he continued. "Everywhere. There were fights, two fights, just today. But no-one did much, we all stood and watched. The first time it was a woman and a man scratching and smacking and bleeding, the second time it was another two, both men. One broke the other's nose."

"Oh."

"Are you going to the meeting?" he asked. I didn't know what he meant. "The meeting. Pilsner ain't happy. He wants to have a meeting, with everybody. Even them. It's around now, actually."

"Why aren't you there?"

"It's not much to do with me. Besides, what's passed is past. Anyway I've been outside long enough. Goodbye, Blondee."

"Goodbye, Fluffed."

He turned, small round arse disappearing into his hut. I poked my head inside our triangle-home, wondering if Burberry had heard about the meeting.

She had, she said, reaching her arms up to embrace me. She handed me the remains of the food she had prepared and I ate, the two of us covered by a scratchy wool blanket as rain battered the window. By the time I had finished water was rushing down the glass and pooling at our feet: with the blanket wrapped around ourselves we made our way to the courtyard.

At the courtyard it was roaring, brutal, beating down the skin of my ears, a deafening monotone buzz. The sky had collapsed, a force of water pressing me into the ground. I could barely see in front of my face but I could hear it, the rush of water on stone. He hadn't seen us. Pilsner stood alone, his back hunched, a shadow through the rain which forced my eyelids closed. I placed my hands to my eyebrows as he raised his arm, waving back and forth. No-one came. Another rush and he was gone.

Burberry left, seeking shelter, asking me to go with her.

Not now, I said: soon.

I stumbled forward, limbs heavy, pulled to the earth, or pushed, or shoved and pressed and crushed. I felt the flagstones against my feet, wet and gritty. Perhaps someone would come. Perhaps someone would come and explain. Explain something. My mouth was dry. I felt the wet metal of the tap on my fingers, pulling the handle upwards. It was lost in the ocean which fell from above. I slumped down, stone against hip, stone against shoulder. I clung to the tap, holding on so I couldn't be swept away, my fingers clutching wetly at my arms. I screwed my eyes closed and screamed. Screaming, screaming, where I would never be heard, screaming until my lungs felt bloody and my body limp and I was lost.

"You're wet, Blondee." A familiar voice in my ear.

Then it was gone.

# i love you

"FREDERICK?"

"Yes—yes, Blondee?"

"Why do you talk the way that you do?"

"Wh-what do you mean, Blondee?"

"The sort-of stuttering, like you have to force the words out. It's like it takes an effort. Does it take an effort?"

"I don't—I don't know, Blondee. I don't remember things being any—different."

"Are you scared?"

"What?"

"Are you scared, Frederick? Are you worried about the things you say?"

"I—I don't know... it's easier to convey—to communicate my thoughts with things—things like models, the things I make."

"But aren't you scared then? About what people will think of the things you make?"

"No. No."

"Why not?"

"I... the things I make... they're not me. People look at those, not at me. If I talk, then, then they look at me—right at me. I don't like that. It would be better if—if no-one ever looked at me. I prefer to watch other people, and listen to them. It's better if no-one sees me. Besides, it's easier to see them."

"I have to go and see Burberry. I love you, Frederick."

"I—I love you too, Blondee."

She shimmered; the lake shimmered. She had no memory of being in water, so I watched her first-time-wallowing in the lake. She had stepped in tentatively, poking at it with her toe, then slapping at it with the flat of her foot, then kneeling, sloshing water over her shins and shoulders. Finally she had waded out, summoning waves with one hand, a box of old blueberries in the other.

Her mouth was stained blue.

We weren't supposed to be there, she and I. It was her idea. She was loving every moment. She took another blueberry from the box and aimed it at her mouth—I pulled myself free of my clothes and waded in the join her.

Once I reached her I placed my arms about her body. She put a blueberry into my mouth. I swallowed.

"Are you happy?" I asked her, juices running down my chin.

"I am." She ate another, chewing it carefully and finishing it before continuing. "I really am. I miss Tanned less. It doesn't feel real any more. I'm happy with you. You thief."

She grinned at me, a stage of stained teeth.

"Were you happy with Tanned?"

She pulled away a little, tilting her head to one side and dipping her dreadlocks into the water.

"I was at first. We got together because it made sense—there we were. We did it because we couldn't really think of anything else to do. He'd go and pick these sprigs and twigs off the bushes for me—it was another thing he claimed he remembered, giving plants as presents, but he didn't ever write that down. But otherwise every day was the same. It was the way he liked it, really."

She pulled me close to her once more, speaking so-so gently into my left ear.

"It wasn't like what we are. It was different to us, and what I feel for you. I felt for Tanned quickly, I mean that I loved him quickly, and then it ended quickly. What I feel for you Blondee, that took a long time—a very long time. Seeing you at the bush and at the courtyard. At first I wanted to get to know you, but then I wanted to know your body as well. After that I wanted you even more, I wanted to be familiar with every piece of you. I couldn't hide that forever.

"There was no room to move before, now there is. I worry Blondee, I worry that I don't have anything to offer—but then I think, why does that even matter? I exist. I don't agree with the way things are done because those memories aren't mine and they're not any better than mine, the ones that I've made for myself. Who can say that our memories all fit together anyway? Perhaps we're all from different worlds, ones which are totally opposite. Like Frederick said. Perhaps our memories couldn't possibly fit together. Why does it even matter?

"And I can talk about this with you, Blondee. There's no pretending. I wish that I had been the one to break the book, that I had torn a page from it. Don't look so sad. You don't control how they act; nothing they do is your fault. They're just scared. We don't have to be."

She picked a blueberry from the box and held it aloft.

"This is it: goodbye Tanned."

She was serious; she dropped the berry into the water. It didn't sink though, it floated slowly away. She placed another berry into my mouth. I was in love with her. She told me she loved me, and that was true. Whatever else may have been uncertain—unreal—that was true. I know that. The look in her eyes was absolute.

I should have sunk the both of us—dragged me and her down to the bottom, my body wrapped around hers, firm and fierce, until all our breath was gone.

*Choosing*

A single word, 'choosing,' spread lower-case across the two pages. In the centre was a bride, staples in her skull, a man on either side. She showed no teeth, and beneath her veil she looked confused. Who to pick? Who would be your ideal spouse? What to look for. Who to look for. When to look.

Medical school? Meaningless words, missing memories. A no, anyway. Long hours, low pay.

Writer? Someone to talk to. No, not a stable job, no planning for the future.

Comedian? Makes you laugh, giggles in bed. No.

The office job may be boring, it may not save lives, but a stable job with stable pay is a must.

But what use is pay in our world?

In the end it is important to look for what will be provided after the wedding. Looks and laughter wear thin. Houses last. Good food and comfort are to be savoured. You might think he's dull now but you'll be the one laughing in fifty years. Fifty years.

But I didn't drag her to the bottom of the lake; she dragged me by the arm to dry land. We lay side-by-side in the sun, water slowly sizzling from our bodies, brushing fingers lightly against one another's: first the edge of the smallest, then two, then three, then interlocking longest fingers, then all in a chaos, caressing and jumbled in one another's hands. Her foot brushed mine and we entwined toes, then clumsy movements of sole against heel, ankle on calf.

"Blondee," she whispered, her voice light with joy.

"Burberry," I replied.

# part five

Burberry.

# a wedding

"I give myself to you whole."

The words left my mouth quickly, slipping from my lips. It was beyond my control. They came so easily, I must have always known them.

Frederick stood before me, shifting from foot to foot. Our neighbours—least and minor—surrounded us, their expressions a mixture of awe and curiosity, envy and fervour. This was the first wedding but there would be others to follow. It was going well.

*Do You Love Me?*

No, I willed the question away. No. I turned my face slightly, glancing through the crowd as much as my view allowed, but she wasn't there. Did I want her there? Did I want her seeing this?

I had to speak, I had to say the next line. He looked on edge.

"To you and to no other," I continued. I needed to clear such thoughts—this was my big day—I needed to be happy.

There was a low rumble from the group. I turned my head again, a tiny pivot to the right. They were smiling. Perhaps they were happy for me. Perhaps they remembered my fling with Burberry.

*Do You Love Me?*

Do you love me? She had asked, and I had answered.

She had never found the magazine, and I hadn't always been careful: I'd even brought it back to the triangle-hut, once or twice. I thought about what would happen if she had found it, what she would say, how it would fit into her breaking of the rules. One afternoon I was lain on our bed of foam, the scent of her skin curling around my nostrils, the pages in my hands above my head. She'd come back early, her face agleam. She was excited to see me. I quickly dropped it to the floor, and her eyes missed it. They were trained on my face.

"Happy to see me?"

And I had smiled and kissed her, moving over so she had space to lie by my side. She'd run her fingertips over my neck, the tips of her nails gently grating. I'd closed my eyes, bringing myself to the room with the mantelpiece, watching my husband. Her lips had then met my forehead and brought me back into our glass triangle. I'd shivered as she moved her hand down my spine, my toes curling, fingers clenching. I'd wanted to taste her.

"To you I will be observant."

Small droplets danced about Frederick's forehead. He coughed, he grinned. This was his wedding too. I tried to cough myself, but my dress clutched at my body, pressing my breasts into my lungs and my flesh into my bones. I looked down at myself, my curves somehow more robust, more pronounced. I had been sewn in—there would be no taking it off until it came away in his hands, filled with a mad lust for soft creamy skin beneath a stubborn cream-coloured dress.

Your wedding night, went the five-page spread. Spread spread spread. Spread rose petals. Spread yourself, spread yourself gently before him. Spread yourself so he may take you. There are techniques you can use but first, first spread yourself and be ready. If you are a virgin take deep breaths. There was a woman rolled back on an elegant bed, the largest bed I had ever seen, her lips smeared red and the boundaries of her body blurred by nearly-see-through clothes which covered bust-to-thigh.

He looked on edge. We had only fucked the once, but soon he would crawl atop me, ravenous and ready. I would feel the bulge of his belly on mine and it would be his breath on my face. He would drive himself into me with unworldly force, my husband, beetroot-scented, filling me over and over. I would spread myself before him and I would be his.

*Do You Love Me?*

I had savoured her taste, her scent, her breath about my chin and cheek as her fingers curled and curved around me. She'd been wild and slow, and took her time with my body. She had always taken her time until I was ready. I would pounce on her in return. I had known when it was the last time, this was the break-up sex, this was it without her knowing. She came whilst looking into me, I love you, I love you, thinking it would be forever. Her breath on my face.

"I will tend to your every need."

What needs would Frederick have beyond sex? Perhaps I could help him with his works, perhaps I could help him rebuild the world. I was doing so myself, with my first recorded memory, one which put all the others to shame. I hadn't even needed to place it in the book. Soon other weddings would follow. I took a deep breath and felt myself expand, the dress a little looser. Breathe. Slowly. Breathe.

The dress was too tight. Each inhale was too short, too sharp. The goo smeared over my lips was bitter and gritty. I wasn't quite the same as in the magazine, but I was close enough.

Now I was framed by two-dozen stares.

I had spent nights watching her, when it was late or sometimes during the rain, watching her as she slept. She was one of the most beautiful women in all the world, her delicate face cradled in strong ropes of hair. So sure of herself. I was special, I was lucky to have access to her, to be able to feel her and hold her. Soon I would have to give her up. I would live my life as I had done before, as I had done outside, with a wedding and a real life. I wasn't going to waste a moment left of her by sleeping. I had rested in the light-hot hours as she went about from chore to chore, resting with the hot sun glowing through the glass. Each time she'd pulled me back into the world with the soft shoo of her voice or the soft shake of her hand my skin prickled as though it was the last time.

*Do You Love Me?*

"Of course I do, shut up." A smile, a joke, her heart filled with hope. She hadn't seen it coming. I'd been angry at her for being so stupid. For having been wrong. She had been sitting on the bed above me, I on the floor by her feet, watching her long toes wriggle as she chewed on red licorice. How could she not know? I had kissed her calf, a gesture, I wasn't sure what kind.

"This will end."

"Hmm?" Her moan, her mouth mushing sugar.

"This has to end."

A pause. A heavy glug of a swallow.

"What?"

"I'm sorry, Burberry."

I'd heard the shuffle of arsecheeks over foam, then seen her face loom over mine, peering at me from the side of our bed.

"Are you feeling all right, Blondee?" she had asked.

"I am."

She'd looked concerned. She'd wanted to peel away whatever was sticking to me.

"Is it what everyone has been saying? The gossip has died down, there's no need to worry. The world will say what it wants, it's nothing to do with us. We are free."

"No," I replied, "no."

My throat was too small to fit through a larger word. Palms slick with sweat.

"Is it Pilsner? He'll get over it eventually," she said, "just you see. He's sour and old. He's just picking fights to he can avoid talking to himself. Don't bother with Pilsner, no-one else does." She'd stroked my hair.

"No. No."

"Frederick? Has Frederick been unhappy, has he said something? Does he need to spend more time with you? Will he not share? It's him. Is it him?"

"No."

"Then what?"

"Burberry."

Upon her name she'd slid from the foam to the thin scuffed lino on the floor, taking my hand in hers.

"Blondee," she'd answered. Confusion had transformed to fear.

"Burberry, this has to end. Burberry and Blondee, Burberry and Blondee and Frederick, Burberry and Blondee and this hut. It has to end."

"I don't understand. Are you not happy?"

How would I know? Perhaps it's different outside, perhaps it's different in the real world. Perhaps it's larger, it's bigger and better, perhaps every heart-jump and belly flutter is a feeble tremor compared to reality. Am I not happy? How the fuck should I know?

"Blondee, please," her voice a slow, low crackle. "Please explain to me."

I didn't want to explain. I wanted to hold her. To hold her or to run as far from the hut as possible. Anything but there, doing that. Anything.

"It's not real, Burberry."

"Fuck," her voice growing, building to a growl, "I don't understand. Fuck. Blondee, please don't do this. I love you. Don't you love me?" Her eyes flooded, her smile wrinkled, crumpling into misery.

I'd kissed her neck. "Burberry, I'm sorry. You're amazing. It's not right."

"Don't do it." Sobs bursting from her lungs.

"I'm sorry. I'm sorry."

I'd pulled her toward me, her face buried in my breast, my nostrils over thick wads of smoke-smelling hair. Deep breaths, I'd told myself, deep breaths. A deep breath to force the clog from my throat, a deep breath to keep my eyes from welling and melting from their sockets, a deep breath to tear away tears, or else I'd cry and wail and never stop. I'd held her cold skin and she'd sobbed and shaken and I'd gripped her arm until my fingers stiffened and cramped and trembled with her.

Then she was gone.

"I will be your wife."

Here we were, in the courtyard, surrounded by guests of two-two-two. Red and green leaves scattered the ground beneath our feet, soft music floating about our rigid bodies. As he heard the words Frederick smiled. He wasn't used to the sounds. Wife. It was new and exciting.

For days after the break-up with Burberry I had waited and longed, alone in the triangle-hut, not eating or wandering, simply feeling the shape of her printed in foam. This was right this was right this was right, I'd told myself. I had given her the coloured curtains and she had given me a rope from her head. I'd placed it under the bed. There was no other choice. Finally I had eaten, then dipped my head in the bucket, sloshing cold water over my armpits, cleaning myself from toe to thigh to neck. By the time I'd stood outside I was excited, my skin tingling from the cold.

What would he say?

It would be fine, I had known that: he would know what was right.

The ground had shimmered, wet below and warm above. My socks scuffed the sand, spraying fine grit through the damp air. The courtyard had stood unguarded, a sight I still had to get used to. Then limp waft of a breeze pressed into me, pressing me back, but I hurried on anyway.

For a moment I'd waited, staring at Frederick's heavy door, unsure of what to say. For the first time I had noticed the faded outline of numbers. Six, seven and—it swung open.

"I have to come in," I had croaked, squeezing his back.

"Yes, yes. Come in, Blondee."

"I have a new memory, Frederick. There's a new way of seeing our world. We can rebuild the old one, for real, we can live as we always should have done."

He had been confused but he'd also been patient. My words ran from my mouth, falling and scattering about the room, ready to be examined and explained. Marriage, companionship, forever, excluding, excluding all others, society, men and women, real roles, a path, a direction.

"Blondee, where were you? Where have you been?"

"Now there's the thing. She's gone, Frederick."

"Why?" He'd drawn the word out, spreading it over three of mine.

"I chose you."

"But you already had me," he'd replied.

I'd slowed down and placed my head on his belly. I placed my story in order and paused now and then, giving the words time to spread out. I had a memory. I had many. In the old world you chose someone, you had a ceremony and you stayed with them, forever. It was marriage. I had had a marriage, I had had a husband, but that me—that person—she had died, wiped from history. We were all married, or waiting, it was a matter of time. No angry shaking tears, no uncertainty, no running to the other end of the world, no averted looks, no awkwardness. It was forever.

He had a hundred questions.

Who was my husband?

"I don't know, he died, too."

What if you don't?

"You live and die alone."

Why didn't you put it in the book?

"It doesn't fit."

I didn't mention the magazine, he wouldn't have understood. There were others, dozens of women, I'd said, and I could see them all. They painted their lips and wore semen-toned dresses and were happy. They lived to make their husband's lives easier. They had roles, they had purpose. It was their job.

"You don't feel like you have a purpose?"

"I do, Frederick. I will."

There were men, bold, confident, straight lines on smart suits. They were given a bride to be happy.

"Do you love me, Frederick?"

"I do love you, Blondee."

"It's what people in love do."

Question, question, question. I poured the pages of the magazine from my lips. I'd whispered and giggled and ranted. I hadn't forgotten a word. We'd lain on his bed and he'd stroked my neck as I'd talked, and eventually his hand had slowed and stopped, his breath the gently buzz of a snore.

When he awoke he saw the truth.

"So, we'll be married then?"

"You will hold and protect me in return."

I formed each sound carefully and slowly. I smiled, tears welling in my eyes. He would protect me, wrap me up in his arms, wrap me up in his home—our home—and shy me away from the eyes of the world. My cheeks tickled and I laughed, his gentle smile answering me. The crowd was silent, they approved. It was time to continue.

He'd grinned. He'd rummaged through a plastic bag and pulled free a wave of cream-coloured fabric. "This is for you."

I had been sitting speechless, running my hands over the cold material. It was the smoothest thing I had ever felt. I pressed my face to it, before catching sight of myself. Less rough, I needed to be less rough. I gently stroked it with my fingers.

"Thank you," I managed to whisper.

He laughed. "Rings will be here soon."

"Did you tell her what it was for?"

"I didn't. We will."

And she'd arrived, a patter at the door.

"Blondee. Can I come in?" She'd been cheerful.

I'd told her she could. The least must all wander in and out of one another's homes, as free and thoughtless as lovers. She might have been minor by pronouncement, but she was one of them.

"You've got a job for me, Frederick?" Her voice sounded far away, as though it wafted from a music player.

"I do," Frederick replied. "It's not—it's really not just any job though, Rings, it's special. Blondee has had a memory. More than a memory, it's bigger than that, really, it is. Do you want to tell her about it? No? Well I will."

So he did, he told her every word I had read and relayed, described every picture I had reported as my own and recorded as memory. He'd missed nothing. Her face had fallen, suddenly serious, weighted by it all. She'd had to sit on the floor.

"It's a lot—a lot to take in Rings," he'd said, "but this is how people lived on the outside. We're going to be the first to live like this here. We'll be the first."

Eventually she'd stood, shaken by excitement. The news had stirred her.

"People should know then, they should know about this, they certainly should."

"I suppose," Frederick replied, or something like it. "But we'll need a dress."

Spinster. The word came to me as she hurried out the door.

Within hours the world knew.

Door by door by door. From the courtyard to every fire tap.

"Blondee and Frederick are getting married."

Salt, sugar, and nutmeg were stirred in.

"Well..."

"Go outside," Frederick had said. "We need some water." He'd handed me his bucket which didn't smell or leak and I'd trotted to the courtyard.

"Blondee! Blondee! It's her, Blondee! Is it true? It's all true, I knew it was. It makes sense, I knew, I always knew that mine was the one. We'll be getting married ourselves, though not before you."

Laughter, playful or snide, and more questions. I told them they must have heard it all.

"Tell us yourself," they'd said, "we want to hear *your* memories. I heard she was married before. What did you say? Is that true Blondee?"

The sun had slipped away by the time I'd carried the bucket back, filled with water. I hadn't even remembered touching the tap.

"Blondee," Frederick had said in a burst of breath. "Here."

He'd handed me a ring. It was woven from old copper wires.

"You shall stay strong for me."

This was the first. There would be more, but we were first, and people we had never even seen, least and minor, were gathered to watch. To watch, or judge, or copy. I didn't care. This was it, my new life. This was it. I peeked at the crowd and for a moment I thought I saw Tie, grinning and happy and not even dead. This was right—if I felt him here I knew it had to be. He was always so steady and sure.

*Do You Love Me?*

There was no time for that. Eventually I would forget her, forget the sticky taste of her skin and the slow, deliberate strokes of her hand. Her words and her sullen sleep faces would leave my mind and she too could start afresh. She would find a husband, or a wife, and she would be happy.

"I will assist you as long as I shall live."

The last words of my vow echoed over the courtyard and two-dozen people cheered. Frederick stepped toward me and pressed his lips to mine, then pushed my mouth open with his tongue and thrust it inside. This was it. This was it. This was it.

# burned

I STOOD BOLT UPRIGHT: it didn't do for a wife to slouch. We had our own cooking-stove, mounted in the corner of our home: it took in a little gas cylinder and burst out a delicate blue flame. We had blue fire. I was even more proud of the fact that we now had privacy: no-one could peer upon what I cooked, and I cooked gladly.

I was cooking a meal for my husband. A recipe. The handwriting of the recipes had improved: that was my doing. I had given a class on that very subject—when writing, it is important for a wife's hand to be as graceful as the rest of her. I had given the class short sticks and had them practice upon the ground, scratching in the dirt: we made sure none of the men saw such rough behaviour. And Ketamine's handwriting had improved immensely: the recipes were now far more legible.

The classes were popular—all the least, minor, and moderate women would gather at the courtyard to learn something new. Almost all, but some things—and some people—cannot be helped, however much you might try, however much you want what's best for them.

I looked over our home. Tables, mirrors, and a pestle-and-mortar. We even had a yellow-skinned plastic chair, without a single crack or sprain. It was surprising what you found in the rations-box when you were the first ones in. The order was changed and not a single person spoke out or complained. Pilsner had stood by, a standing scowl, but when a new-married couple shouted 'those two first,' nobody had spoken against it.

I brought the rice to the boil. Salt, sugar and nutmeg were stirred in. Nutmeg was my favourite—I was glad the recipe had called for it in great quantities. The rice went white at the edges and brown in the middle, so I stirred it vigorously until the colour was even throughout the pan.

I chopped three mushrooms and a cucumber with my new knife. It had no rust and fit snugly in the palm of my hand. We even had our own block of wood for chopping the vegetables. Frederick had told me that we'd earned it.

I glanced at the door: he would be home soon. The apartment was clean, I had made sure of that before cooking, and the coloured shapes shone brightly. He would be pleased, wherever he had spent his day.

I told them not to nag their husbands, as the magazine had told me. One of the women asked if she was allowed to nag, as she had a wife, not a husband. Her wife was seated next to her. I told her yes, she could nag, but those women with husbands must leave them be. If you are concerned, draw a circle around those thoughts; keep them contained, where they can't cause any problems.

Three powdered eggs were sifted over the rice. It was looking perfect.

It may have been young Ketamine who gave out the recipes, but I was the one who taught the others how to cook with grace. I saw the perfect woman behind my eyelids, stooped gently over a pan, her wrist firm but not rigid, her expression cool but not absent. They stood in rows and I helped them form their imperfect mimicries. Some did well; others poorly. I couldn't control such things.

Where was Frederick? He wasn't making artworks.

I needed to contain such thoughts.

An acrid smell: the rice began to burn—now the edges were getting too brown. But I couldn't turn off the stove: this food needed to be served hot. I stepped carefully to the front door and opened it, peeking out just a little.

There he was—lumbering toward me looking pleased with himself. His shirt was buttoned all the way to the top: your body is for your spouse, no-one else, not even the flies.

I quickly stepped back toward the stove. I was stirring when he came in, but I walked over to him and gave him a kiss on the cheek.

He told me the food smelled burned.

A circle.

I had a class to give that very afternoon. I sat in the corner of the room on a purple and gold cushion which was embroidered oh-so-delicately, and closed my eyes, envisioning a pristine married couple. At first all I saw was darkness and a dance of dim colours, then they swam into view. They were the couple from page 32 of the magazine, an older couple, with matching grey hair and slippers, dancing together in an 'old-fashioned minimalist apartment'. The couple were having a conversation, their voices identical to Frederick's and mine. I listened.

I held on to the scene for as long as I could before it dissolved. I delicately stood from the cushion and opened my eyes. Frederick lay on the bed, one hand over his eyes, his face scrunched tight and tense. I walked over to the bed and delicately kissed him on the cheek—no response. I told him I loved him and made my way out the door to the courtyard.

They were already there: almost all of them, as always. They waited patiently, wordlessly, in rows. The least women were on comfortable chairs or varying shapes, sizes and colours; the minor women on some rickety chairs or stools; the moderate women on crates or small stacks of bricks.

Least, minor and moderate, their demeanour was the same. They looked at me with equal expectancy.

This was our time at the courtyard: the rest of the time it was full of men. Men went to get the water, that was their task. Frederick would go to the courtyard for hours at a time, talking to the others—in some small way he had the same role as me, but the men didn't need so much guidance, it came naturally to them.

I took two deep breaths—the same two breaths I always took beforehand. They did the same, though I never told them to do the same. In the third row was Ketamine, alert—one of the most attentive.

As always I looked for Burberry, as always Burberry wasn't there—though I knew she would come eventually. She would want a spouse of her own.

I told them that today we would examine the topic of conversation: what should a wife say to her spouse? What was appropriate? I made it clear that this was not the same as addressing the husband, that this was the 'small talk'; the little conversations that make up a day.

Nodding. Forty nodding heads.

I reminded them to avoid questions: questions can make your husband tense. You want to soothe. Avoid gossip and hard, metallic topics like the length between rations, or memories, or things that affect the whole world.

A hand was raised: I had taught them that too. It was Ketamine's hand.

She asked what they could talk about.

I told her that was a good question. There was the weather—though that should stay light, its best to talk about the good things the weather brings: how wonderful the snow looks, or how nicely the sunlight shines through the window. If you like the sound of the rain, then tell him.

Another hand: a woman with short hair asked if there was anything else?

I told them that of course there was. The rations themselves made a good topic of conversation—talking about food always being satisfying. I suggested asking which recipes he wants to try—Ketamine beamed—and to talk about which things tasted good, and what they appreciated, to let him know he made the right choices.

Another hand: a woman said she had a wife—what should she talk to her about?

I told her she should talk about the same things: If one of them picked the rations then the other should let them know how good they were. Perhaps it was even easier for them; they didn't have to distract their spouse from harder thoughts, they could both talk about how much they loved the sound of the rain and the home they had together would be lighter than air.

She really should be hearing this, I thought. What was the point in her sitting alone in the triangle hut?

The class was over in no time at all. Each of the women lined up to thank me in turn. The wives were full of appreciation: I had given them something to talk about. Eventually Ketamine stood before me.

We each told the other how happy we were for them. She had married Jay the casinoist. They were good together, she said so. They worked as a team. She would write the recipes and he would take them to the casino night, handing them out along with the alcohol. We would then all chatter over them whilst taking small sips of drink—sometimes Jay would stay for a moment. He was the only man—other than Frederick—I had directly spoken to in a long time.

Ketamine asked me how Frederick was. I told her everything was wonderful. She asked me if he was still making artworks—I told her no, not at the moment. Perhaps he was forming something in his mind, working his way to something big. Ketamine said that she hoped so.

Two women passed by: thank you, thank you.

Ketamine thanked me and made her way back to her home. I waited for the rest of the women to leave, then did the same.

The sky was dimming at the window. It seemed to be getting dark early, but I knew Frederick would be home soon. I had busied myself by picking at frays from the carpet-circle near the door, being careful not to damage my nails.

I wandered over to the box by the bed. Inside were all my clothes, soft and some shiny, clothes which suited me and flattered my figure. At first I had been excited to try each new dress or shirt or skirt on, swaying in front of a mirror, feeling the pull of my own body. I was less excited now, and learning how to sew properly myself had robbed them of their mystery.

I went over to Frederick's box. The fabrics were firm and dull, course and stiff. In the days after our vows he had wanted to take a jacket or trousers and have Rings sew on something shiny or silky, but such things didn't fit, and I knew that if brides were to behave a certain way, then the grooms were too. He had wrinkled his face. It was the last time I'd told him to do anything.

I picked up a brown-grey jacket.

Blondee. What're you doing with that? Frederick's voice was met with the clunk of the door falling shut.

I told him I was just checking it was straight. Softer, I needed to be softer.

Frederick asked me how the class had gone and I told him that it had gone very well, then thanked him for asking.

He sat down, pulling his shoes from his feet. He told me there had been a scene.

I wondered if I should ask.

There had been a scene at the courtyard, after the women had left. Two men, both had beards. Frederick said one was called called Gut, and that they were shouting at each other, right in front of everyone. Gut hadn't even had a shirt on. They were shouting and shouting.

I told him their names were Gut and Green. He looked irritated at my interruption.

He continued. He told me that they were shouting, but Gut, he started crying. Actually crying, in front of everyone. People were whispering about how he should act more like a man, and they didn't look pleased. Green didn't like it either, and he spat at him. On him. Right in his face.

Frederick gestured to his nose, his words rushing by more quickly.

Eventually Gut stopped crying and said it didn't have to be that way. He said he didn't want it, he didn't want marriage—he wanted Green, and for things to be the way they were before. Then he started crying again, in front everyone. He just told him he loved him, over and over, until everyone ignored them. Pilsner had then taken him away somewhere.

I felt sorry for Gut.

Frederick didn't—he was sure he would come around and have a marriage of his own, eventually.

Frederick collapsed onto the bed, a small putter of dust spilling into the air. I slowly took off my clothes and lay with him.

I watched the darkening sky and felt his bulk on my body. In my body. I groaned, it was important to make sure I made the right noises. To move properly, to writhe. I writhed beneath him. He enjoyed that, it made him go faster, more little beads of sweat formed about his shoulders.

He pulled himself out and kissed my neck, his tongue slopping against my skin, leaving wet trails behind it. His mouth almost met mine, but he moved it down to my breast, sucking at it. I gave him another groan and lifted my arms above my head. He brought himself back up and entered me again.

*I was in the yellow room. There was the mantelpiece, there was the stone woman over to the side. There was the bucket of soapy water.*

*The door was open. A sickly light drizzled over the carpet, the carpet which was the softest thing my feet had ever felt. The door was open. I could leave the room. I called for my husband, and stepped over to the exit.*

*In the hallway everything was different.*

*The surfaces were bare wood, smoothed and varnished to a fine shine which was slippery under my fingers and toes. At regular points along the hallway were paintings, paintings of nothing, paintings of paint, exploding into a hundred colourful swirls.*

*Five paintings later there was a staircase, leading downwards. "Husband," I called, "husband where are you?"*

*There was a grunting from downstairs, furious, mad, the sound of a pack of animals swarming for food. The stairs were as slippery-smooth as the hallway, and I took each slow step one-at-a-time, placing one and then the other firmly on each ledge. There was another painting, and I reached out to touch it, but my shoulders fell forward and my legs gave way—a step slammed against my elbow, another on my hip, then my head, and knee, my hip again, clenching closed my eyes as I reached the floor at the bottom.*

*The grunting was everywhere, all around me. Cries and moans and whispered words—like that like that ohhhhh like that.*

*I opened my eyes to a white-lino floor, and pressed myself up, waiting for a twinge or shriek of pain. Nothing came. I stood amongst a dozen naked bodies, bodies in heaps and around one another, some slow and serious, some quick-quick-quick with giggles and big haw-laughs. In pairs and threes and four and more. The walls were made from glass, and light shone on every dip and pit.*

*I called for my husband again,*

*"Hermee, come over here," called two men, both dark-skinned and wide-grinned. One waved as the other kissed his jawbone.*

*I called for him again, but he wasn't there.*

*"Hermee," a woman behind me breathed into my ear, her dreadlocks on my neck. "Why do you look so startled? Come and cuddle me, we'll talk about it." She looked like her, full breasts and lazy gaze, given up for the sake of a marriage. I had known her body, languid and sleeping in a triangle. I had felt her tongue many times. How could I leave her?*

*I turned to her. She stared at me in concern, and I stared back. I knew her. I'd known her for years.*

*"Hera."*

*And she took me in her arms, and I in hers, as I stroked the thick ropes of her hair.*

No. No no no. It didn't fit. The memory was wrong—I shared the house with my husband, I had known that. What were all those people doing there? I didn't know them, I couldn't have known them.

It was a false memory, a fiction—I had never lived in such a place and neither had Burberry. I had fallen asleep, like Frederick, there next to me—we had both been asleep.

I huddled myself close to Frederick—he grunted and rolled away.

# miss a stitch

*The big glass doors were open, the warm air soft over the farmyard. Everyone was naked as before. There was a fence, rickety, built by one of us; below it the furrowed earth and green shoots, prying their way upwards. Beyond was a smaller house made of glass, a tangle of green leaves inside, a few with plump red fruits bursting from the stems, plants I didn't recognise. To the side was another hut, this one made of wood, straw spilling from the small entrance, a cluck-cluck-cluck echoing from within. On from that were more shoots, climbing upwards—all to be picked, chopped and eaten. Some to be smoked.*

*The group were sat on logs eating from bowls and plates, skin bare in the pale sunlight. The last breaths of a fire were gently puffed into the air. For some moments I watched them unnoticed, then a woman called to me:*

*"Hermee, come and eat."*

*A fat bird clucked and cooed about my legs, stabbing at the ground with its face. Come here you, one of the men called, grasping it as it flapped its wings and carrying it to a small wooden hut. Hera shouted through full lips, her dreadlocks flowing, but I couldn't hear her words.*

I awoke to bright sunlight, blasting in through the window. There was another class scheduled, they were becoming more and more frequent; the women were hungrier.

Frederick was already gone. I had failed to make him breakfast. I would have to make it up to him later. I slipped on, then buttoned up, a shiny-silk shirt and made for the door.

They were all there, waiting for me. Row after row after row, each on their own seats. Each turned to me and gave a smile of relief. A sigh or two drifted through the evening air. All watching and waiting.

This time I walked in amongst them. They cleared a space in the centre, between legs and wide eyes. There was a clattering over the stone: chair feet and boxes, wood and metal and plastic. I picked my way through, careful not to catch the flutter of my skirt under heel. I closed my eyes and flicked through each page of the magazine, searching for something to talk about. I opened my eyes and kept them lowered, careful not to meet with any expectant glares. I was surrounded by legs, bare and poised.

A bride was sat on a log, surrounded by stick-thin trees. Her hands were clasped in her lap, one leg hung limp over the other.

I introduced the day's topic: sitting. Then I coughed, ready to continue. I told them that sitting properly was important for a woman.

I paused, expecting a murmur to ripple outwards through the crowd. It didn't.

A hand held aloft: then what is the proper way?

I needed to demonstrate with someone.

There was a scuffle of limbs.

I made my choice, running my hand over the shoulder of a young woman by me. She nodded, her head bouncing quickly.

I told her how to position her legs, feeling her soft skin and the light fuzz of hair. I wrapped my fingers around her calf and planted her foot down. She trembled, her hairs prickling.

More scrapes of metal and stone. I looked up. Some at the back had stood to see better.

I whispered, remembering to soften my speech whilst hoping I could still be heard, telling her to hang her other leg over it.

I placed both hands over the quiver of her thigh and lifted it, placing it over the other. A soft scuffle of words scattered about me.

Right, I moved behind the woman, my nose nearly nestling in her hair. I took each of her arms and placed one hand in the other, both into her lap, my head balanced on her shoulder.

I stood up. The two women next to her copied, then the two next to them, then the next and then next, outwards and onwards until each was sat the same, on stools and deckchairs and crates which once held cans of cucumber.

That was that. I began to pick my way through the perfectly-folded legs perched on ramshackle seats. I had done enough. I wanted to go straight back home, but instead I waited at the front for each to come and thank me.

It was dark when Frederick returned.

Frederick had terrible news.

Terrible news and I had to prepare myself.

I was sewing. Whatever could be so important?

He told me Burberry was dead.

I didn't miss a stitch.

"Oh," I said.

Thread under, thread over.

He asked me how I was. He asked me what I was thinking.

I told him I was thinking about sewing, so we left it at that.

There was no sex. That night I lay in bed, eyes closed, watching her naked body spread before me, tasting the salt of her skin, tasting sugar on her mouth. I watched her lying next to me, sleeping peacefully and without dreams. Somewhere far from me came the dull clunking thud thud thud, at first in its usual near-nothingness, but growing stronger, reaching nearer and nearer until it was almost in the hut with me, almost until I could touch it or taste its dull earthy flavour. It entered my skull and curled around my brain, pounding the back of my eyes, working its way into the depths of my ears. I almost expected to hear her voice. Instead I heard Tie's.

"It wasn't just you."

And I wasn't surprised to hear him. His voice was there: he had burst from past to present, soft in my ear.

# the triangle hut

The bulk of my husband heaved over me, blocking the light, him a heavy mass, cloud-like, dripping sweatlets of rain. He was inside me—I had to remind myself that he was inside me.

I groaned and shifted and did all my usual positions and patterns, in order, running through the process in my head. Reminding myself to enjoy it. I placed myself several steps away; there, that was better, now I could see clearly—husband and wife, one atop the other. The wife performed with grace.

"What're you doing, Blondee?"

"You know what I'm doing, Tie. You told me you did it yourself."

"Not like this."

"I've done it many times."

"Not like this."

I gripped the sheets and tugged them to my ears, to muffle his voice, but I kept hearing it, dull and fuzzy through thick fabric.

"Go, go, go," I moaned, stretching out the final 'go', long and orgasmic. Frederick humped with more hurry, over, over, over.

"Are you enjoying it, my dear?" Tie's voice was sure enough, caring, cooing and soft. Full of judgement. I wanted it to go away.

"I enjoyed it before."

Had I said those words out loud? Frederick hadn't noticed, his face scrunched in ecstasy.

"Are you enjoying it, my dear?"

I wasn't enjoying it, but it wasn't so bad now, now that I was used to it. It was true, I had enjoyed it before, before magazines and gowns and total-world celebrity. But it was just once, a one-off, a fluke.

"That was the only time you had sex with Frederick."

"What?"

"That was the only time you had sex with Frederick. That's your husband inside you right now."

"Shut up, Tie."

"Mmmnaaargh," my husband groaned, his face crumpled, his cock exploding inside me. I smiled and brought my lips to his.

He fell asleep before long. I lay on my side, facing the rest of our home. Luxury, luxury, luxury. The best furniture in all the world. Tie had no comment. He had other things to say.

"Go there, Blondee."

"Go where, Tie?"

"You know where, my dear."

So I quietly slipped on my so-smooth clothes and slipped out. I made my way to the land of the minors: to the triangle hut. I made sure Frederick didn't hear a thing. He wouldn't approve.

Don't look at it, don't look at it, don't look at it.

I couldn't help myself.

There it was: a window propped against a wall. A piece of damp foam inside. She died in there.

I pulled back the fabric of the door. The dirty lino—which covered the worst of the dirt floor—was crusty with old blood. She was here, and she would never leave. I wondered if I could touch her. Running my finger over the brown scabs of clotted pools didn't feel much like touching her, but I did it anyway.

Burberry had dropped dead. It wasn't that uncommon a thing to happen. Could it have been foretold?

The lino was cold. I wiped the gunk off my hand and onto the foam. She'd had so much blood, coursing through her, coursing from her.

Burberry was dead, Tie was dead. But it was Tie who had come back.

I had never seen Tie's blood. He'd died alone, and it was all cleaned up. Pilsner had made sure of it.

Tie had had a new lover, and I never even knew their name, or what they did together. But I saw this new person when he'd smile or laugh. He'd talk about them endlessly, being careful not to give away too many details, not even saying why. He declared himself in love, his face bright red. I even saw this new person in his bright red face. Then I'd see them when he cried, and I hated to see him cry, as though everything was ever-ending. I said that it wasn't so bad, and he'd said he'd never been loved at all. I told him that wasn't true, that they do love him—haven't they said so? I always stopped the tears and got him to smile. I could do that.

But the last time, that was when I couldn't get the tears to stop. Nothing would work. I told him over and over that they loved him, they loved him, I was so startled. Haven't they said so? No, he'd said that they hadn't. He'd said 'I love you' and they didn't say it back. He should have known, he cried, he should have known it would never happen. Why would it?

I'd left to get him some water and when I'd returned he was gone.

No, it wasn't uncommon for people to drop dead. Tie had dropped dead, with a sliver of metal in his hand and criss-crossed wrists, he had dropped dead. And Burberry had dropped dead. She'd gone back to the triangle-home. She had used a shard of mirror hanging from a string, yanking it from the window-frame and plunging it into her neck, spurting herself over the floor, collapsing in a grunt, with a shudder, and a moan, on her hands and knees, trembling, then face to the ground, panting, panting, panting. She'd grown weaker, and who knows what she'd thought of, lying there, lost and sleepy, tired and alone, as she'd spread her last breath across the lino.

I lay on the stretch of foam. I traced her outline with my finger. I clasped a rope of her hair in my other hand.

"You're thinking of her, Blondee."

"Be quiet, Tie."

"I'm just saying."

"Be quiet, Tie."

I shuffled my body across the foam, over until I was resting in her outline. I inhaled, deep as my lungs would go, hoping to taste her. I spread my hand wide, hoping to feel her fingers entwined with my own. My toes, her toes. My lips, her lips.

Nothing.

I mumbled her name to myself. Burberry. Burberry. It wasn't me, Burberry, it wasn't my fault. I couldn't have had both of you. That's not how things are done. I did this to help. Burberry. I never stopped you, you could have found a husband yourself, you could have been happy. I'm not responsible for you, it's not my fault. I never stopped you.

I loved you.

Why did you leave? Why were you so stupid? You lost me, not yourself. You don't understand the world, you never did. I am building something that will last. We were in the way. That wasn't your fault. It wasn't mine.

I never stopped you.

# spinning won't help

I SWIVELLED AROUND ON MY YELLOW CHAIR. Around and around and 'round, the hut blurring and my head spinning. Frederick was still sleeping and I was bored of Tie. I could ignore him if I spun.

Until I had to stop, my head lighter than the air.

"When will you be giving your next lesson, Blondee?"

"Be quiet, Tie."

I didn't want to go to the courtyard and teach them.

"Is this how you lived?" Tie asked, "In these shiny shirts with those long nails?"

I nodded. It didn't matter.

I went to inspect our rations. Rice. Salt crackers. Dried peas. Mustard. I hadn't seen mustard before. I glanced at Frederick, seeking permission, but still he lay motionless, blocking out the room with his hands. I unscrewed the jar, gently dipping in my small finger, the one with the shortest nail. It tugged at my tongue. It tasted expensive.

As it had filled with ever-new items, the hut had lost colour. I had loved running my hands over the new furniture, feeling them crinkle or slip under hand. The last thing my husband had come home with was a large roll of mirror-sheet, crumple-crackled and metal-coloured. We'd hung it ceiling to floor. I had spent hours watching it. He even entered me in front of it. I'd been fascinated by the thousand tiny Blondees staring back.

The floor was covered in rugs and rectangles of carpet. Burgundy, maroon, a little navy blue, some red. No part of the floor looked empty, not even—

"It was there."

"I know it was, Tie."

"I'm just saying, my dear, it was there."

"Great."

"Mmmm. Blondee? Are you all right?" Frederick stirred, his throat filled with sleep. I had been talking out loud. Talk inside, Blondee, keep the talk inside.

"I'm fine."

"Mmmm," he groaned, drifting away.

Tie was right. He was dead as all fuck, yes, but he was right, that was where it had been. So it wasn't there any more. The towers, the offices, apartments, the silly little bricks. It had all been in the way. It was his idea, we need the space, he'd said. I just smiled and said of course, or something like that. Had I used a soft voice? Probably.

"So when will you give your next lesson?" he repeated.

"Be quiet, Tie."

"What's that?" Frederick sat upright in the bed. His eyes were pink. He lay back down before I could answer.

"What will you teach them, what will you show them my dear? Do you have anything left? Is there anything else you claim to remember? Any other womanly tips? What will happen when you run out, when you can't help them any more, when you don't have anything else to do? When you can't pretend you're not enjoying it any more?"

"Just fuck off," I shouted, throwing the dried peas.

"Blondee, what—what are you doing?" Frederick sat up again. "Pick them up will you, please, I'm trying to sleep."

*We were outside again, the naked group, the farm: but this time no-one was eating. Some were in pairs, sitting on logs and talking, some were running to and fro with thoughtless throaty laughs spilling from their mouths. I was on the ground, feeling firm flesh and nuzzling a neck. The man pressed against me and groaned, reaching his hand back and running it over my arse, pressing me into him. My cock was so stiff it ached. Someone whispered in my ear: you are so young, so young, just a boy, and the man whose body was pressed so warm against my own took me in his hand and guided me into him. I shuddered, and gently eased forward and back, each push making him moan, and I kissed the back of his neck and ran my fingers over the fuzz of his chest, pushing, pushing, pushing, over and over, each groan growing to a roar, and I took him in my hand, gripping him hard, thrust after thrust until he shook and spilled, until I burst, balls aching, the sweat running down my sides. The world was a blur, a soft panting rush.*

"You had a penis, Blondee?"

"I don't know, Tie."

"You were sure, so sure, my dear—you were a wife."

There was nothing I could say to him. These memories weren't mine; they were from someone else, from another world. I was a wife and I had been married to a husband.

But I couldn't remember his face.

"Perhaps they are stories, just stories—ones you remember from the old world."

Burberry would have agreed that they were fictions—that imagination is stronger than memory, maybe even that I was deluded. She would have said that it doesn't matter anyway, that only right now is important. But she was gone.

I hadn't invented either: husband or farm.

They were no longer night memories, either. They came in the morning, in the middle, in the dusk. Tie always saw them—I had the feeling that he was showing them to me. Perhaps he had always been showing them to me.

*There was the farm again. I hadn't seen it from the front, not yet, but I knew where it was. Who was I now? I reached inside my stiff navy-starched trousers. No, no penis. I looked down but my breasts blocked the view. I was big and sturdy and my limbs felt heavy. I had a bag over my shoulder. I swung it round to my front, which took a couple of tries, then rifled through. There were parcels, and letters, all with a small stamp in the corner. Dart Delivery Ltd.*

*My name was Helene, and I was delivering the post, with thick frizzy hair and rings about my ears. I stomped toward the door, which chimed as I approached it. I hadn't even been close enough to knock when it opened.*

*"Helene."*

*There he was, the man I had been not moments ago, forever ago, the penis I had thrust with now hanging limp. "Here with mail already? Come in, go on, fuck policy."*

*"Hermee," I greeted. He was young and naked, a little hair and a little belly that didn't match the rest of him. He smelled of root vegetables.*

*An earnest smile, his cock once flaccid, now hard, demanding. He had said he was an artist in the old world, but no—he lived in this place, naked, exposed. My quiet husband had always been in charge, despite being so young.*

*He turned and wandered down the hallway, his firm body weaving a little as he went. I nodded, feeling my chin against my neck, then followed.*

*We were sat at the table, cheery yellow Formica, a mug of Veg-Quickmix each. There were three letters spread between us, each addressed to the farm. Hermee picked them up. I could see groups of naked people eating, outside the window.*

*"Listen to this, listen to this one," he commanded, pointing at the letter.*

*"Dear occupant—" he made a face, "—Occupant? Anyway—dear occupant, la la—your organisation is in violation of social behavioural orders."*

*He laughed. "It'll be them down the road complaining, that church, the one I told you about. Always moaning. They could do with a trip here themselves. Anyway, here, it goes on—This has been your third notice. Please evict all occupants not belonging to your immediate family or spouse."*

*He set it down on the table. "We're all family here, they really should know that. We're all here to get away from that. It used to be fine, down in the city, but—" his voice trailed away before building again "we need this place. You understand that right?"*

*"Hermee," I soothed, "I just deliver the post." I smiled, trying to get him to smile back. It worked.*

*"Look," he grinned, "they've sent the same letter twice. They can't even get that right."*

*I giggled for him, but I knew I wouldn't be delivering the post to the farm much longer. It was a shame, they were a friendly lot. Who knew where they'd be taken?*

"You can't be more than one person, Blondee. And you certainly can't have been him, your husband from this world."

I saw him, inside and out.

My arms were empty. My hair was getting wet.

I snapped my head up, getting it away from the chlorine-scented waters which trickled down my neck. My back was bare. So was my front. My leg was tickled by a twig as my arse rested on the soft clammy earth.

I was by the lake. I was in a circle. I could taste morning on my breath. I was losing track of where I was—I'd be in one place, and then another, then back again. Where had I been? It was a dream, it wasn't a memory.

"Can't it be both, my Blondee?"

"Why do you talk like that? You didn't talk like that before."

"Before what?"

"Before you cut yourself up."

"So what do you think it is, Hermee?"

"Don't call me that, Tie."

"Do you prefer Helene?"

"Shut up, Tie."

"That's what you were called." He sounded hurt.

"It was a dream."

"It was as real as that husband."

"How did you even see those memories?"

I knew he wouldn't answer that one. He hated questions about himself, and I thought I heard him growl. It served him right for calling me Hermee. It was a stupid name, and it had never been mine. They were stories then, either ones I had been inventing or ones I had simply remembered. I had filled them with people from my world, to try and make some sense of them. That was it.

Right then my biggest problem was getting back to the hut without being seen. It was wrong to be naked when not on top of a bed.

So I set off, covering myself with my arms.

Between the lake and our hut, there was a woman.

"Blondee."

I didn't know her name. She had an unwomanly figure. I nodded.

"I got married just before the last rations."

I nodded again. I had no idea why she was telling me. I wondered if she was bragging. She didn't seem to notice my nudity.

"The wedding was everything you said. There weren't many people there, people were busy. It was beautiful though, just like you described. It was beautiful, it really was."

"That's good." I spoke so softly I only mouthed the words.

"I went to all of your talks. I learned everything. It worked—I have a husband of my own."

"Good," I mouthed.

"I just—"

"Go on." I found my voice.

"Will I stop thinking about her? I was with someone else when he asked me to marry him, and he was the first to ask, so I said yes. I thought I'd stop thinking about her. I don't know why I'm talking to you about this—I'm sorry, I really am, I just don't feel like I'm doing things right. It's the walking, I find it hard to walk like a woman should walk and I think there's something not right with me, really I'm sorry to say this to you—I'm sorry, I just don't seem to be getting any of it right. Will it get better, is it normal to feel like this—is it right?"

My voice came louder than I expected. "Just keep going." She nodded as though she was shaking and scuttled away, her hips swaying oddly as she did so.

I reached our hut to find Frederick crouching by his box.

"Blondee." He stood, still facing his clothes.

"Frederick."

"Where did you go?" he asked, his eyes narrowed.

"To the water. It looked peaceful outside."

"You went naked? And isn't it peaceful in here?"

"It's peaceful plenty. I just felt like going outside."

He looked suspicious, but he knew I couldn't have been with her—she was lying under the ground by the courtyard, where Tie used to be. He had no reason to suspect that I was being unfaithful. I had been good to him.

"I love you."

# severe

Before I knew it the hut was gone. The book's hut—which had stood since the start of the world—was gone. I wandered along a chill breeze, which had gently guided me to its location, but there was no location—it wasn't there: only a flattened patch of smooth earth and brown-limp grass. It had left, it had escaped. Where had the book gone?

Even Frederick knew.

Pilsner, he said. Pilsner took it. It had been left, unread and untouched but he wanted to keep it. He'd take good care of it. Frederick said he didn't mind, and none of the others cared.

I asked question after question, forgetting myself, and he grew bored, more and more, with each one. His voice turned hard. The hut had been taken down, no use any parts going to waste. Only the least really knew, but no-one else had noticed. "No, no, no-one at all. For fuck's sake, please, don't look so worried. None of it is needed. We changed everything; we changed it all for the better. That thing isn't wanted, he can have it. Quiet, please, I want to think."

I left for the lake. The world was still. Each hut I passed was silent and not a single flame jumped or danced. Each hut seemed abandoned, empty. I wasn't sure if it had ever been so dark.

I had some relief, mixed with anxiety: the classes were over. I had failed in my duty. There were no more lessons to tell. Frederick offered to let them know via their husbands, quietly, one by one: though the women with wives would find out last.

"No-one would mind," he'd said. "We've done enough for everyone, we've remade the world. Think about that."

I was trying not to.

By the time I reached the water my eyes had grown used to the darkness. It was warm, and as I smelled the streaming stench of chlorine a trickle of sweat tickled my armpit.

The lake was at peace. Some of Frederick's twigs had been blown away by two days of wind and gush-heavy rain. The forest—leafless and in tatters.

It had rained when she died. She liked to sleep when it rained.

I pulled up a twig, then another, and another, throwing each onto the water, scattering them about the gentle bob of the waves. A few steps away was one lonely twig, the last one left. I took it in my hand as it grated the skin of my fingers, and threw it into the water. I watched them all slowly circle, toward me, then away, and back. Each edged further and further out, until eventually they vanished, carried out to sea.

Perhaps there was a way out. Perhaps I could swim out, under the wall, and follow the twigs to the old world.

"Perhaps there's a way, Blondee."

"He said there was a pipe, but that it was too small to fit through."

"Too small for him."

"Tie. There's no point. I remade the world. It'll be the same out there as here."

Perhaps I was Hermee. Perhaps I was that man, but it seemed more likely I had been a bride, with a smile and a slush-toned dress. There would be no way out. The water might drain away, but wherever it went no person could follow. It started to rain again.

I decided to go and look at the courtyard—now the lessons were over it was almost exclusively the domain of the men, and I wanted to see how it was. The dusty row of vacuum-tubes which lined the flagstones had barely come into view before I was spotted.

"Blondee."

"I turned by head just enough to see him. "Tanned."

"How are you doing?"

"I am good, Blondee, I am good. I see you've been good too." He slanted his head slightly, watching me at a diagonal.

"Yes." I couldn't see how he had been with her. I couldn't imagine her planting her face on his, their hands tearing at each other.

"Things have changed."

He righted his head again and we stood in front of each other. I had never noticed I was taller than him. It didn't feel right, so I rested my weight on my hip.

"You got married too, then?" I asked. He must have married.

"No."

"What?" I asked, my voice a little more shrill than it should have been,

"No, I didn't get married. Thespie married someone else." He looked sad, sadder than I thought was possible.

"We haven't spoken in quite a while, have we?"

"We haven't."

I could have found out the details of his life, his giddy excitements and slow, long heartbreaks, but the conversation trailed and there was nothing worth knowing. Sooner or later he'd have mentioned her name, or I would, and there was the risk that everything would collapse, that the walls would fall down but they'd fall in on us, that everyone would be buried in an endless crush of rubble, falling ever inwards, until finally it mashed us two here in the centre of the world. It wasn't worth it. I wished him well and, with a glance around, even kissed him on the cheek. He was alone, he'd have time to think. Perhaps he'd even copy her and drop to death. But there wouldn't be any talking.

He left for the land of the minors.

*I was in a different place, and I couldn't see the farm anywhere. Who was I now? I looked down. I had clothes on: that was something.*

*A tattoo spread over my arm.* Pilsner. *It had been a joke at my expense, a drunken stag party gesture.*

*I was pacing the room, from chintzy china ornament to tacky glazed decoration. The walls were wood-brown, and I was surrounded by tiny faces, hand-painted and sold in magazines. I was waiting for the door. Where was she? Where was she?*

*There it was, there was the chime. I knocked over a girl, her face and her parasol shattering on the floorboards. Fuck fuck fuck. I pulled the door open, almost hitting myself in the face. What did my face look like? There was a mirror in the hall, but no time to check—*

*"Minos," the post-woman greeted.*

*"Helene," I replied, my voice heavy and solid. "Helene, how is he? How is Hermee?"*

*"I don't know if I should tell you," she answered.*

*Was she joking? Was she?*

*"Helene."*

*"If he's not responding to your messages—"*

*"Helene."*

*I tried not to cry, I tried not to let my eyes fill with water and burst in front of the post-woman, but I couldn't help myself. "He's my brother, Helene," I managed to choke out, "He's my brother."*

*She ignored my outburst. She was good like that. Helene had an honest face, and was the first delivery person I had ever spoken to. Usually delivery people were invisible, there one minute and gone the next. You could never ignore Helene.*

*I took a deep breath and wiped at my eyes with a used tissue.*

*"Would you like some tea, Helene?"*

*"Oh all right. I could do with some tea. People are sending one another lead boxes for a joke, I'm telling you."*

*We made our way to the kitchen. I made the tea in silence, silence aside from the whine of the kettle, and she waited with equal quiet. Porcelain figures stared down from the shelves at the top of the walls, right near the ceiling.*

*I needed to hear about Hermee. There had been nothing from him in so long. I hadn't meant for us to be on bad terms—I'd just wanted him to be safe. The farm wasn't safe, the farm was being monitored. I had told him that he could still see the others; he just had to be discreet. He had told me that there was nothing more important than living the life you chose. The world had changed but he hadn't.*

*We had still been speaking, even after he'd left, but I'd wasted my messages trying to convince him to come back. You can love everyone you want, Hermee, but you must keep quiet. The world is watching. Eventually he had grown sick of my nagging and stopped responding entirely. I couldn't blame him for that.*

*I worried about him.*

*I poured the tea into two delicate cups—ordered from the other side of the planet, no mean feat—and placed one by her, the other at my place on the other side of the table.*

*She took a sip of the tea before she spoke.*

*"They're going to remove them. You knew that'd happen, Minos, you don't need me to tell you. That's just what they're doing. That's life."*

*I covered my face with my hands. I must have knocked my cup off the table because I heard it burst over the varnished floor. That's life. I wondered if I could convince him to leave, if it wasn't too late. But I couldn't. He would stay, he would stay until the very moment they came and took him away, along with all the others. Hot tears stung my hands. My lungs burned.*

*When I looked up Helene was gone. She had finished her tea.*

"The world is unravelling, Blondee."

"Is it, Tie?"

I didn't know if that was true: the world was simply going through a change. 'Things change', that had been written somewhere in the book, and that was the rule we had broken the most. Nothing had ever changed, not really, not before the magazine. We changed the world, Frederick had said. He was wrong, it was me: he had been innocent.

Now when I wandered from hut-to-hut in the lands of the least, the minors, and the moderates, I did so without Frederick. He said he was going to the courtyard, but when I hid and watched from a distance he was never there. There was Green, there was Fluffed, and Tanned, but no Frederick.

He was away with Pilsner, that much was obvious, and the right thing to do would have been to break down Pilsner's door—and then?

Instead I explored.

The world was quieter: many of the huts were now empty. The others were louder, raised voices and accusations. It was the same in each of the lands—least, minor, and moderate. Accusations of penises in foreign vaginas, foreign mouths, foreign arseholes. Defensive manoeuvres: questions, counter-accusations, pleads.

"The world is unravelling, Blondee."

"They just need to get used to it, Tie."

Of course they didn't argue in every hut: some were quiet but clearly had people inside—some were at peace. Each of the three lands was the same—only the size of the huts really differed.

But there was one more land, the land of the severes, where they lived all in one hut, the hut made from the dregs of the world. There they lived together.

Had they married? Had they heard my advice from afar?

I needed to see.

"Leave them be, Blondee."

"I'm only going to look, Tie."

"You can do a lot of harm just by looking, Blondee."

I went anyway. I took my best shoes, ones which almost fit my feet, and my best bag, filled with some of our choicest rations. I took the long way around the courtyard, and journeyed to the land of the severes.

The usual dusty concrete. No trees, no huts. A glint of the metal fence at the far side. the sun was setting but only my body threw shadows.

There it was: there was the hut, a new mound of earth beside it, marked with a small row of broken bottles. There was no-one around; they were all inside. I took off my shoes and placed them into my bag, padding my feet as softly as I could over the concrete. There was smoke rising from the hut. They must have built it around a fire tap, clinging to the wall.

I reached the hut. I pressed my ear to it. It vibrated.

It vibrated with a half-dozen conversations. There was an argument, one which stopped my heart, and I listened for words, 'unfaithful', 'betrayed', 'matrimony', but they were fighting over nothing, a fight they would forget in a matter of moments. There was a laugh, someone telling a joke, a multitude of chuckles, together a roar. There were quiet murmurs.

I had to see them.

I could see a gap in the wall, high on the hut, and so I climbed it: I climbed over parts of old bikes and rickety planks of wood. My body was light and the hut stayed strong. I peeked through the opening.

There was the fire, in the centre, and there they were: clustered around; some eating; some sewing. They were clung in groups of threes and fours, threes and fours and not twos. Three of them were naked, running their fingers over one another, the middle one trembling. Another crawled over to join them.

They were different.

"The world is unravelling, Blondee."

"Not all of it, Tie."

I walked back home, over the concrete. I wanted to dance.

# watching

It was warm. Should I take off the fuzzy purple pullover? There wasn't time. I could see him—him across the street.

I was talking to Norna, miles and miles away, through fibre-optic cables. The world is a funny thing, it is.

Norna enjoyed watching her neighbours too.

I was giving a running commentary. This was our game: we would watch our neighbours and we would report on what went on. People lead the most interesting lives, much better than the kind of things that were broadcast. This was real. People have dramas, and you don't even need to hear them to be a part of the experience: you just need a window, and the quick-wits to glance away if they suspected you were watching. Watching events can influence them, that's a rule of science, it is.

It was my turn. She had spent all of last week talking about the young family who lived across from her, and nothing even happened. They just had breakfast and did the same day-to-day things anyone did. Norna wasn't very good at picking neighbours to watch. Norna wasn't really very good at anything.

I could see the people opposite, sitting in my chair by the window. My neighbour was sitting on a sofa, reading a book. "He'll be interesting though, Norna," I'd told her, "just wait." I knew because he had all these ornaments, all these little figurines all over his walls. What kind of man had figurines all over his walls? That would be worth a watch. I was good at picking which neighbours to watch, see.

Norna had said it was all down to luck, but that's Norna for you. She daydreams. "How can you pick your neighbours?" she'd asked. I told her it was an important skill.

I could see the post-woman arrive, her van stopping on the street outside. I told Norna. She said that was no more interesting than what her neighbours got up to. Her voice was echoing, and arrived too slowly: her connection was bad. Norna couldn't get anything right, she couldn't. I was even prettier than her—I have long dark hair and big eyes. It's a hassle—men chase you. I never trusted men.

I told her to wait. I checked my messages: I'd no new messages. Only things from

*Norna. Norna could be a good friend, when she wanted to be, even though she lived so far away.*

*The post-woman arrived at the first floor of the building opposite and pushed some letters though the box. The neighbours there had their curtains drawn. What were they trying to hide?*

*The post-woman arrived at the second floor, but there was no mail. That was too bad: the old woman inside had heard the footsteps in the hallway and looked up, expecting a visitor. I could see, even though her windows were grubby. She didn't have any letters.*

*I don't pretend I'm popular and important, but I have Norna.*

*The post-woman arrived at the third floor, his floor. I could see her rat-tat-tat on his door. He ran to the door and opened it quick enough. The woman below him turned on her television.*

*I told Norna, I said, "he's talking to the post-woman" Norna didn't seem very excited: she could never sense when something was coming, one of her faults.*

*"He's crying, Norna, he's crying," I told her. I must have shouted it. I could hear her breathing fast, she was excited too. This was more than her boring neighbours had done. My neighbour was crying: what kind of man cries at the post-woman?*

*"She's ignoring it," I told her, "but she's not leaving either. What do you think they're talking about?"*

*"It'll be an affair," Norna said. She could be daft sometimes. That man wasn't having an affair with that big old post-woman—he'll be a homo and she'll be lesbian. "You should know that, Norna." Norna said she couldn't even see them, so how could she know? I didn't answer such a stupid question.*

*There was a crackle and Norna was gone. Her bloody connection.*

*It was time for a ketamine break. She had recommended it—she had even bought me a t-shirt with the word splashed across the breasts. She thought it was funny. After a few minutes I disconnected and reconnected, just in case, waiting to hear her voice. It broke through, tinny and smooth.*

*I repeated myself, told her again what he'd done. "He's making them both some tea now—who has the post-woman around for tea? It's a strange old world, Norna. Maybe they were up to something: he'll be thinking of the mischief they could get up to, him and the post-woman—not an affair but something just as devious."*

*Norna said I didn't know that. She told me I should stick to what I could see, and I couldn't see inside their heads. She said I was crazy. She was no judge, she hadn't even left her house this month. I had, I'd gone out to get milk. And a paper, even though it was too expensive and it never said anything interesting. Of course I'd been harassed by a guy with a tacky tan: that's men for you.*

*"Norna," I said, "Norna! He's crying again, he's got his face in his hands and he's bawling his eyes out!"*

*"What's the post-woman doing then?" Norna asked.*

*"She's just drinking her tea like there's nothing the matter at all, like she's by*

*herself in her own kitchen. Did I tell you he had his ornaments in there as well? It's a strange man collects ornaments, I can tell you that right now. There's something afoot."*

*I was winning the game, but then I won every game Norna and I ever thought of. She wasn't very good at games, but she liked losing and I liked winning—that's companionship, that is. Two people fitting together, even if they've never met in person. Especially if they've never met in person. Who wanted to deal with people, with all their smells and strange noises? I feel sick whenever I talk to the newsagent—I can see the spit foaming in his mouth and the gunk in the corner of his eyes.*

*"Oh, Norna, she's leaving, she's gone, the post-woman's left."*

*I glanced over at Norna's emulated face. She was nodding, up and down, up and down. As though she were simple. There was nothing going on between them, he was too much a coward to be doing any plotting, and the post-woman was too sensible. "Norna," I told her, "she's left and he's still crying—who'd have thought it?"*

*"He should pull himself together," Norna said. It was the first sensible thing she'd said in ages.*

I drifted in the darkness between that world and this, in the space where neither was real and nothing true. In the space without the weight of the past. Without anything. For once his ghost was not with me.

Rebels on a farm, the anxious brother, a lonely neighbour watching and watching. I knew their faces, their bodies, their smells.

I slowly returned to my bed, my husband snoring to my side, a long-lost ghost in the corner.

# orange

She screamed for me: she screamed for me from the rations. I found her, in the corner amongst the furniture. Frederick had said he should go to the rations alone, but I told him that, just this once, I had to go with him. And there she was.

The stone woman.

Just as I had seen her. She was poised in the corner of the big metal rations box, a hands-length tall, dogs at her feet and arrows at her back. When I picked her up she stopped her screaming: I had found her. She could watch over us.

She wasn't all that came with the rations—there was a new drink: *Antee-Freeze*. This was the new booze, Casio had announced it. It smelled sweet. That night would be a casino night.

I changed into a newly-made green silken dress whilst the stone woman watched me with her stern eyes. I stared back, trying to sense if she approved, or even if she knew about my strange memories from so many different lives. Either way, she was keeping her thoughts to herself. Frederick ignored her entirely.

The casino night was cool and dry, though my armpits were warm and wet, and I wanted to shake my soft green dress to let the air in. Instead I walked without moving my legs too far apart, wondering what the booze would taste like this time. There was a rapid chatter—not only had it been a long while, but some had said it might be the last time at the casino, that booze should be saved for weddings. There were still some unmarried, and they would be the real cause for celebration. I didn't hear anyone disagree.

Jay was actually sober. There had been a large amount of juice with the rations and, he said, the booze would be better with it, it was obviously strong. Try not to drink too much of the juice, he said, there'd be little enough left for the minors, and none for the moderates—they would have to drink it neat. Ketamine stood by his side, her arm in his.

People were placed in pairs. It had been dark early the evening before, but that night the clouds were only starting to darken as we gathered two-two-two. The lessons may have stopped, but I was still the centre of attention. They were happy, they told me with their looks. Each was happier than the other, and they could prove it.

Jay was busy slinging back his head and draining the *Antee-Freeze* down his throat. He retched and tilted his head back again. He didn't offer any to his wife. A man with curled hair grabbed at his collar and held up his glass, which was already half-filled with juice. A bottle was thrust into my hand and Frederick took it from me, carelessly slopping pineapple liquid into my glass.

Jay began his journey step and semi-stepping around, weaving between chairs with women sat perfectly cross-legged and men poised anxiously, holding up their glasses.

I only got a small splash of the booze, and I was going to complain before I composed myself. If anyone should complain for me it should be Frederick, and he hadn't noticed, he was busy rubbing his knee and telling me how it ached. I raised the glass to my mouth and stabbed at it with my tongue. It was sweet, sticky and sweet.

"Pace yourself dear, you don't want to look unwomanly," Tie uttered, his voice a wet whisper. He was making fun, but he was right. The other women were sipping theirs, watching with unheard envy as their husbands gulped from their glasses and held them up for more.

Jay made his rounds and staggered out of the tent, Ketamine following behind. They were greeted by a roar of applause from the minors. He had left us with most of the juice, but had taken a little for the minors as well. Dice appeared, green mats were laid and cards were strewn about between us. Frederick placed our spare rations—which were better than the others—into the middle of the group. The tent was grand, with enough room to lie down if I wanted. One or two of the men did, or rested on their elbows. One or two wives glanced over at me, wanting to know if it was acceptable, but I kept my eyes lowered.

The Queen of diamonds was smeared with purple lipstick.

"What do we have?" Frederick asked, a little too loudly into my ear. "Shall I hold them?" he mouthed, but I was already placing the rations into his hand.

Everyone had put on their best clothes, and so it was easy to spot which of the least were first in line for rations, and which were further back. Some even wore multiples of layers, something which would never happen in the sweat-stained heat of the minor tent.

"Ah, we need better luck soon," Frederick groaned quietly.

I nodded, running my fingers over olives, wrapped tight in clear plastic. I finished the rest of my glass as the booze passed nearby.

"Blondee," Tie warned. The other women had barely touched theirs.

The tent grew louder and we lost more hands than we won—though I was sure some were trying to help us—and the air warmed.

A man in the corner looked pale, his wife was feeling his forehead. They weren't noticed until he staggered from the tent, her giving a small, stunted wave goodbye.

We won some hands, and the rations were piling up by our knees. Much of it was chocolate, and I wondered if I could place some on my tongue without looking rude, or ruining the game. I decided I couldn't. I also wanted the swirls of cheese, but they too were forbidden until the end of the game. I was feeling hungry.

"See, we'll see if we can win another," Frederick gasped, his lungs heavy, his breath sour. He held up his glass, but the man opposite held the bottle of booze upside-down, exaggerating his unhappy face.

"I'll wait," Frederick said, "I'll wait until he, Jay, gets back."

Jay didn't come back. More and more people looked ill,

a man,

a man,

a man,

one woman,

another man. They left in pairs, concerned wives taking their husbands to bed. The one ill woman staggered out with her husband, the two of them leaning against the weight of the other. As soon as they were out of sight we heard a loud retch from beyond the tent.

Frederick leant his face against mine. It was cold and wet.

More people left, two-by-two, manly stumbles and womanly waves. There were worried looks on faces, and cards were held with trembling fingers, but no-one said anything. Husbands and wives whispered to one another, wives cooing and shushing, with gentle kisses on the cheek or hand.

"Do you need to leave, Frederick?" I whispered. He shook his head.

"We're winning."

Soon there were just a half-dozen of us left, the other two wives staring at the ground, their hands clenched to their husbands, each husband growing pale.

The green mat, covered in discarded cards, was splattered in orange, all shades of orange, a loud heaving filling the tent, before being silenced by a shrill scream.

We stepped from the tent as carefully as we could, following each cry, following the violent chatter. Screaming.

I felt fine. I felt fine. Frederick's hand was slimy.

The screams came from the moderate tent, and we were joined by frightened minor wives and ill-faced minor husbands, all of us stepping as quickly and as gracefully as we could toward them.

Frederick and I entered first. Ketamine was screaming, over and over, endless. In the centre, spread amongst cards, in amongst mouldy bread and bitter chalk-sweets, there was Jay.

There was Jay; his orange-splattered face and sprawled body.

There was Jay; his eyes half-open, half-closed.

There was Jay; the tips of his pubes poking up from his trousers; his skin white as paper.

# part six

THE WIND HOWLS HERE LIKE A GHOST. I can hear small leaves sliding over the tarpaulin.

Jay was first.

Jay was only the first.

Life was expelled, forced out from every orifice: a pale husk remained.

The shrieks of frightened wives were everywhere. You couldn't avoid it. The stone woman watched it all. Her face remained unchanged.

Did I tell you she's here with me, here in this hole?

She's in my hand.

Her face never changes, I can tell you that. Whatever happens she looks the same. I don't envy it.

Wax-paper skin. Frederick too was forcing life from himself.

But I didn't shriek.

# fluttering

She watched over us, and sometimes I liked her and sometimes I wanted her away. Either way it was my fault, I had brought her indoors. She never changed expression, and never looked very happy or very sad. She didn't have eyes, or lips really, perhaps that was why. She was stone. Still, sometimes she seemed nearly real, and I'd offer her a luxury: something rare, a little packet of mustard, or red licorice. She never took it.

"She's not real, my dear."

"And you are?"

Frederick grew worse. He'd stopped speaking now, and his eyes stared in blank confusion, unseeing. Once or twice I'd left to get more water, and I'd left her next to him, hoping he wouldn't be too afraid. It was better to be watched over, even if it was only by the small stone woman. He didn't seem to notice.

"Do you think he'll die?"

"Shut up."

"Sorry," Tie whimpered. He had been saying that a lot recently. He had been less rude in general.

My arms ached and creaked when I moved them. I had been filling the bucket several times a day, getting more water, back and forth to the courtyard. At first he had been sick, over expensive fabrics and even in his box of clothes. Now he lay naked, curled up, like a fleshy stone. He had even been sick at her stone feet, even *on* her feet. She didn't look angry.

At first he'd kept running out of the hut, behind it, and I'd hear the hurried scrape of earth as he frantically dug a hole, and then a groan. He'd left more and more often, until there weren't any scraping sounds, just another groan. That was when I started going for water. Water would help, I had heard that somewhere. He wanted it—he'd gulp it down, droplets racing down his neck.

"Frederick?" I tried, shaking him a little. He turned his head, opened his eyes and stared for a moment, before letting them fall closed again. I thought about climbing in with him, wrapping my arms around him and telling him he'd be fine.

I'd been sleeping in the yellow chair. He wasn't leaving the bed to shit now, and I cleaned it up as best I could, but the satin sheets were stained. I brought a cup to his lips and tipped water into his mouth, before collapsing back into the chair, my arms stiff at my sides.

My back hurt. I stood to the sound of my bones clicking. I scavenged the kitchen to see what I could make for breakfast. I wouldn't be able to give him any. I shoved some poppyseed crackers in my mouth and wandered over to the bed. I noticed we were out of water, and went to get more, preparing my arms for the work.

"Are you ready, Blondee?"

"Ready for what, Tie?"

There was a furious buzzing. I let the door slam behind me and tried to cover my ears. It came from everywhere. The air was thick and dirty—rancid and soiled.

"People are sick, darling Blondee, everyone is sick."

"I know that, Tie."

I pulled my shirt over my mouth. It smelled of my own sweat. My stomach was exposed but I didn't care. One or two wives were milling around, their faces twisted in confusion, obviously unsure what to do with themselves. I passed them without a word.

The courtyard was quiet, pristine. Pilsner stood by the water tap.

"Blondee."

"Pilsner. Could you step aside, I need some water."

He stepped over slightly, watching me as he did so. "Are you ill?"

"No."

"Is he ill?"

"He is."

The water fell in a sickly trickle. It would take ages to fill the bucket. I sighed.

"Some are worse than others," he stated, flat and matter-of-fact.

"Worse?"

"Go over there," he motioned to the moderate land, "go over there and see."

I hesitated.

"No-one will stop you. You've been there before, we both know it. Go on, I'll watch your bucket."

Over the embankment I couldn't see anything different—perhaps there was more vomit on the ground, mushed into the gravel. I wandered, not sure what I was looking for. Near the huts the buzzing was deafening, but there was a silence, a quiet I couldn't work out. It was as I was running my knuckles over the spine of a dwindled tree that I realised. There were no voices. No cries, no shouting, no whimpering or retching or grunting. There were no frightened wives. I had to leave. I returned to the courtyard.

"It's—"

"They're all dead. Pretty much. Most of them are, I haven't checked everyone." Pilsner kept his voice still as ever.

"It's not—" I mumbled, kneeling down to the bucket.

"It was the booze. But you know that, right? It was the booze. I've figured it out. The moderates, they drank it raw, without anything to mix it with. It was the booze."

"Right."

"But you're giving him water, that's good. I think a lot of people will live—but more will leave before it's done. They won't get help you know, they believe all they need is each other. But you helped, Blondee, you helped make it that way. Most of them don't even know to fetch water. It's probably just as well, there wouldn't be enough to go around, not all at once."

"It was that way before."

"I don't know how many people will live, Blondee. How could I? The severes didn't drink anything, no-one gave them any. Perhaps there will be more of them than there are of us, when all's said and done. We'd be in trouble then, Blondee, I'm telling you."

"There must be something we can do," I choked, my voice rough and coarse as wood. Even without enough water, there must be something to do, I knew there must.

Pilsner didn't say anything.

The book, the book must have something, it must have some answers.

"The book," I pleaded, "there must be something in the book."

"There isn't."

"Let me see it," I had to see it, "let me see the book. I can help, I can find help I know I can."

"You've done enough, Blondee."

"Pilsner—"

"Enough."

The bucket was overflowing. Pilsner turned the tap off and handed it to me. There were tears, I couldn't stop them, I just had to keep them from falling into the bucket.

*And all the world was gone, but I watched her. Fibre-optic cables over miles and miles.*

*This was our game: I lost and she won. She said that was companionship—of course I let her win. I was in love with her. We had never met. She was beautiful: long dark hair and big eyes.*

*My heart wasn't in the game: I was watching her as she watched other people. It was an excuse, of course, all an excuse. She called me Norna, and that wasn't even my real name. Why did she call me that? Well, she wouldn't know better. She had never even seen my real face. I wasn't Norna, I was Loke, and I wished I was thin, and maybe even a woman, but I was fat and I had a short stubby penis that people laughed at. But I always kept myself smart, I always wore a tie. Even by myself. Even with everyone gone. It pays to be presentable. At least, I thought, it might.*

*I wondered, perhaps I could show her myself. My real face. It wouldn't matter anyway, beggars can't be choosy, and there were so few of us left.*

*Imagine that, I told myself, romance because of plague.*

*This was our game—it was all we had. There were no neighbours, not really. It was all pretend. We'd sit, and pretend to watch others, we'd pretend that the kitchen opposite her apartment was full of people having tea, rather than corpses turning colour. We'd sit and pretend to watch others because there was so little else to do. Wait for rescue, they said, wait for rescue. I'd been certain it wasn't safe to go outside, though she had gone, once or twice. She had found drugs in her neighbour's apartment, and a diary. We read it together, hundreds of miles apart. I told her how to take the K.*

*We'd sit and wait for rescue, she and I, pretending to watch the world. We couldn't even admit to one another that the world was dead. I laughed about it, late at night, when I'd gone offline. I laughed so hard.*

*How long had it been? It didn't do to count the days. The messages they sent told us not to. I had shut myself away from day one—I saw a body on the street, skin black and face twisted: it was one of the kids I dealt to. I decided the street wasn't for me. I told her about it, but she doesn't like to think about the pain of the world. She talks about her neighbours like they're real. She must believe they are.*

*Day by day I'd stopped hearing any noises from my own neighbours—they had run away and died or they had stayed and they had died. The ceiling in the kitchen started leaking—the bathtub upstairs had been left on. I tried to call the superintendent but there was no phone signal. There wasn't any phone signal anywhere. But the internet worked, so I emailed him: there was nothing else I could do.*

*At first people hurried by the street outside—frantic cars racing to safety; bicycles; even carts. Everyone rushing somewhere and I stayed at home. I mostly avoided listening to the official announcements on the radio, though they had some way of sending them to every email address in the land.*

*Websites stopped being updated. Blogs went silent. There were fewer and fewer videos being uploaded, but I didn't care, the videos were depressing. People filming their dying moments. Hundreds of thousands of them, like they were original. So many videos and so few people viewing them. Maybe they watched each other—maybe it was like dying together. That would make sense.*

*All I'd worried about was her—every day we met online at ten in the morning, and every day I was relieved to hear her voice. I'd ask her if she was sick, and she said no. She asked me if I was sick, and I said not yet.*

*Neither of us got sick.*

*I didn't care what we talked about, I didn't care if she won these games. She told me the man opposite her apartment was crying at the post-woman—she was triumphant. I was glad she was still alive.*

*Eventually the ceiling in the kitchen collapsed, but I'd stopped using the kitchen anyway—I'd gone through the rest of the building to find food, there was no shortage of that. I was no longer so scared of leaving the apartment, if I was going to get sick I would have by now. It's in the air, they'd said. Pray. The news channels had actually told us to pray.*

*I laughed so hard.*

I had to ask.

"Was that you, Tie?"

"A world dead of plague? Probably not, Blondie. But how would I know?"

There wasn't time for these stories, stories that didn't even fit together. Who cared what happened before? My world was dying.

It was after taking the water home and wiping the last drops from my eyes that I decided to find Tanned. I had to find Tanned. We hadn't spoken for so long—this way there was a chance I could help him. We had been friends once, we could be again.

Tanned was a minor: maybe he'd downed less of the fatal drink, perhaps he'd drunk just enough to leave his insides intact—discomforted but intact. I stumbled through the cries of anguished wives, terrible sirens surrounding me.

In front was a woman, her husband doubled over, his cheek on the floor, his arse in the air.

"Crisp. Crisp. Crisp," she cried, her husband's name pounding through her, her body rigid. What else could she do? Where else could she move? She may as well scream his name.

Her voice faded.

I reached Tanned's hut. He wasn't inside: his patch of foam was untouched, his rations were properly stored away. I had to find him.

I called his name, over and over. "Tanned. Tanned. Tanned."

I walked without direction. What else could I do?

There was a buzzing at the minors' fire tap. The buzzing of a thousand flies. The air was thick; putrid and sodden. I covered my mouth with my fraying pullover. Beneath the flies were bodies.

Pale skin and open mouths. Eyes unfocused.

Had they gone there together, to the cooking corner, trying to find solace there? They were piled five high, near-all men, the gentle arm of a woman poking through the mass of clothing.

I gagged.

"The wives brought them here, Blondee. This is their place. They didn't know what else to do. You've deserted them."

"Tie, you need to shut your fucking face right now."

"Do you see my face, my dear? Do you see his?"

I looked. I pulled at shoulders, rolling them over, to the ground with a soft heavy thump. I wasn't careful—I didn't need to be careful. They wouldn't know, not now. I was rough, not gentle. The eyes of these husbands didn't see me.

I saw old neighbours: faces wrenched in agonies, mouths lined with red-orange sick. One was clutching his bare hairy belly, swelling with gas.

There was Green—his beard crusted in vomit, his skin smooth, the texture of wax. There was Gut, his old lover, the one who had cried for him. But where was Green's new wife, why wasn't she with him? How could she be alone?

I pulled Green by the arm, pulling him free from the pile. Beneath was Jay, the first. But his wife—where was Ketamine? She couldn't desert him now, could she? Do your duty Ketamine, keep watch, wipe away his cares.

I pulled and pushed. Arms, legs and bellies.

And there he was. Tanned.

The same as the rest of them. I don't need to explain.

I stepped back. Panting. The effort hit me like a gust of wind. I gagged again. A woman was watching me. She was stood over to the side. I hadn't heard her arrive, she had been stood there the whole time. I knew her face, her sturdy, manly figure. I didn't know her name.

"Did you bring them here?" I asked.

"I did," she replied.

I'd had enough. I wanted to go back home, back to caring for Frederick. As I went to leave the words tumbled from her mouth.

"I brought them here. You know me. I met you—I told you I didn't know how to walk like a woman. I wasn't sure about anything. Well I'm still not sure about anything, but I brought them here. I dragged them here—it wasn't womanly, but then it seemed right for all the men to be in the same place. I couldn't take them to their place, to the courtyard—where would we get water from? I had to bring them here, you see.

"At first I just took whichever of the men were just lying around. I lay them side-by-side, but they were taking up too much room, so then I placed one atop the other. I went everywhere for them. Some were hidden in places you would never think to look—some I only found because the flies led me there. When those were done I went door-to-door for more. The other wives gave them up without a word. They didn't know what to do with them. I do—I'm going to make a fire. I had a memory, about piles of bodies burning in a fire. I can't write it in the book though—the book seems to have gone.

"As for my own husband—he's not in the pile. I've still not found him. He ran away when he was sick, with his hand over his mouth. I lost him in the dark. But I'll find him. Eventually the flies will lead me to him. I'll take yours too, when the time comes."

I nodded my thanks, but she never noticed—she was already trotting away, scouting for more husbands to add to the pile. I went home.

# the book

I EXAMINED MY SICK HUSBAND. At first I used my eyes: his hair, dark and greasy, a tangle above his too-pale face. He wore an expression of empty pain, of thoughtless discomfort. His mouth had fallen a fingers-width open, teeth stained, jaw coated in black stubble, the trunks of dead trees poking through snow.

I pulled back the covers, the skin of his shoulders snow-pale too, long strands of hair spread over them, spreading over his chest, surrounding the dark mounds of his nipples. Beads of sweat shone. His belly too as mass of dark hair and pale skin, but deflated, emptied of everything.

I pulled the covers further still, revealing the limp sag of his cock and balls, slung over his thigh—on his thigh there was pale skin and brown streaks.

I examined my sick husband. I used my hands—the clammy forehead, the delicate unopened eyelids, the furry cheeks and dry lips.

Down, down, to the down of his shoulder hair, his chest hair—soft on cool wet skin. His nipples hardened, fleshy mounds into hard pebbles. His belly hollow.

His limp cock, thick and heavy in my hand. This was Frederick's. My husband's cock was always pushing, always hard and ready for the attack. But Frederick's was soft; unassuming and gentle. I pulled back the foreskin, purple head and creamy lines.

I dipped a cloth into one of our water buckets and I washed him—away the clammy skin and dried oils, away the brown stains.

I didn't wash him as his wife. I washed him as Blondee. I was rough. Rough as I liked.

Now he smelled better.

I pressed my lips to his, cracked and dry, with the scent of stale sick. I poured water into my mouth and brought my lips back to his, flooding his mouth with it; mouth on mouth, water to water.

If she and I had drowned together, what then?

He didn't wake up. The sun upped and downed and he had slept. The low rumble of his breath. The rise of his chest. I watched for these things. This wasn't duty. This was love—grotesque and humiliating.

Blood spurting over lino and forming claggy pools. We just can't help ourselves.

This is how we love the body—not through thrusting or the lust of licking. It's the blood and the sweat and the shit.

She pooled upon the lino and so I loved the pool. Her bones in the ground.

I loved them both. Grotesque and humiliating.

Soon I was having a feast. I had taken all the food from the shelves and boxes and had them spread before me, like my very own casino night. I was alive, I was here, and I would eat. There were oatcakes, hoi-sin duck flakes, sugar grains, the olives, cocoa-powder, sweet-scented sweets, rye bread, rice (which I hadn't cooked), soya-butter, two types of cheese and three packets of ketchup, which I was saving for last. I was sat opposite the stone woman. She was looking at the food but she wouldn't want any. Between us the rations were spread out on a beautiful off-white silken cloth, which I had taken from my clothes box.

I could spare the food. It wouldn't be long until the next rations anyway. I placed an olive and a piece of cheese into my mouth, my tongue curling with the flavours.

"You have to help them, Blondee."

I was going to help them. There would be something in the book. I was going to find it, no matter what Pilsner said. He would be back at the courtyard most of the time, dispensing wisdom to people who didn't want to fucking hear it, and then I could go get it. There would be something. Besides, I had already started helping. So far I had found three wives, each wandering in a daze, and I had told them: water, water, water. Keep getting water and keep giving it to the sick. The first had been pleased to be told what to do, to have help. The other two had nodded, their faces grey, their bodies slouched.

I covered the oatcakes in the butter and coated the result in cocoa powder.

There had been no recipes in days. There had been no anything. It would take a long time to get everything back together, to get everything back to normal, but it would happen. Eventually it would happen. The book had been taken away too quickly and we still needed it. When we had the book back we'd have the world back.

*There was a woman, down by the newsagents: she was on the ground, mumbling to herself, milk to one side and a newspaper to the other. She was beautiful—long dark hair and big eyes, a t-shirt with* ketamine *emblazoned over it. I said hello.*

*She held the newspaper aloft, high above her pretty head.*

*"It's too expensive and it never says anything interesting," she said. She let the pages fly through the air.*

*She was crazy. Who could blame her? The world is a fucked up place. I went home. I went to my room and looked at myself in the small mirror on the desk. I didn't look crazy. I looked normal, good even. I have a firm jawline and tanned skin—I always have a tan, even during months of rain. My friends called me Tan, though it's not my real name. It helped me when I needed to sell my body, to sweaty older guys with fat fingers. I always kept my mouth closed, hiding my one grey tooth. They always enjoyed themselves.*

*Now they buy boys full-time, in handcuffs from Russia. They wouldn't hire the locals any more, there was no need.*

*I took whatever I could get—those my age, we have no choice. No jobs, no money, no future. I wouldn't mind the first, but they demand the second or else we freeze and starve. Then there's no third. The bank had called me that very morning, demanding that I pay them more money, but there is no more money, don't they know that? What can I do? They left us with nothing.*

*Worse than nothing. They took what little we had and gave it to those in opulent mansions and smart penthouses, then had those same people threaten us for yet more money. They say the welfare state is dead but it's worse than that—the welfare state is twisted, undead, devouring those it was supposed to protect.*

*Bankers attacking homes. Governments holding you down while they raid your pockets.*

*I had to do something. I had to find money.*

*But my rage, my rage that had built over months and years, it got in the way—it fogged up my eyes and made my hands tremble. The rage—the powerlessness, the impotence—I couldn't help it, I couldn't control it. All I could do was scream, alone, in a room by myself.*

*That's what I did.*

*The neighbour thumped on his floor. I got a broom and thumped back: thud thud thud.*

*I couldn't go stay with friends, my friends are all in jail. Imprisoned for protesting, for carrying signs and shouting that we had nothing left to give. Leave us alone.*

*They were wrong, though. We do have something left to give—they found something more that we had, and something they wanted. Something that all the penthouses and luxury vehicles in the world couldn't bring. The very core of us—they wanted the very core of us.*

*I screamed.*

*I had to calm down. I drank a bit of whatever was left in the cup on my desk and opened the drawer. I had a collection of old photographs, ones of naked people. You might say I collected them. I liked pictures people took of themselves, pictures which were honest. There wasn't anyone telling them how to pose, how to act: they just did what they felt like. The pictures were old—from a happier time. They helped me forget myself.*

*I had one in my hand: a man and a woman posing together, and he looked bored. I found myself getting hard. That's what I liked, honest looks like that. He looked bored. He wasn't looking at her, and she looked interested, kind of excited. Perhaps it was her first time, the first time she'd taken her clothes off for the camera, and he'd done it so many times he was bored, his cock half-limp half-hard. He was half there. She was smiling, her nostrils flared, and I gripped myself. Maybe, maybe it was the other way round. Yes, it was his first time, and he wasn't bored, not really, he was covering his anxiety. He looked bored because he was scared. She knew that, deep down, and it excited her, it turned her on, and I came. It was quicker than I expected.*

*I stumbled into the hallway, looking for a towel. I still had the picture in my hand. Do it, the man said.*

*But what would I have left? It was the very core of me.*

*The adverts were everywhere. Sell your memories. It's quick, it's easy, it's painless—so they say. That was it, that was the one way I could make money. They were desperate for them: the rich wanted a vicarious thrill, to live the life of another. They even have testimonials from other people who sold theirs: there's plenty of time to make new ones. The adverts say that as well. If I applied for a trial, if I sold some of them, just a few, I could pay my rent. I could pay for any insurance money could buy: health, life, fire, police. Anything could happen to me and I'd be invincible.*

*Make some money now! Make someone happy! Do your part. Quick and easy.*

I drifted in the dark between the worlds. The worlds that didn't fit together. Worlds of order, worlds of plague.

He was once my friend. Had each of us come from a different world? Had we met here, between these walls, at the centre of them all?

Fiction, stories: books and films and radio broadcasts. Would it matter?

A bright flash of colours as Frederick's hut swam back into view. I clutched at the chair, but my hands were sweaty and slid right off. Each time the worlds grew bigger, and each time it all made less sense. There was no time for any of it, I had to fix *this* world, whilst I still knew which one I was in. I was still Blondee, I wasn't a tubby post-woman or a spy across the street, or a fat man pretending to be a woman in the midst of a plague. I had shown the world marriage, I had shown them what it meant to be a man and a woman, and they had gone in pairs to die. But I would fix it. I would gather everyone at the courtyard, or go to each hut in turn if need be, book in hand, ready to help. I didn't need any more time to think.

I would just go; right then and there. I was making the decision as I pulled on a thick jumper, scratchy but warm. I put the stone woman in my pocket—she was so heavy she almost pulled my skirt down. I put my copper ring on Frederick's finger.

Outside it was cold and dull; as though the sun had shrunk into a tiny ball, pathetic and small and unable to warm anything. The ground was slippery and the slush about my feet was crusted like snot. The tickle of flies hit me in the face and I batted them away, only for more to try and land on my cheeks and chin and chalk-make-up skin. My face would be covered in black dots and I could feel them in my hair. I couldn't see anyone outside, there was nobody about.

The courtyard was empty. Water was frozen in little pools. It didn't matter. I would still go. I would still try. I told it to myself over and over, I would still go, I would still try. I said the words until I was at Pilsner's door, ready to knock. I peered in through the window instead. There was no-one there.

I could even see the book, in the middle of the hut, on a multi-tiled table.

It was warm inside his hut. There was a strong smell of berries. The book was in front of me, under my fingers, then pressed to them, dry against my hands. I pulled open the front cover. I could hear my breath.

And there was the page.

Not the ill-fit reproduction, not a rough-scrawled copy.

The real page.

The one I had stolen, smeared with soil.

And a finger prodded my back.

"Blondee."

"Pilsner." I didn't even turn around.

"You're in trouble, Blondee. You're in the *shit*, Blondee."

"The page is here." And what else was I to say?

"I found it by your hut."

"My—"

"Your old hut. Three feet away from where her body was found."

"Her—" The hut blurred, the world blurred.

"We were happier to say it was her. She was dead anyway."

"It wasn't her." Where was I going?

"I know. We know."

"I just want to help. I need to help."

"Put it down."

So I did. I put the blue fuzz of a shape down to where the table once was.

"It was you. It was you. You're the thief, and we should have known." He paused for a moment. "I was just by your hut, as you came to mine. I've seen him. I've seen him, Blondee. Frederick—"

His throat seized up. Then he lost control. I sat on the table, blinking to make it all right, to see everything properly, and words were shouted, word by word: bitch; cunt; fucking bitch; fuck; fuck you; fuck everything you've done; you fucking; fucking cunt. Over and over and over and soon they had no meaning, washing over me, a wreck of sounds, smashed to smithereens.

Pilsner looked afraid: his face white, his white eyes large, white all around his pupils.

"Blondee. You're in trouble."

And there they were, Casio, and some of the others.
"What will happen?"
"You'll go back to the hut, for now."
And I even knew which one they meant.

# luxuries

THE HUT WAS COLD. There was no food. There were no blankets, save for the brown-black wallpaper which had peeled from the wall and which lay on the ground like bedsheets. I was glad I had brought the heavy bulk of jumper with me, and at night I chose to use it as a pillow, until the painful prickle of my skin forced me to put it back on. Even at night I could see, I could see the shadow that was waiting outside the window of the triangle hut. Sometimes the shadow changed a little in shape, but it was there to make sure that I wouldn't leave. It would make sure I stayed there, in the hut, where I couldn't do any more damage. I couldn't blame them.

"Can't you, Blondee?"

"No, Tie."

I did have water. They made sure I had that, though it tasted a bit funny and I knew they probably done something to it. What did it matter? I drank from the bucket even when I wasn't thirsty. They just poked it back through the cloth-door, freshly filled every time. I drank and drank until my bladder would burst. I pissed into the corner, hoping it would mask the smell that covered the world. It did, quite well, and I was pleased by it.

The stone woman kept watch.

I slept across a dark brown stain: a pool left by Burberry. The last of her body. I slept on top of her, and she under me.

By day I watched from the window, but there weren't many people past the glass. I stared, waiting for the gentle gamble of the minors. There were so very few of them. Once or twice I saw my neighbour—Fluffed—sloping this way or that, and I made certain to wave. He never looked in my direction. He was alive. He hadn't spewed or shitted away his life.

"Tie. How many do you think have gone?" I pressed my fingers to the bare glass. It was filthy, and a slick layer of grey coated my skin.

"Who can say, Blondee?"

"Try, Tie."

"Try, Tie?" I could hear from his voice he thought he was being funny. I was silent until he spoke again. "Well, a lot of the least are alive, you know that much. How many died? Some, some of them will have, my dear. Less of them though. We're a naturally better breed, less guilt. We have more of a reason to live."

"That didn't stop you—"

"Quite, Blondee. And quiet. There are more women than men now. Perhaps now people will marry whoever they like, as many as they like. But not likely. That's not how you shaped the world is it? Perhaps the women who lost their husbands will pine and mourn and live and die alone, watching from the outside. You don't want to hear about that? Well no, it's depressing.

"Then there are the moderates. They're all dead, near as fuck it. Don't look like that, you look as though it's your fault. I wouldn't go peering into those huts nowadays. The smell alone would knock you backwards. Do you know what happened to me when I died? My belly filled, absolutely filled with gas, and it eventually exploded. It wasn't a sight for a lady, but then you're better than me at saying what is best for women. Are you crossing your legs properly right now?"

I deliberately uncrossed them.

"And you can see the minors for yourself. It's quieter than it was, that's certainly for sure. Especially for a day like this, not too hot or too cold. It's too dry for me though, I didn't like going out when it was dry. You knew this area, this was all you ever knew. I used to worry, leaving you alone with this bunch."

Tie laughed. I never heard him laugh much before.

"I should have worried for their sake."

"I thought you said—"

"I'm rambling, I know. I'll stop."

And he did stop, for a while. But I needed company. I asked him a question, the one I'd always wanted to ask.

"Why did you leave, Tie?"

It was a few minutes before he spoke. The stone woman watched.

"I was tired, Blondee."

"No, really, how could you leave?"

"I couldn't cope. I looked to the future and saw nothing. And there was nothing. I know what you're thinking: you're thinking that you should have been enough to save me. You were. You weren't. I may have gone sooner if not for you, Blondee—I was able to help you and you could distract me. You saved me for a while, and that's all any of us can ever do: help each other for a while."

"I thought you left because your heart was broken."

"You distracted me. This lover of mine—I'll never tell you their name because I want you to stay—this lover reminded me. When they ended the relationship I could do nothing else but look ahead—and see nothing. It's not their fault—they just reminded me, that was all."

"What will happen to me now, Tie?"

"You have no future either, Blondee. But you never did. You were just good at distracting yourself."

There was nothing more to say to him, not for the time being. I stared down at the lino: I stared at her. A series of brown shapes, jagged together, light-brown, dark-brown, shit-brown. I watched the shapes with real focus, staring and staring at them and waiting for them to move. They didn't.

My legs were cramping. I had crossed them again, and shards of pain swelled through them in screams. I stood up, and looked for the shard, for the mirror glass which had pierced her neck.

I felt my neck. I couldn't remember how long the glass had been, but it must have been big, to make her bleed like that.

I fell to my knees, looking out the window. Had that been her last view? Facing the world? Or had she been the other way? I spun round. Perhaps she had been facing our bed.

I lay down, my neck over the big brown stain. She had either been looking at the window frame, or under the bed, the edge of the lino where I hid the magazine, and a t-shirt, and her hair. I pretended I could feel her.

*My clothes are of significant quality—you can tell quality by touch. They fit my form well and—I can feel—I have expensive jewellery about my neck and ears. They cause my skin to tingle, each and every time I place them about my person. I appreciate such things—things which others with money so often fail to notice, and which renders them vulgar. They buy larger and larger cars, build a cinema or a large swimming pool right into their gaudy house, or even buy up exotic animals to play with. Modern-day barbarism. It's the little things that matter: the fine cool lining on a well-cut jacket, or a properly-bred hound. Such things are priceless.*

*In their vulgarity they say that there is nothing new that riches can buy. Some people, and by that I mean my friends, say such things. They grow bored. Their husbands leave to go hunt prostitutes in some evangelic third-world nation (as I say, modern-day barbarism) and they simply do not know what to do with themselves. More specifically they have not learned to appreciate the small things.*

*I was having lunch with two such friends of mine: Lamia, whom I met on some charity drive the two of us have long since forgotten, and Callidi, who happened to live nearby. Our three husbands were likewise friends with one another. The lunch was going well and we were even eating on the terrace: something I had not dared do when the horrifying collection of nudist neighbours had purchased the farm next door, but which I now did for the first time since I'd had them removed.*

*Instead I was to grapple with other concerns. Lamia had drunk one cocktail too many (I had attempted to distract the staff from attending her, but to no avail) and was moaning once more about her husband's absence. Callidi and I listened patiently—Callidi's husband likewise being called away by that vague cliché, 'on business'—as Lamia grew redder and redder in the face. We hadn't guessed it, but there was a purpose to this rant.*

*"We need to get away, girls," she announced.*

*I hated her referring to us as 'girls'. I didn't much prefer the prospect of a holiday with the two of them—I had been on holiday with friends twice before; the first time being terribly boring and the second an unbearable chaos. I was determined to let the idea die gently. I would deliberately take the wrong meaning.*

*"A wonderful idea, we should go out for the day. Somewhere we can take a good walk and find somewhere nice for dinner. I would very much like that."*

*Callidi agreed, but Lamia would have none of it. She swung her red face from side to side.*

*"No, no, no," she whined, repeating herself like a child. "I don't mean that at all. I mean we should go somewhere for longer."*

*"Yes," Callidi agreed, "Two weeks away somewhere carefree and warm. It's a lousy summer here and it's been so long since I took a vacation anywhere."*

*"No, no, no," Lamia said again. I ran my fingers over my bracelet. She was irritating me. "I don't mean for two weeks."*

*"So," I began, "you do not mean for the day, and you do not mean for two weeks. How long, then, do you mean?"*

*Lamia calmed herself and reached for her handbag, carefully withdrawing a leaflet and placing it on the table before us.*

Forget Yourself.

*"I mean longer than two weeks, though how much longer depends on certain factors. It says it all in here," she said, motioning to the leaflet. Callidi collected it from the table and began reading. I was left to twiddle my thumbs.*

*"What exactly are you talking about, Lamia?" I asked her. Her madness had intrigued me—perhaps I have lied to you in my implication that I am never bored myself. And if I am honest I hid beneath my clothes to hide my clumsy frame, the fact that I didn't feel I was doing any of it right, that I couldn't even walk as a woman should. I was never good at just* being, *not like Lamia.*

*"I will tell you girls, but you must promise me no further interruption. Can we agree on that? Good. Well this is like nothing you've ever seen before. I found the leaflet in my husband's desk. Don't look at me like that, Merope, I have to know what's going on or else how am I to keep it all together? Anyway, I didn't want to read it at first—I presumed it was one of those 'alternative' holidays organised by one of those sinister Russian organisations—but something about it piqued my curiosity and so I began reading.*

*"It's like a vacation, but the amount of time depends on certain things. They take you away to a remote part of the world—without telling you where—and they wipe your memory clean. That is the point of the whole thing. They wipe your memory. Merope, do not look so horrified, it's all temporary. It's the way to see the real you. They place you into this encampment, with no recollection of the outside save for the very basics, and from then on it's up to you. What sort of person will you become? What might have been?*

*"And they record everything for you to view afterwards. Behavioural reports, video footage, simply everything. You can learn anything you want about yourself. When it becomes too much you're removed from the programme. As simple as all that. You get to lead a whole new life and view the results afterwards—it's the sort of thing that the Christians dream of."*

*I would be lying to you once more if I said that the idea held no interest for me—but it was simply too extreme. I had a whole life—my husband, the houses—there was no way I could leave it all behind until it became 'too much'. I conveyed these concerns to her, hoping that it would be an end to the matter. Besides, she couldn't very well leave her husband behind, could she?*

*She listened carefully and slowly, as though she were now at the peak of sobriety, before giving her response.*

*"My husband, dear Merope, is already in the programme. He left without telling me."*

*"My god, Lamia, how terrible for you," Callidi comforted, placing the leaflet back down upon the table. "We are both here for you, of course, for as long as it takes for him to return. Surely though, we simply can't go ourselves. I have my own husband and he—"*

*Lamia interrupted her.*

*"Your husband has gone too, Callidi. I found the receipts in the desk along with the leaflet. Yours as well I'm afraid, dear Merope. It seems they left early this morning. Don't look so shocked, the two of you. You know I'm telling the truth. I'm certain letters from them explaining everything will arrive tomorrow. Are you angry? I'm actually quite excited. If we go ourselves not only do we get our revenge on those insensitive, thoughtless men, but we also get to meet them all over again and see what happens. We will never have another opportunity like this for as long as we live."*

*I opened up the leaflet.*

Pilsner was coming. I knew he'd come, I knew it. I heard the footsteps outside the hut. I could hear everything that went on—there hadn't been any rain, or loud storms, or even much wind to batter bits about and muffle those going to-and-fro. There weren't many footsteps around, and I knew that these were for me.

"Pilsner," I uttered. It wouldn't do to be impolite. Whatever happened it wouldn't help.

He said my name. There was nothing to the way he said it, and I searched the sound for clues, but nothing.

"How long should I stay?" I asked, without moving from the floor. He stood stooped before me, careful not to hit his head on the window-frame. His trousers were torn to the back of one leg, and I thought of touching his calf, feeling the prickle of hair and bare skin, but I didn't.

"Blondee," he said my name again. "Blondee, Blondee, Blondee." He shushed them out in a sigh, all in one breath, Blondee-Blondee-Blondee. There were clues that time, clues in his voice. He was worried—he was tense, he wanted sympathy. The world was going to-and-fro without me. Sometimes I had hoped it would, and sometimes I wanted it to stop, and to wait for me to come back.

"Pilsner."

He asked if he could sit down, sit on the foam where we had lain together, perched above where I had hidden that magazine, the strange memories of a past that didn't fit, one shattered shard scattered and surrounded by a hundred others. He asked again: can I sit down? His voice made of wood this time, not foam.

I nodded. "Sure. Yes. Of course. Go ahead." What else could I say?

And what could he say? At first he said nothing. He stared from the window, and Fluffed walked by but no-one else, and Pilsner stared until he placed his face and hands together. His hands and head were shiny, and sunlight bounced from his pores.

In return I sat in silence, as I had been. I returned to the cycle-swirl of thoughts which I'd filled the hut with, to thoughts of vomit and blood on lino, the masses of skin stretched over one another in pleasure, of bad news from post-women. Of computer networks—networks!—what they'd have done with that information. I'd have filled five books over. But it wouldn't have made sense to them, it never could, they wanted truth, they wanted to glue all the shards together, but they were from different mirrors, and they'd never fit. There was no single outside.

"Blondee," he said. "Do you know why you're here?"

I wanted to ask him what was the matter.

"It's the severes," Tie whispered to me. I nodded. Had he ever told me something I didn't already know?

I answered Pilsner. "I'm here, because I'm a thief. It's why I was placed in the world."

"Why," he asked, "are you in this hut, right now?"

I answered Pilsner. "I'm here, because I'm a thief. But you knew that already, we all did. I committed a crime I'm already being punished for." And I remembered Burberry's words, of how we were guessing, guessing at things we couldn't know.

"Blondee," Pilsner said, "you stole from us, you stole from everyone. You took all they had. You took their memories." For a moment he stopped. "Frederick."

"You took our guilt, or you tried, my love," Tie mouthed.

"And I gave them new memories," I replied.

"It was never yours to take," Pilsner told me, his voice strong and ordered. "Where are you looking, what are you thinking about?"

"I was thinking about Tie."

"Never heard of him," Pilsner told me, his voice weak and confused. He was lying, or had forgotten. Nobody was ever mentioned much, after they'd left.

"And what're you thinking about, Pilsner? It's not me, I know that."

He paused, a reluctant tut from his tongue and teeth.

"It's the severes," I said. "Isn't it?"

And Pilsner nodded. "It is. It's the severes."

He told me how there weren't as many of the least now, how there must have been as many severes as were the others, as there were of *us*. *Us*, he said it like he meant them and not me. I didn't care, he could say *us* how he wanted. Soon they would come for us, he said, they'd come and, well, who knows. Their crimes are worse than ours, they're capable of anything, considering what they'd done. A horde, a swarm, a mass of angry uncontrollables. The worst thing in all the world.

I listened, patiently and silently. I might have fallen asleep. At some point he left.

*I had to hurry, and these legs were too short. Everything was empty, the shops all shuttered, and most of them hadn't even bothered to put up notices explaining. They didn't need to.*

*A young man sporting a heavy tan knocked me, the both of us stumbling.*

*"Sorry," he called, scurrying off. For a moment I felt my skin tickle with anger, but I couldn't blame him. He had somewhere to be. Everyone had somewhere to be. I caught a glimpse of my face and blonde hair in the dark glass of a closed store. I looked so scared. It made me laugh.*

*The city centre was depressing. I had thought of gathering some more supplies, but I couldn't see much point. Thorgeir, my husband, he had sorted most of that out, but I had wanted to help. I had left it too late as usual.*

*I would go to the park. The trees and bushes wouldn't have left, they'd still be there to enjoy. It wasn't too far away, and I was glad to be leaving the quiet dark streets of empty offices and shuttered shops. All the cafés were closed. A bakery had a bin through its window, an alarm screaming to no-one. Even the police were hidden away. What the hell do they do at a time like this? Some war zone. It was like everyone was already dead.*

*I knew even as I reached the iron railings of the park that it was a no-go. There were raised voices and shouting, rage-filled roars and barks. Barks from large dogs. They were somewhere to the other side of the trees and bushes and I could see them without looking, our pointless thuggish defence. Perhaps they were sympathisers, for the other side, ready to keep order for them. That made more sense. Some of them were already here.*

*So I would head home. The rows of houses were quiet, and some had the same grey metal shutters as the shops. There were fewer cars than usual cluttering the street. They must have been gathered into garages. Then it was raining paper, paper from the sky. One white square was carried in the air into my face. I clutched it away from my lips and nose and pressed it into my pocket. Home first. I'd get home first.*

*Home was quiet as everywhere else, our poky little house as silent and still as if it were abandoned. I took off my coat and remembered the sheet of sky paper. I took it from the pocket, smoothed it against my palm and read.*

*They were letting us know they were coming. I giggled at it. The giggle grew. I laughed, heavy, gasping gulps of laughter. How could we not know? How could we not know? I laughed until I was dizzy.*

*When I was calm I called his name. I called it again as I headed up the stairs.*

*"Thorgeir."*

*He was in the middle of the room, with the yellow wallpaper I always hated, doing some cleaning. He had a bowl of water by his knees and was cleaning my statue, the one of Artemis.*

*I know why he was cleaning—why he was cleaning in the middle of a war zone. He wanted to be ready. If they burst in with guns aloft, the house would be spotless for them. They could never say we weren't clean.*

*But he was scrubbing her too hard, my Artemis figurine. He was scrubbing her like he wanted to remove her colour, he was scrubbing her like he wanted to make her pale as a ghost.*

*Stop! I cried.*

*He looked up at me with his gentle smile, the same he had given me when he'd decided we wouldn't run. It made me feel safe. It made me feel as though I were being patronised.*

*He handed me my stone woman and I clutched her to my chest, a wet patch spreading across my blouse.*

*She was the only protection we had.*

I stepped out from the triangle hut. No-one was there.

This was it. This was it. This was it.

I walked along beside the wall until I found something I could use: a steel bar.

I picked it up and walked back to the triangle hut. The one Tie had built.

I struck it.

The window shattered.

Where I had lived when Ketamine arrived with the rations, a carrier bag over her arm.

I struck it again.

The frame splintered.

Then Frederick and Burberry. Here Burberry had lost herself, spilling to the floor.

I struck it and struck it.

Where I was waiting, the last piece of me.

It collapsed, a rubble. A pile of litter.

You could never have guessed it had been a triangle hut. Not now.

"This is it, Tie."

"What do you mean, dear Blondee?"

"You know what it means."

He was so close I could almost see him. His belly, his blotch-puffed cheeks, the squint about his eyes. I could smell him, even over the urine and the tang of my body, there was him, the odour of stale sweat caught in folds. I would miss him, but he was gone and soon I would be too.

"What're you thinking, Blondee?"

"Many things, Tie."

"The world isn't as empty as it looks out there, you know. You know that."

"Perhaps, Tie. You used to say things that made more sense."

"I ramble these days."

"You do. Yes, yes you do."

"So what are you thinking, Blondee?"

"I was thinking about you."

"I'm touched."

"I was thinking about the severes."

"They won't come."

"What do you mean?"

"I mean they'll stay where they are. They won't come—they won't change a thing. If I were still around I'd talk to Pilsner about it. When he's figured out that they're not even coming, they'll come and do what they'll do with you."

"Should I be scared or something?"

"Do you feel scared, my dear?"

"Not really."

My limbs kept jolting, painful shudders like they were forcing themselves awake. My clothes stuck to me. There was no more water. My tongue stuck to the sides of my mouth.

"Blondee?"

"Yes, Tie?" I missed the next word.

"… me Blondee, what do you mean, this is it?"

"I'm saying goodbye."

"You're taking a long time about it. This isn't how to go about it."

"How do you know?"

"You're sounding like her."

"Thank you."

It hadn't been light or dark for what must have been days. The sky was caught, in between, unwilling to move one way or the other. I couldn't remember if it had even last been night or day.

"What did it feel like, Tie, when you left?"

There was a sharp silence before he spoke. I could hear the smack of his jowls. "I can't give you any answer you don't already know."

"Did you feel the same things as her?"

"I'd imagine so. The thrilling rush of blood, that sort of thing."

"I can't help having to leave you, Tie."

"I know that. I know that."

"Though you left me first."

"I know that."

"Well then, I'll say it, though you never gave me chance that first time. Goodbye, Tie. I hope if you've been reborn you're happy. I mostly hope you haven't though. I wish I'd known you better, and that you'd stopped all this somehow. I kind of wish I'd felt enough to fuck you. To fuck you and treat you decently. But it never should have mattered, and maybe it wouldn't have helped anything. Do you think you need to fuck someone to love them? You'd still have left, sooner or later, you wouldn't have been able to help it. I missed you, I really did, but who could I have told? You've gone again, I can feel it, but I'll carry on if it's all the same to you. I wish you'd had the guts to tell me what was going on, or tell me their name. I wish you'd told me more about the start of the world, or why you thought we were here. As long as I'm Blondee I'll hate you for leaving.

"He's here, Pilsner's here and I have to go, but once again you've left first. Bye then, Tie."

Pilsner looked at the rubble I had created. He said nothing. Sunlight streaked his face. He seemed pleased, more pleased than when I had last seen him. Slivers of rusty razors shot from the music player he had brought with him.

"This is it," he told me.

"Did they come, Pilsner?"

He asked me who I meant. He grinned. He knew who I meant. I wasn't in the mood to play, I had equally important places to be. He continued. He feigned surprise, "Oh, oh," he said, "The severes, you mean the severes." He said they weren't coming after all, his grin growing, growing over his face like a plague.

"They might. They might be waiting." I didn't believe it but I wanted to scare him.

For a split of a second it worked, his face flickering into worry before his teeth returned. They were crooked, the ones at the front, and a bit yellow. Mine were better. He started talking again, about how they hadn't come, how they never would, how they, unlike some, knew what was right, how we should live.

I wanted to shock him again.

I started stroking my chest, small motions at first, and he glanced for a moment, just a moment, until I pressed both palms into my breasts and caressed them, careful and slow. He glanced again, a second longer this time. It was working, he had stopped talking. I wanted to laugh. I had shut him up. So easy, so easy. I played with my left nipple, teasing it, even rubbing my thigh with my free hand, slowly bringing it to my crotch. I groaned a little, just for effect.

He asked me what I was doing.

I ignored the question and leaned back a nudge, undoing a button on my shirt.

He asked me if I wanted sex.

Then I laughed, right at him. "No, no, no. No I don't want to fuck. Why would you ask that?"

His face flushed with blood, his eyes white and small in the centre of his purpled face. It made me laugh more.

He told me I was in trouble. He told me I had no idea how to act. He told me I had no sense of order, of what was right, or wrong, for that matter. He told me I used other people for my amusement and he had no idea who Blondee was, not really.

I was tired of listening. I added words to the notes from his player. I sang his words back at him: Blondee you're weak, Blondee you're corrupt, Blondee Blondee Blondee. And Blondee it's your fault, and Blondee you prove us right, Blondee the thief. The worst one. Stop that, stop that, sto-o-o-o-o-op it, stop, you fucking fucking freak. That's it, there's no point, no point, no point in talking any more. No point. This is it, Blondee, this is it. It it it. Time to go. Time to go-o-o-o-o, oh.

I drifted in the dark space between worlds, falling through each, choking on stories.

*He kisses me and we lie down on the grass, a chicken clucking near my ankle. I can't stand the waiting, the post-woman always brings bad news. Rebels on a farm. And now I'm fucking, him, I'm fucking him, I'm fucking him so hard it feels like my cock it going to explode. What did she say? That I was young? Why need to tell me that, I know I am. I know I am. And I'm close, I'm so close, and I'm gonna—*

*The bag is heavy, so heavy today. I don't want to bring them bad news. It's not my fault, it's just how things are. I'm even going to get myself into trouble, talking to his brother like that. He'll be on some kind of list, they'll be watching him, that's for sure—for certain even. Don't shoot the postwoman, I used to say that to people and they'd laugh. Too much bad news is delivered these days, and the bags are so heavy—there must be a better job but what am I to do?*

*I need my brother. He's the only one I ever needed. He looked after me, and now I'd look after him. Those fascist fucking pigs won't get at him, I won't let them. They could round me up and stick me in a prison camp somewhere for all I care. As long as I was with him it wouldn't matter. Then we could always look after each other. We'd remind each other who we were, who we really were, like we did when we were teenagers. Smoking spliffs and ignoring bad news. Now he's in the countryside, a place I daren't go.*

*I've lost the connection again. Fuck it. Perhaps I'll go outside. No, no Norna will wonder where I am. She might be stupid, quite stupid, but she'll wonder where I've gone. Besides, the neighbour will be back soon, that one who's always on the phone.*

*She might be able to guess what they're actually on about. But, but it's doing my back no good sitting in this chair all day, no good at all. I've never noticed the window is so dirty. Perhaps I can suggest another activity, one which involves less sitting and spying. Perhaps we can go somewhere together, somewhere where we can actually leave all the busy world behind and be alone, just the two of us. Do I really feel like that?*

*The connection is gone again, but who has been keeping it going anyway? Who's keeping the electricity running? They must have finished putting the turbines on the roof before the plague peaked. They'd better come for us, take us somewhere where it's safe, where there's no disease and plenty of food. I'm wasting away. Where has she gone? I need to talk to her. It might be through a fake face, through a woman's lips but it's better than nothing. With her I know I could be more. More than some sad old man in a shirt and tie who sells drugs to neighbourhood teens. Neighbourhood teens who'd eventually vomited their lives away, along with their brothers, sisters, along with their parents. We might be the last two left on Earth.*

*I looked for the pretty woman again, the crazy ketamine one outside the newsagent, but I couldn't find her. I was just distracting myself. Truth is, what I'm doing is scary. I never knew anyone who did this, who sold their memories for hollow cash. And the building looks so normal from the outside, so fucking normal. It might have been an accountancy, but for the logo. It's a different one from the ads online. It has a man, with a floating black ball for a head: like on toilet doors. But his head is glowing, one colour to the next, all the colours that exist, all in turn. Is that a good thing? Do I want my head to glow? It doesn't seem like the type of thing that'd be good for you, after all, selling your memories. Enough distraction, I have to go inside.*

*It would be utter madness—and this plan is one of Lamia's more extravagant lunacies. It cannot be possible, surely? Yet her idea has wound its way about my mind, weaving its way into my thoughts. She is right in saying that my husband has left, and she was correct in her premonition that he would send a letter the very next day. The letter said all the usual things, about how he loves me and cherishes the time we spend with one another, and that I mustn't be too angry at his absence—he had even bought me a car to cheer my thoughts. Modern barbarism. The letter gave absolutely no clue as to the length of this apparent absence. In truth I have absolutely no idea what I will with myself while he's away: especially if my two friends and their husbands have left as well. Forget Yourself. That is tempting. The opportunity to live one's life afresh. Who is to say that there aren't some invaluable experiences to be obtained? A chance to see oneself from the outside. It is tempting, certainly tempting.*

*And there he is, my husband, my ever-cleaning husband. I don't know how he could clean at a time like this, the calm before the storm, the silence before the scream. Will there be screaming? The scream of jets overhead, well we've already heard that. Will they come and round us up? Enough questions. Wait and see. I lean over and kiss his salty lips, and in return he's running his tongue down my neck, to my chest. He giggles, and I giggle, and for one moment there is no war. No shutters, no mobs, no paper from the sky. We collapse to the floor and I pull him on top of me, feeling the weight of his body press me into the ugly pink carpet we've never changed. I pull off his shirt, then my blouse, feeling skin on skin, our pulses pounding, firm, hard, rough and a crash. A burst of sound, an explosion. It has begun, but we carry on anyway, just more gently, the light touch of fingertips, the soft nudge of a forehead, soft and quiet, careful not to disturb anything.*

# epilogue

YOU SHOULD KNOW I AM BLONDEE. For the last time, I am Blondee.

This is the last time I can talk to you. After this I won't be Blondee, not any more. Who shall I be?

First I'll tell you what they did with me. I'm alive, but who I am isn't consistent, if it ever was. They took me, talked, they lectured me, led me, and left. And here I am, at a different wall, at a place I saw only once before. It's not too bad. I am in a hole, the ever-rustling blue tarpaulin above, soil below. At times it's lovely here. At times like this how could I want anything more?

They gave Blondee a new label, one of her very own. I suppose they were trying to give it to me, but like I keep telling you, I'm not a stable entity.

Now there were least, minor, moderate (species extinct), severe—and me. Pilsner had a proud gleam in his eye as he announced it. I'd laughed at him.

*Isolation.* This was an elegant word they gifted me. Blondee was to be placed in isolation. That was why they gave me this ramshackle shelter. That's why they keep leaving me rusted tins of food and mush-sloppy fruit. If I died I wouldn't be alone, and who knows where I'd be? Or who? They keep me here so I can be by myself. They don't know anything.

This is the end of my story. But there are so many more. Now I'm by myself I can see them all. See and touch and taste. A million worlds outside our walls, all leading here. I had known each person—my dreadlocked lover and beetroot-scented husband living on a farm; my lost-long friend who cut himself up but who had lived a life behind a screen watching the world die; the man I hated, who only wanted his brother back; even the clumsy husband-gathering woman who lived bored and rich. Different worlds, different stories. All had been brought here, refugee or prisoner, vacation or torment. I saw them all.

Yesterday, for example. Yesterday I was Timon, whose friends had called Tan. Tanned skin and one grey tooth.

*And I was scared. It wasn't just the logo, sprawled all over the walls, a man's head glowing blue then green then purple. I'd found a cigarette on the floor, a whole unsmoked cigarette, and I took it as a sign. I was doing the right thing, there would be a tomorrow. I smoked it as I watched the colours in the logo-man's head change. A drag and he went blue. A drag and he went red. A drag and I threw the stub to the floor.*

*I was scared, and it wasn't just the receptionist, her face firm as her breasts, her voice clipped short of compassion. I was scared, couldn't she see that? But she must have seen it every day, a hundred sad and lonely people a week selling all they could possible have left. She was bored and had no empathy. But I couldn't blame her—she was just trying to make sure she had her own future now. Better her side of the desk than mine. There's no more money, and we all know it.*

*"Just a few," I told her.*

*I wouldn't want to lose them all, not all my memories. Nothing on her moved even a millimetre, she was poised and placed, official like a statue. Eventually she handed me forms, a hundred signatures and I went into a little room which smelt of nothing—of nothing at all. It was dark in there. I'd always known clinics to be bright as a headache.*

*There were two men in the room. One was a lawyer, one was a doctor. I couldn't tell which was which. They wore near-matching designer suits and they handed me more forms. The medical and the legal ones looked the same. Rows of incomprehensible words. I have a degree but I'd never understand.*

*"I only want to sell a few," I told them.*

*I wasn't wearing a suit. I was wearing the same t-shirt I'd been wearing since yesterday. I could feel the little damp circles under my armpits. They nodded and talked about procedure. There wasn't much for me to do. The doctor/lawyer told me they could do it the same day, and it was a statement, it wasn't a question. I just nodded, nodded and nodded and hoped they didn't notice the sweat-marks on my clothes.*

*There were more rooms, dark and hot, and there were a few more people, all in suits.*

*This was it, the very core of me. This was all I had, and now I had surrendered it to them. Once I had sold my body, and that was nothing. Now I sold my past, so that I could gain a future. Was that possible? He who controls the past controls the future, that's what they say. Oh gods I hoped they were wrong.*

*"Leave my mother," I told someone. Leave her. She was gone and if they took her I'd never get her back. Leave my mother.*

*They weren't even listening by then, milling about, pills and wavelengths and sterile beds. The forms were signed and they had no further need of niceties. I belonged to them—most people are law-illiterate, they can't speak or read what they lawyers write, and I was one of them.*

*Banks and lawyers and politicians—they need us, you see. They need every part of us, so that they can grow fat. Without us they are one of us, and that's worse than death for them—for we have no future. They jabbed at my arms and pinned me down.*

*And so they took everything. They took the very core of me. I couldn't scream.*

*I slept. I went to sleep and I woke up somewhere else.*

*I woke up here. Naked to the world. A new world, one I didn't recognise, and I couldn't recognise anything, especially myself. People were gathered around, ready to name me.*

How could I have been Timon if I wasn't by myself? Without the luxury of isolation? With someone there, watching my performance. They'd grab on to me, hold on and not let go. Preconceptions and expectations would weigh me down, and I'd be trapped, Blondee, Blondee forever.

*I am Timon, known as Tan, and I sold my memories for rent.*

*Is there a better reason? Of course I didn't get to use the money myself. Read the small print, always read the small print. Bring a lawyer to help you wade through the endless meaningless syllables uttered by sharp-suited men. My family would get the money, but I would never remember who they were. Leave my mother, I'd said. For all I remember I could have been born in a tube, surrounded by goggle-eyed scientists. And someone somewhere has Timon's real-live memories, which can never be copied, never duplicated, only moved to some squishy new organic home. Memories of beaches, of winter presents, memories of kisses and crosses and first cars. Did the rich read the small print? All the money in the world can't buy a lifetime. Did they know how they got them? They'd be able to afford the lawyers.*

This place isn't so bad. Here in my hole I have space. Not too long ago there would have been people scattered about, with questions and statements and thoughts. Now all I can see are one or two empty huts. Sometimes even, when the wind is blowing the right way, I can barely even smell death at all. But the distant dizzy hum of flies is always there unless it rains.

A day after I was brought here I heard someone. I could hear the panting. They wanted to come and see Blondee. Their footsteps were all around me, I could hear them above the rain.

I hid away until they left. They had been watching me. I knew who it was.

I couldn't see them. I couldn't see anyone.

Can I hold you?

You might not be real but that doesn't matter. I will still hold you.

Will you think of me, holding you? I have blonde hair that reaches my shoulders and I am of an average stature—though of course my definition of average will be misleading. I have the long fingers of a thief.

These will not change, even when I'm born anew.

*And I was Loke. Years of watching women on a flicker-happy screen had given me thick glasses and a gut. But I always dressed smartly, I always wore a tie. I had watched the world die, a plague like in a bad film. I watched my neighbours panic and collapse, one by one. They ran constant broadcasts, and I saw more than one presenter die right on air. Sometimes the cameramen were dead too, so the image was frozen on the body, and then I'd change the channel.*

*There was nothing good on. The radio was the same, they'd be sick on air, all would turn to static, aside from the emergency broadcasts. It's surprising how much they mentioned god. I thought we were a secular society. They're cowards, turning to a tyrant as a last resort.*

*There were thousands of videos online they had made, their last films, all of them dying like they thought they were original. They didn't need gods, the young ones, they had the videos of one another passing on. They all died together and that was all they needed. It soothed them.*

*Why would we care? We were still alive.*

*There was only her left, and so I watched her, like I'd always watched women. It's not like I was proud of the fact, and I know how creepy they found it (one of them even sent me a virus which somehow scorched circuits deep within the hum of the box). I enjoyed it though and the only thing which would have stopped me was the death of every woman on Earth.*

*But she didn't mind, not this one. She'd gone a bit mental, pretending to watch her neighbours, pretending their bloated boils of corpses were walking and talking and making tea, but she was company. She would win and I would lose. That was companionship, she said so. She could make up any game she wanted and I didn't mind, so long as I could watch her. I loved her.*

*She didn't know much about me, and she wasn't even surprised when I told her how to prepare the K. She thought I was a woman as well. But that was our romance. A crazy woman and a mask, the last two humans on Earth.*

*We weren't the last two of course. It might have been poetic—fucked up and poetic—but it wasn't true.*

*Some people had survived, hidden at home like us, hiding behind net curtains or Venetian blinds, listening to radio static and wondering why the internet still worked. Dotted up and down the land, we were immune, protected by the god of genetic predisposition.*

*So few of us left to watch the bodies turn black and blue.*

*Eventually they came for us, dying men in rubber suits: a group of government zombies. But I can't pretend they weren't friendly, a message to my box and coming right to my door to bring me to the bus. They didn't even notice my kitchen ceiling had collapsed, with a bathtub in the middle.*

*They gave us coffee from re-seal cups. Taken to safety were the buzzwords. We're taking you to safety. You're being taken to safety. Each new person on the bus, from city to town to hamlet. You'll be taken to safety.*

*I had my own buzzwords: where is she? Where is she? Where is she? I only knew her first name and I wasn't even certain where she was. She wasn't on this bus, which snaked over litter-streets and past silent dead-eyed buildings. I looked through the caged glass, ignoring the jabber of the woman to my side. Waiting for her.*

*We slept right there in the seats. The bus never stopped. Well, only now and then when another rubber-suit man gargled and slumped and was then left by the roadside.*

*Then there she was: three bags and a suitcase. She got on the bus asking for Norna, looking for her pre-rendered face. I wanted to grab her and clutch her to me, but she hadn't known any Loke, just a Norna, with flawless skin and a well-designed smile. She perched at the front where I could watch her once more.*

*It made me cry. She was so close. I sobbed gently, my head resting in my coat as I pretended to sleep. I sobbed until I slept for real.*

*I awoke when it was night, the bus moving and the road so dark, with a dozen heads bobbing about. I watched her hair, her head lolling to and fro. She was asleep. And I was happy. She was alive, and while she was alive I could know her. Or just watch her.*

*Ages passed and finally the bus stopped, a hiss of contentment. We're here, they said, and I waited for 'at safety'. Instead they told us to step down from the vehicle. There was a wall, a big endless yellow-grey wall, with the word 'Hyboria' plastered like an advert. One of the rubber-suit men had a speech.*

*He told us we were the last. He told us we were lucky. He said that we were the only ones. He said this was home now. He let us know this was our world.*

*And people shouted and sobbed and looked curious. They asked what it was, where it was, how long they'd be there for.*

*The questions weren't answered. The rubber man went on. "You will," he said, "need to forget the old world. For your own sanity. You mustn't know you are the last." He and the others were backing away, onto the bus. "You'll forget; you'll forget it all. You'd thank us for it if you could. You'll be new people. You can start afresh. There's nothing as bad as nostalgia. You'd thank us. You'd thank us."*

*And I felt tired. I felt so tired.*

*"Sleep," they said. "All of you, sleep, and we'll bring you in when you're good and when you're ready."*

*So I lay down and I got ready to sleep. I heard some of the others throwing themselves at the caged bus. I didn't. I'd be with her. Nothing could make me forget her face. I was ready. Ready to join the new world. Ready to be reborn.*

*I woke up here.*

And I was Blondee again.

I spent a while tidying up the area around my living-hole. I made a trench in the sand all around, and decorated the ground by the wall with shards of coloured plastic. There was no harm in leaving an imprint.

I licked mush from my fingers and planted the squidge-fruit seeds in the chalk-barren ground of my corner.

I was Blondee, and it wasn't long before my visitor was back.

This time I stood up and saw a face.

I wasn't surprised at who it was, I wasn't surprised at all. They looked hungry, and tired, and so, so desperate. What did they want? What could they possibly want now? They looked, and turned, and left.

I wasn't sure what to do, so I gave a little wave to the back which got smaller and smaller.

I dug the trench a little deeper, hollowed with my hands.

*I am Loke, one of the lucky few. A new world, a new start, free of the burdens of Armageddon.*

*And I'm lucky, I won't pretend otherwise. My guts stayed inside me, part of a tiny fraction of all the guts in the world—those not vomited up into sinks or onto carpets. The world had stopped, cars never left driveways, trains static in stations, milk souring then curdling then crusting in cappuccino machines. We were told we were lucky, over and over, though most of them didn't believe it—the luckiest thing, one of the others said, would be to have no plague at all—to have loved ones alive and neighbours to smile at.*

*But for me it was a fresh start, a new beginning, a chance to be with the woman I loved. But who was she? Who was she?*

The book doesn't exist here, my world within the trench. Would Pilsner put the book back? He had always believed in it—not the memories, he believed in the power of it to bring people together.

People don't need words to bring them together.

I always thought he was stupid.

I'm not one person.

And the outside—well, it's not one place, how can it be?

Everything in the book is as true as everything else, I suppose, but it's irrelevant. She said nothing was true, but nothing is not true, here under my blue tarpaulin.

I told you love is all I have left. And that's true. But I have no-one left to love, no bones or shit, so I have no choice but to love everything.

Grotesque and humiliating.

It spills from me like blood. It's killing me, but I don't mind.

Tomorrow I will wake up someone new. The same damp earth will be under the same toes; the same fingers will clutch the same food and bring it to the same lips.

But someone else will taste it.

The same eyes with someone else's vision.

The same brain with someone else's thoughts.

*There were no sirens. When I think of war I think of sirens, screaming to shut the windows, screaming to hide in the basement, or under a table. But there weren't any sirens. We didn't need them, but a little part of me felt cheated.*

*It was an odd thing to be thinking about, as my husband and I were making fuck for the last time, curled together under the gaze of the wet stone woman. Perhaps I wanted it to be more dramatic, love-making to the shrill shriek of the world's end. It wasn't even spectacular: there weren't any fireworks or head-rush dizzy pleasure. I didn't even climax.*

*Afterwards he lay on me, cold and clammy and panting, and I thought of the hundreds of young men marching down the high street. I thought about their firm bodies beneath their uniforms, the perfect-round pecs of the enemy.*

*He kissed me, and I was grateful to have my thoughts interrupted. He lay, his clammy sweaty-bulk on top of me, kissing my lips then my neck. He loved me, he said, so I said it in return. I did love him, but there was so much to think about. Was I the only one? Had everyone shuttered their windows just to head indoors and make love to their partners, their minds empty of the war?*

*There was an explosion somewhere else. I waited for screams or fire-sirens, but nothing came. No commotion, no attention, nothing at all. Then there were more, pointless echoes of the first, a rain of meaningless noise. Still the husband lay there, as if he was shielding me from the dull horror, something he had never bothered to do when the newspapers were ranting with panicked faith.*

*He was asleep. Each breath was deep and even. Outside there was a double-bang, two bombs bursting side-by-side. I hoped the window wouldn't shatter, spraying us with a rain of glass. But the bombs were far away.*

*I had imagined this moment. For months before the war. I imagined feeling terror, of sheltering bravely, of crying noble tears. But I didn't want to cry. I wanted to feel something about what was happening, some kind of rage, some kind of loss, but I was too calm. Things were changing, that was all. Routes planned, borders redrawn, religious icons painted. They were changing now and they'd change again, and why feel sad for something that wasn't permanent?*

*Fucking shit. Utter wanking shit. Existentialist nonsense. I should have cared, and I wanted to, but I couldn't. We can't help our minds, I told myself. We can't help our minds. My husband Thorgeir snorted and pressed his hipbone into me.*

*We lay for hours.*

*There was a crash downstairs. A door flung from hinges. There were voices. More than voices, there was chanting. "We're the defence league, defence league, defence league, we're the defence league, de- fence—league!"*

*There were footsteps up the stairs, heavy boots on our new carpet, and they burst in. They gripped my husband by the neck and flung him away from me, his limp cock flapping uselessly. One of them lay on top of me, as my husband had done, and giggled. He stank of cheap lager. They carried on their chant, de and fence and league, and when the lager-stench was lifted from me I saw my husband was gone. Get up, they screeched—get up and come with us. I lay there, looking at the rose on the ceiling, until they gripped my elbows and hoisted me to my feet. They grasped at me, all over, until one shouted that there wasn't time, so they grasped my blonde hair and dragged me downstairs instead.*

*"It's time for a new life," they said, "you'll be helping heal the sick."*

*So that was it. We'd be guinea-pigs, lab rats, hamster-test-subjects: just like the papers had warned. Don't worry, lager-breath whispered, you won't even know it's happening. You'll be in your own little world.*

*I still didn't feel anything. Nothing at all.*

*I am a wife and the world fell to war.*

*Dramatic isn't it? But it wasn't, it really wasn't. It was quiet and grey. Numb, that's the word, it was numb. There weren't any heroes, nor any villains, not really. There might have been explosions but I never saw them. There were kisses on carpets, sweat over formaldehyde-soaked sterility, but after that there was waiting. It wasn't even exciting as they took my mind, and it was near-normal to wake up in here. Experiments, poisons in the food, poison to end it all.*

*Without knowing who or where we were we'd never resist: we could be watched. And I couldn't answer why me, they picked our house, number 67, and perhaps there were more, mini-worlds up and down the land, each filled with experiments. Maybe we were the only ones. And forget the drama of romance, the last thing I saw of my husband was his flaccid prick wobbling away. And he farted as they took him.*

*I woke up here.*

It rains. Thunder over the blue tarpaulin.

I'm lying down now, staring at the ripples and waves of rain on plastic.

The mud is in my hair.

Water flows down into the hole, over my fingers, over my arm.

My eyes prickle with tears, tears of relief.

I enjoy the feeling of them welling in my eyes, flooding over my face.

These are the last sensations I will have.

Tomorrow they will belong to someone else.

The rain is falling heavier, the tarp beats like a dream.

*The three of us waited at the ferry-port: Lamia, Callidi and myself. Lamia cheered us up—remember, we're following our thoughtless husbands on a great adventure. Eventually a smart black car arrived and some men in suits stepped out. They asked us our names and then asked to see our identification. We gave both willingly, though we were tired and, I may hazard, each a little frightened at this undertaking. Then men sent to greet us did little to alleviate our concerns: they did not smile, nor make any attempts at reassurance. I told myself that perhaps this was simply the manner of their professional capacity. In reality I was cold and rather hungry.*

*We were directed into the car. It was large, warm and with plenty of snacks, and so our spirits were indeed soothed. Lamia opened up a bottle of complimentary liquor and poured it into the glasses provided. She called a toast: to our adventure. Callidi and I repeated her words with less vigour.*

*We drove for many hours. Having endured an extremely lengthy journey and then eaten, the three of us eventually drifted to sleep. As I drifted off it struck me as somewhat odd that the men in suits hadn't said a single word to one another—not once. I confess that I slept heavily.*

*We each awoke when the car reached a halt. The men opened the doors and we found ourselves outside a plain white building surrounded by a thick forest. It had been newly-built and seemed of little expense. Lamia loudly asked them if this is what we had paid for. It was a fair question—after all, this experiment was costing each of us a considerable sum. The response of the man she had asked absolutely shocked me.*

*He took hold of her arm and slapped her across the face. Lamia burst into tears. As did Callidi. He told her that he did that because she simply would not remember. He went on to inform us that we were in absolutely no danger in his presence, but he was tired of 'all these rich cunts lording it over us when their own lives are so fucking shitty they'd rather forget them', and that if we were to speak out of turn we would receive a slap.*

*I was Merope, clumsy and unwomanly. I was talked into handing over my memories at the other side of the world.*

*Perhaps if I had been blessed with something of a backbone I would have mustered the energy necessary to saying no. No to Lamia, no to my husband. Instead Lamia, Callidi and I were led into the unassuming white building and gruffly informed of what we already knew and now had no control over. Our minds would be wiped clean and we would start afresh. When it all became too much we would be removed, informed of how we did, and given our precious results.*

*I have lied to you again. I just told you I have no backbone. Well I must have at least a small backbone, for I asked them a question.*

*"How do you know when it is 'too much'?"*

*They each laughed at me. They said that they would do their best to prevent any suicidal actions, but that they were not omnipresent, and could do little if we were to really put our minds to it. Callidi started crying again.*

*It was Lamia's turn to ask a question: "But the conditions, the conditions are appropriate?"*

*"They certainly are appropriate," the men replied, "you shall be living in squalor. That is appropriate. You wish to forget your old lives—if we were to place you in fine and very nice conditions then you would be repeating the same lives over. We want to try you with something new."*

*Then, to our greatest surprise, it was Callidi who stopped her crying and asked her own question: "Why won't you let us leave right now, if that is what we really want?"*

*"Because, there are greater interests than your own at stake. You could say you're assisting in a great research project. Besides, we would really rather you forget our inhospitality since your arrival. It would not be a prudent way to keep our jobs. Or our heads, for that matter."*

*We were led into a room with three clean beds. Lamia told us not to worry—remember the adventure. This is the type of chance you only receive once a lifetime.*

*Yet by that point I was beyond comfort. All I had left were questions—where would we be living? How would we recognise one another?*

*And most importantly: what will I become?*

*I woke up here, no memory as to why.*

The visitor came back—back for the last time.

I'd stood, we'd faced one another. They were here for me, they wanted Blondee, they wanted to end the isolation.

Mine and their own.

They had a look, filled with hunger, starving for touch or maybe even taste.

They were alone and looked so pitiful, standing there in a corner with the fading smell of death. They opened their mouth, ready to talk, but if they did I'd be trapped. Air pushed from lungs, vibrated by voice-box and spread over me.

So I picked up a rusted can of apple-squares and threw it. That was that. They ran away and I knew they wouldn't be back. I was alone.

*I was surrounded by people, and I had always liked it like that, even before we all moved to the farmhouse. We had to go somewhere, there was no room left for us in the city—the farmhouse was my idea. No-one else was using it. They all remembered my suggestion, and I'd become some sort of leader. I never liked that as much: I liked being around people so I could merge and meld and melt with them, not so I could sit atop them all.*

*Well, not like that anyway.*

*We didn't have much longer there, and the responsibility was mine. All mine. Not many of the others seemed to show much concern, though I had told them over and over, as we were gathered on logs outside chewing breakfast with fat chickens clucking about our knees. So far I hadn't even received anything stronger than a 'we'll be fine'. We'd always made do, sure, but that didn't mean everything would be fine, not forever.*

*We were in trouble—why couldn't they see it?*

*So every day I waited for her, our handy post-woman, the bringer of bad news. She was a nice enough person, though I could tell she was bored by our situation. To her, we were a bunch of immoral hippy-types who spend all day fucking. Still, I liked inviting her in for tea, of sharing some space with someone from the city. She lived in the city, she told me, in a small apartment near the sorting office. She was very matter-of-fact and didn't ask many questions.*

*I missed living amongst the towers and the hurried bustle of people, shoving one another and spilling down stairwells, into subway stations, up into office blocks. I liked wandering round and round in circles, getting lost in a mass of strangers. Sometimes they looked at me funny, in my natural dyes and unironed hair and jewellery I made myself. I'd look at them funny back and feel a strange sort of pride. I was different to them.*

*We all were, dotted about town, bad seeds scattered in a society which wanted some kind of order, in a world of new-found faith. If I wanted to play in the shower with the hottest redhead I'd ever known I'd go see Athers, down the diagonal street and past the New Life Celebration Hall, where chastity-ringed teens would glare. If I wanted to have Heph's skilled tongue curl and thrust into me I'd head past the moral office, with the purse-lipped men and women in suits who stared past the hippy, the pagan in hemp.*

*Eventually they wouldn't put up with us. There were less and less of us for a start—friends suddenly married, stopped taking calls, brothers or sisters or aunts found faith. Then there were bricks through windows and notes through doors. We gathered together in my lounge, too tired to fuck, and I suggested the farmhouse. We talked for two nights, eating meatless stuffing and Mumbai Mix.*

*My brother told me not to go. He said whatever happened I was better where I was. I gave him an ornament I made, I kissed him on the cheek and I told him to swing by any time. I missed him.*

*But it was a fresh start. We fucked of course, and we talked, and sang and even grew food ourselves. I brought chickens and we named them the first names which sprang to mind. We saw no programmes, we had no net, it was us, our bodies and the post-woman.*

*And the letters started coming. I crumpled the first ones up in front of the her, but later I smoothed them out and kept them. We were in trouble, we were deviant, and so I told the others. But there were no bricks thrown, there was no graffiti over doors, and so for them the world was fine. We had each other and that was all that mattered. Nothing could convince them otherwise.*

*My brother knew what was wrong—he told me in message after message after message. He thought I could go back. But I couldn't—to give up my freedom, that is to die. I couldn't stand his pleading, his reasoning—he wouldn't understand, I'd already gone over it all in my head. He was trying to protect me—I couldn't even protect myself. I stopped answering him. He would be better if he forgot about us and the farm. Memories of what you've lost are painful.*

*That's what I said to him, the last time I wrote—you are my brother. You must forget me.*

*One night they came. Three vans filled with men in uniforms. There was shouting, from us and from them, screams from both sides. Heph laughed and joked at them. They shot him in the face. The kitchen walls were sprayed with the stuffing from his skull. After that the others were quiet, they were led into the back of the vans without a fight. I was led in last, the rough grip of fingers clamped to my shoulder. In the van it was dark. We were silent, all of us, as they took us away. We didn't know where we were going, but it wasn't our world. It wasn't our world.*

Once I was alone long enough I knew that Blondee would be left behind. No expectations, no desires, no idle conversations. No love.

Pilsner once told me that I needed more lovers than most, a validation of all that is me.

It isn't true.
It just isn't true.
Without love I'll be free.

The wind has stopped: everything is quiet. The ground is starting to freeze beneath my limbs. The hole is getting cold.

*I lived in a commune, I'm with the ones I loved. Of course I warned them, I warned them so many times. Now we're here, away from the public, isolated, where we can't contaminate even the sturdy post-woman. We were happy enough to leave by ourselves, to hide ourselves away—but this was on their terms. Without our deviant memories perhaps we could even be cured—perhaps we'd learn the worth of marriage, perhaps we'd learn our real-moral-roles. Woman as women, man as men. We'd be reborn, but between dusty walls, not in baptism. Contain what is queer. The others were right, I can understand, enjoy what you have, enjoy it whilst it's there. We were the ones who knew love.*

*There were times I had no worries.*

*How can I worry whilst surrounded by affection, how can I worry when my mind is filled with pleasure and my cock feels as though it'll explode? How can I worry when I can kiss those I love, when they can run their hands over my body with pure affection. Affection without possession. Whatever happens, whatever happens here, I'll always have this instant, this point, this time of pure pleasure. Them and them and me.*

*She whispered in my ear, she told me I was young. I know what she meant, she meant that I should worry. I should be on my guard, that we should barricade the house, or flee, and run—somewhere else. If they come they come. One person licks my neck, their breath on my skin, whilst another plunges me into their throat, enveloping me with a deep driven kiss. There is only this, there is only this, and if we run we'll miss it.*

*An arm I love, breasts I love, legs and balls and cocks.*

*I'm gonna cum, I'm gonna cum. I am here, I am here and I can smell the scent of sweat and feel the tremble of soft skin against my chest. How can I worry when I'm about to spill all I have, spill for those I love, how can I care about anything else? I'm here, I'm here, I'm here, and it's now—now. There.*

*I woke up here.*

The rain has died a little; I think I can hear footsteps.

I cannot tell. Perhaps, perhaps not. I'll shout anyway.

No, nothing.

So I stole: I am indeed a thief.

But I wanted to give also.

If you are prevented from giving, then what is left but to take?

Doing nothing was not an option. Doing nothing is death.

And now I'm doing nothing. The wind howls here like a ghost. I can hear small leaves sliding over the tarpaulin.

I am Blondee, for the last time, I am Blondee.

There was someone else before and there'll be someone else again. I knew them all. They come from different worlds. I don't know if the worlds are real.

Someone else will run their fingers along dusty walls afresh, someone to wonder at the weather and watch plants grow in frigid earth.

Someone to eat the afterthought rations, to munch on mould-coated bread and slurp sour milkshake.

Someone to lie under blue tarpaulin and listen to the rickety pound of rain.

Someone to remember.

I'll close my eyes, I'll lie down, I'll close my eyes and lie down and I'll sleep. I'll sleep and be reborn, and the whole world will be presented to me like new. Who else could I be?

Who else could be so lucky?

# about the author

REDFERN JON BARRETT is a writer and polyamory rights campaigner armed with a doctorate in literature. Author of *The Giddy Death of the Gays & the Strange Demise of Straights*, his works have exhibited in seven countries and been translated into five languages. His writing has featured in *PinkNews*, *A cappella Zoo* (and its tenth anniversary 'best of' edition), *Strange Horizons*, *Heiresses of Russ: The Year's Best Lesbian Speculative Fiction 2014*, as well as *Shaped by Time* (National Museum of Denmark, 2012). He currently works with *Guernica* magazine as a fiction reader, dividing his time between Britain and Berlin, where he lives with his two partners and plays too many board games.

Lightning Source UK Ltd.
Milton Keynes UK
UKOW03f0615030517
300391UK00001B/149/P

9 781590 213643